Emo Reality

The Biography of Teenage Borderline Personality Disorder

Jerold Daniels

SINGAPRESS

Warning: Inside are the words of a teenager whose mental health collapsed in her teens. Her life has not been easy to live, and so her words are not easy to read. They are painful, raw, obsessive, clichéd, and sometimes offensive, but that's because they're real; only her most outrageous millennial labels have been edited for modern readers. If you require trigger warnings, this book is not for you.

Our insulted and ridiculed mouse becomes absorbed in cold, malignant and, above all, everlasting spite. It will remember its injury down to the smallest, most ignominious details, and every time will add, of itself, details still more ignominious, spitefully teasing and tormenting itself with its own imagination. It will be ashamed of its imaginings, but will go over and over every detail, will invent unheard of things against itself, pretending that those things might happen, and will forgive nothing.

—Fyodor Dostoevsky
Notes from Underground
1864 [abridged]

i realized today
while crying in the bathroom for hours
that
i'm never going to be able to live 100% for myself until my dad is dead
even if i move out and never talk to him again,
i wont be able to be completely for myself until he's dead
part of me is dedicated completely to spiting him
even it if means ruining my own life
—Lina, 15
Notes from Singapore
2008

To make a lady, you start with the grandmother, and to make a schizophrenic, you start with the grandmother, too. ... Father may impose the controls, but it is mother who gives the pattern.
—Eric Berne, MD, Psychiatrist
What Do You Say After You Say Hello? The Psychology of Human Destiny
1970

Author's Note:

This book is probably not what you expect. It's not a traditional novel where creative prose tells an invented story. It's not an academic textbook about mental illness for mental health professionals. And it's not a guide on how to help people who have borderline personality disorder.

So what is Emo Reality? This is a biographical memoir that showcases the inner world of Lina, a living sufferer of borderline personality disorder, in her own words. Through Lina's reflections, diaries, and correspondence you'll discover first-hand how it feels to suffer from acute mental illness through childhood and into adulthood.

This book is a case study, as true a reflection as possible of how a teenage mind worked in the throes of mental illness: it can be inconsistent, clumsy, and obsessive. You might feel irritated by Lina or even offended by her in places. But that's because the book offers a unique and true insight into borderline personality disorder, revealing directly what Lina did, thought, said, believed, experienced, heard, and dreamed.

Although identities and some details are obscured for privacy and ethical considerations, the people, events, thoughts, and dialogues in Emo Reality *are genuine and derived from primary sources. They are condensed from fourteen million words of Lina's writings and those of her family and friends, preserved in digital family archives and available online.*

The only exceptions to the book's primary-source nature are Lina's post-therapy reflections and the forward-looking final chapter, "Recovery Journey," which is partly fiction. These introspective and mature insights depict my sincere hopes for Lina: a healthy, happy future, self-understanding, and to start loving.

Why so much hope? I am Lina's father.

My role for Emo Reality *was mainly that of curator and compiler, and I have done my best to honor Lina's words and meaning. Integrity is critical in biography, so I included everything Lina and her sister said about both parents, even accusations and false memories arising years later. It took years to compile, sequence, and merge all of Lina's thoughts into one linear narrative, and my mentor, S.M., a retired psychologist, reviewed all drafts to ensure that I avoided distortion and selection bias. My only edits to the original material were to condense it, anonymize it, and reduce offensive language.*

This is Lina's story, so it does not contain my voice except in the final chapter and her post-therapy reflections. Although I witnessed the destructive impact of borderline personality disorder on Lina and our family, I wasn't present when Lina had her most extreme experiences, many of them solitary, and at the time I naively thought nothing was wrong. Telling a child's story from her father's observations and viewpoint would limit its depth and require interpretation of her hidden feelings; instead, I decided to present Lina's point of view directly using her own words, as faithfully and respectfully as possible.

Emo Reality *is about—and for—Lina and others like her. I hope it encourages teenagers struggling with disordered thoughts like Lina's to seek early therapy; I hope it helps those who are going through this to understand their pasts, take control of their futures, and move forward; I hope it offers insight to families of sufferers and allows them to speak up and encourage their loved ones toward the right help; and I hope that other people with borderline personality disorder can find a way towards the positivity that we see for Lina in the final chapter.*

You are about to read the thoughts of a teenager and young adult experiencing the progression of borderline personality disorder; Lina speaks through the pages of this book in her own words.

I hope her words speak to you.

To S.M.

Contents

Pre-Teen Years

CALL ME LINA. I WAS A GIFTED CHILD who lived and traveled around the world. I grew up with every advantage, surrounded by material luxuries and educational opportunities. But in my teens my home became a battlefield and my life fell apart.

My sister and I were born in Europe. I had to be induced and was born two weeks post-term, jaundiced, and in the 97th percentile for weight. Post-term children often have more behavioral and emotional problems than term-born children, so my problems might have begun in the womb.

My dad was a British engineer for an international company. I liked to imagine that he was a secret agent because it made him seem a lot cooler. My sister and I are British too. People always ask if we were military, but we weren't. My introverted dad is thirty-nine years older than me; old enough to be my grandfather. My extroverted mom is a Filipina who was born in a bamboo *nipa* hut. She's twenty-seven years older than me. Her father was a construction worker in the Middle East who remitted enough money to put her through school, and she was the only family member to go through college. My parents met when my dad was traveling in the Philippines. They got engaged a week later, and they married three months after that in a big wedding in Manila. My mom moved to Europe right away. She wasn't lonely, because her sister lived there with her European husband and their baby.

My dad had a contract that gave us a cosmopolitan lifestyle

with private schools, health care, club memberships, and business class travel allowances. In return, we were required to relocate every few years, so I grew up in cultures that didn't belong to either of my parents, like almost all the kids I went to school with. My dad worked hard and usually came home from the office too late to eat with us, but he walked us to school in the mornings and read books to us at bedtime. My mom never worked outside the home. She spent her spare time keeping fit, painting, and socializing, especially after she had children and met lots of other moms. It was easier for me to relate to my bubbly mom than my serious dad. Our family of three girls and one older man made it hard for my dad to understand us, and us, him.

When I was one year old, we moved to Japan. We lived in the center of Tokyo for five years. I was a pouty child, unlike my sister, who is two years older. My sister obeyed my parents and could be bossy to me, like my mom, but I did things my way. Our neighbors called me *mignon*, which meant cute, but I hated being called cute. We went to church on Sundays and prayed every night.

By three I didn't smile as much as my sister. I can see it in the family photos. Among my many happy childhood photos are some melancholy shots of me. It wasn't the household, my family, our neighborhood, or my kindergarten that caused this sadness, because there isn't a single childhood photo where my sister looks sad. One day I tried to run away, but I didn't have the strength to carry my toys so I decided to stay at home so I could play with them.

At four I wanted to be a unicorn. I said clever things like, "When you pee-pee in the bed you turn the mattress over, but if you pee-pee in the bed again you have to sleep with

Mommy and Daddy." Once, in an amusement park, our boat drifted under a dinosaur.

My dad winked. "I hope it doesn't eat us."

My sister laughed. "I hope it doesn't step on us."

"I hope it doesn't pee on us," I replied thoughtfully.

At five I went to kindergarten. I wanted to be a ballerina, so I took ballet lessons. I started looking for shortcuts to get the things I wanted without having to work for them. I once asked my dad to buy me a stuffed toy by pointing out that if he bought it for me now, that was faster than me praying to God all year for Santa to bring it at Christmas.

I started to hate my dad and thought he didn't deserve my mom. I loved my mom, and I didn't want my dad to share her love. My dad had a photo of my mom in his wallet, so I wanted to steal the photo because I didn't want him to have it. But I thought he'd get mad if the photo was missing, so I stole his whole wallet. When he and my mom were searching the house for it, I showed them where it was and told them I hid it as a joke. He never again left it in a place where I could find it.

School was easy and fun—no homework yet—and I had lots of friends. I loved the ramen in Japan. We lived in nice houses. We took holidays and got to travel around the world. We drove all over Japan and stayed in *ryokans* and soaked in *onsens*, the outdoor hot spring baths. We went to Tokyo Disneyland three times. I used to say, "Thank God for computers, videos, sleeping, and books."

We moved to America when I was six years old and halfway through grade one. The school year was six months different, so my sister and I skipped the second half of our school year and moved forward to the next one, to grade two for me and grade three for her. A few months after we started school, the school contacted my parents to say my sister was invited to join the state-wide enrichment program for "gifted children," in addition to her regular program.

I was smart enough to skip a grade but not *mature* enough. My maths and reading were good, but I wasted writing time drawing fonts, not writing words. Halfway through grade two I was moved back to grade one. A sense of failure stayed with me—a feeling of not being good enough compared to my sister, who was now two years ahead of me. No one could have foreseen the consequences of that small change on my later life.

Our school auditioned everyone on strings; it was *that* kind of private school. My sister played cello, I played the violin, and we both played piano. While my sister didn't have much of an ear for strings, my music teacher wrote on my first report card (the italics in all citations and quotations are mine):

> "Lina demonstrates a *great deal of potential* as a string player.
> With practice on a daily basis she has the potential, and the
> ability, to become a *very fine violinist*."

The school recommended I receive private violin lessons, and I got them, in addition to taking piano lessons like my sister. We loved to play piano-violin and four-handed piano duets. We took horseback riding lessons and did canoeing and camping. Our school had summer camp. We had a pool in our backyard, traveled around the country, and went to the beach a lot. We drove to so many places for holidays. My childhood was luxurious.

At seven I became jealous of my sister attending the gifted children program and wanted to join her. My dad figured I was as smart as she was, so he had our IQs tested. Our IQs were identical: performance IQs of 140 (99.5th percentile) and full-scale IQs of 130 (98th percentile). My psychologist report said:

> "Lina is a well-adjusted girl. Her *very significant intellect* should be acknowledged and nurtured; otherwise, she is a *potential underachiever*. She should be extended across all areas of the curriculum and enrolled in gifted children programs. Lina has the potential to have an *outstanding school career*."

My sister's report was similar. Our reports led to our parents putting me into the gifted children program with my sister and giving us all the extracurriculars we could handle. For many years it was fun, and I was proud of all the things I did. We were privileged to have all those classes, lessons, and instruments provided to us, and I'm grateful for that. But luxuries come with an expectation to try to be all you can be and not settle for second best. When I became a teenager I would feel that pressure for reciprocity and find it very difficult.

When I was in first grade and my sister was in third grade, my mom made us watch a movie about young girls who got raped and murdered by the good-looking family man in the village. His victims included his daughter. My mom warned us to *be wary of our own dad* because he could do this to us someday. My sister was in tears at the end of it. All my mom had to teach us was to scream if *anyone* ever touched us "down there." She may not have meant to single out my dad—life can be rough in the Philippines—but this was only the first time she wedged us away from our dad with a secret conversation.

I began to feel incredibly disturbed, and my dreams became nightmares. From my bed I could often see shadows on the wall when people stood in our kitchen, and in my dreams these ordinary shadows became my dad killing my mom. I dreamed our house was haunted and the ghost was trying to convince me to kill my mom. I dreamed about a "chopper": a giant, rusty machine armed with chainsaws, knives, serrated blades, every manner of slicing device. It slaughtered my parents in front of my face. I dreamed I worked at a place that tortured and killed people. I had to tie people up in horrible machines and watch their insides being torn out. But if I tried to quit, they'd kill me in the way I was forced to kill others. I still can't watch gory movies. I still cry when I see stuff like that.

I loved chocolate and normal ice cream, which was what I called vanilla. I quit ballet lessons because I wasn't good at dancing and I was convinced that everyone was judging me and whispering behind my back, thinking I was fat because I wasn't skinny. Quitting because I had enough of the skinny ballet mentality was normal, but quitting because I believed people were whispering behind my back was abnormal; my paranoia was an early sign of the issues that would trouble me my whole life. I began to push away anyone who liked me.

MY SISTER AND I HAD OUR EYES TESTED almost every year. My sister didn't wear eyeglasses, so I tried to cheat on eye tests so I wouldn't have to wear glasses and look like my dad. Whenever I got a bad result I would be retested, and my next result would be good so everyone thought my eyes were fine. No one knew I was developing "lazy eye," where the brain starts ignoring the weaker eye. By the time my amblyopia was diagnosed in middle school, it was too late to treat it. When my horrified dad then gathered all my eye tests together, from Japan, America, Europe, India, and Singapore, he discovered my right eye had tested good-good-bad-bad-good-bad-bad-good-bad-good, while my left eye had always tested good. The doctor said I must have been peeking between my fingers. My cleverness left me with a blurry right eye, even with glasses. That's why I never read any book that anyone gave me. When I started having trouble in school, the discomfort of reading made things worse. It's hard to be an academic success when it hurts to read.

My dad printed Christmas cards with my artwork on one side and my sister's on the other every year for eleven years, and we would write our greetings inside the cards. Every year he made CDs of us playing our instruments, singing, reading stories, and just joking around with the family. He stopped making the Christmas cards and the CDs when I broke down.

I began to bully others because I had no self-esteem, I didn't feel loved by my family even though they were good to me, and I hated myself. I felt better when I mistreated others. I mistreated them to make them feel as terrible as I felt about myself, to make them feel as alone as I felt, to hurt them for having what I thought I didn't have: love. I bullied someone every year for seven years. The only way I could be happy was to ruin other people's lives.

In first grade I met a girl who had a best friend, and I was jealous because I'd never been anyone's best friend. So I turned her best friend against her, so my friend had no one. Then I told my mom that she was bullying me.

In second grade I met a girl with a pencil case with secret compartments, and I was so jealous. I became friends with her and I stole her pencil case. I couldn't even use it because someone would recognize it. But all that mattered was she couldn't use it either.

In third grade I bullied a girl who was overweight and an

easy target. I'd quit ballet lessons because I was convinced that others saw me as fat, so I focused on her weight.

In fourth grade I treated a girl like garbage. I told her that her clothes looked like snot and the color looked like puke, and I invited everyone to my birthday party except for her—I passed out my invitations right in front of her. I was punished for bullying and had to apologize. She cried to hear my apology, and when she had her birthday party, she invited me.

In fifth grade I bullied a girl because she was popular, and I got caught and punished.

In sixth grade I had a crush on a boy. I couldn't handle it, so I stole his binder that had all his schoolwork and ruined his school experience. I got caught and had to write him a letter of apology.

In seventh grade I tried to turn a popular girl's friends against her and take her place, but there was no way a vile, petty, manipulative bitch like me could ever replace her. After she moved away, I bullied a girl because I was jealous she had a boyfriend. I posted hurtful things on her Bebo account for everyone to see.

I targeted all these kids over the years because they had what I wanted: love from everyone. I thought I was a horrible child, but most people thought I was fine, including my parents. When my dad's company had a "Bring Your Daughter to Work" day, my dad brought me. I drew pictures on the whiteboard in his office and behaved so well that one of his staff actually said, "When I become a mother, I want to have a daughter like Lina."

My first job was playing Christmas carols on the violin, with my sister on an electric piano. We made hundreds of dollars playing "Jingle Bells", "Silent Night", and "Away in a

Manger" in front of the supermarket, wearing Christmassy outfits. We donated half the money to charity and split the rest. I was eight years old and she was ten.

We were creative because we played together so much while growing up. And when we weren't playing together, we were drawing and narrating as we went along, doing the voices. We moved through the story faster than we could draw, so we'd wind up with stacks of unfinished doodles after the first hour and our mom would get upset by the paper waste.

After two years in America we returned to Europe. My mom couldn't stay there until she got her visa, so my dad went ahead to start his new job and our family was separated for six months. My dad flew back after three months to take us on a driving holiday.

We lived in hotels while our furniture was being shipped, and sometimes the four of us shared two large beds. No one wanted to sleep in the same bed with me because I kicked so violently in my sleep, thanks to the torture nightmares I kept secret from everyone.

Once again, my sister and I had to go forward or backward by half a school year. This time we both went forward by half a year, so I was back in the same grade I would have been in if we hadn't moved to America, but my sister was two years ahead of me, not one.

We went to an outdoor exhibition on my ninth birthday, where I ate my favorite food and got gifts. It was the hottest day of that year, and my emotions were all over the place. I got really tetchy. I remember it as a terrible day. I hated my dad that day, even though I look happy in the photos and videos my parents took.

My dad got our family the rare breed puppy my sister and I

wanted. He wanted to make our second stay in Europe a happy one: when anyone asked for anything, she got it.

Two months after my ninth birthday, my sister got the rollerblade set she wanted for her eleventh birthday, and then I wanted one too. So my dad took us back to the sporting goods store, and I got my own set, in addition to my birthday gifts. Her set was $200, but mine was $400 because it had to be expandable. We are smiling in our rollerblading videos, but we only rollerbladed a few times.

My childhood memory began to be distorted and even creative when I reached my teens, as if it was determined to find reasons to blame others, especially my dad, for anything imperfect in my life. In my teens I remembered, bitterly, that I'd wanted a fifty dollar *skateboard* when I was nine, not a set of rollerblades, because I'd become obsessed with Avril Lavigne and wanted to be a cool skater kid, but my dad bought me a set of rollerblades instead of a skateboard *because he didn't like skateboards*. In reality, her song "Sk8er Boi," about skateboards, was released several months *after* I got my rollerblades, I didn't talk about skateboards to my friends until I was fourteen, and I never bought a skateboard.

I corrected this false memory at almost thirty, just before I began psychotherapy, when I received from my dad my digital archives and his memoir. I also remembered that, for years, whenever my sister or I asked for something that we might not use, he grumbled about our rarely-used rollerblades—but that was not a false memory. It was justified.

We loved our school in Europe. I loved playing the violin and I loved my violin teacher. I joined the youth orchestra and I enjoyed it, at first. The conductor directed me in English, but most of the kids in the orchestra couldn't speak English or didn't want to speak English to me, so sometimes I felt lonely. But I was proud to be the only violinist in our family. I'm smiling in my first semi-annual youth orchestra concert video.

My dad bought my sister and me robot kits from the neighborhood hobby shop for Christmas. We put them together with pliers and a soldering iron. I built the Moon Walker kit and my sister built the Hyper Peppy kit. I was proud of my robot, and I'm beaming in my robot videos. But anything could depress me. For Christmas I also got the Vanessa Mae CD *Subject to Change*. When I listened to her song "White Bird" I would get depressed and bawl my eyes out.

I started writing songs in a little notebook that I loved. The cover had a drawing of a woman holding an electric guitar. She looked so cool; I wanted to be her. I started writing lyrics with guitar chords. My family knew I was writing songs but I told them not to read them. I'd written a loving song about my mom, and she overheard me singing it. She went into my room when I wasn't there, and she read my lyrics. When I found out, I tore out all the pages and threw them into the fire. My mom broke my trust and taught me that I couldn't keep anything safe for myself.

My second youth orchestra concert was in a cathedral. Pride was written all over my smiling face during the ovation. I also performed in school concerts as a soloist, in duets with my sister, and in duets with my violin teacher playing jigs and reels.

The whole family loved Europe. My mom had a small car, took art and swimming lessons, and worked out in a gym. We traveled through Europe in my dad's big car. We drove across eight countries with our dog in the back. I loved the Eiffel Tower.

Things at school were going well, except that my bullying

got so bad that the school complained to my parents three times and they had to go to the school with me. I got punished and I stopped for a while. My grades were high, like my sister's, and my reports were full of positive remarks. I got A's in music, art, and French. My nightmares stopped, and I began to control my dreams like I could watch a movie: a list of dreams would come up, and I could pick them.

But my mood would change. Before the Christmas concert, my third concert, my mom did my hair and put me in a red dress, stockings, and shoes. I hated all of it. When my parents called me to the car to leave for the concert, I wanted to kill everyone and myself. I hated them for turning the beautiful instrument I once loved into hell by putting me in a youth orchestra. The thought of seeing my parents in the audience—the people who did this to me—was too much, so I hid a knife in my shoe. I had no intention of using the knife, but I wasn't supposed to have it and that was exactly why I needed it: it was the only thing I could control that night. In that video I'm not smiling like I did in the first two concerts, and I have a faraway look in my eyes.

I started taking guitar lessons, in addition to piano, violin, and the youth orchestra. But three instruments were too many to practice every day, so after a while I gave up piano to focus on violin and guitar. My parents let me quit the orchestra. I asked my dad for an electric guitar and an amplifier for Christmas, and I got them.

For almost twenty years I believed my dad gave me a *child-size* electric guitar. I was embarrassed to hold it in high school because it looked so small. Yet it was the standard adult size that every electric guitarist in my high school played. It wasn't even a false memory; it was totally wrong from the start. I was so misinformed by my reality that I couldn't see what I held in my own hands.

After two years in Europe my dad's company transferred him to India. He left my sister and me with our mom to finish the school year and went ahead to start work, so we had our second six-month family separation. My mom resented my dad for our having to leave Europe. She told my sister and me that she wanted a divorce but not yet because we were too young, so we had to keep her divorce wish a secret. My sensitive sister felt our mom's secret as a burden on her shoulders, but I began to see my mom as a partner because I already hated myself and my dad. Today I realize it was totally inappropriate for a parent to share psychological baggage like that with ten- and twelve-year-old children. It would lead to our depression—and worse—in the years to come.

My dad and my sister loved everyone; they couldn't see what was going on in the family. My mom and I liked to rant together about how much we hated my dad, but sometimes when he was away I thought I loved him. My sister and I wrote him letters and poems telling him how much we loved him. He flew back every two months to see us, and we took more European holidays.

At eleven I was tall enough to reach the toys on the top shelf where my sister hid them from me, and I was tall enough to go on the giant rollercoaster at Disneyland Paris! I have been to Disneyland five times in two countries.

India was amazing. My best childhood memories, by far, are of fighting with my sister with bamboo staves in our huge backyard, pretending we were in a fantasy land. We lived in an awesome mansion near the sea. We had a housekeeper, a maid, a driver, a gardener, a pool cleaner, and a security guard. Not only did we have our own bedrooms, we also had our own bathrooms and walk-in closets and balconies. The pool and garden were huge. We were always in our pool.

I loved India and *Monster Isle* and playing *Age of Empires* and my mom's packed lunches our driver brought so we didn't have to eat the school food. The maid and her husband, the gardener, lived with their two children in the servants' quarters, where I saw them fucking. One time she ran around the kitchen with a carving knife, chasing a rat. Another time our dog killed a chipmunk, so my sister and I hand-raised her babies. I sometimes played my instruments with my chipmunk on my head. I even liked the Prime Roaster chicken restaurants they had there instead of KFC.

What I didn't like was the international school, the music teachers, and the power failures, when we had to turn on a noisy generator. Sometimes I got nostalgic for Europe. One day I looked at my old school's website and saw my smiling picture featured on the home page, and then I didn't want to be in India anymore. I could feel my emotions becoming uncontrollable. I would be happy, then something would happen and I could feel myself tearing up inside. I started hallucinating animals.

When I was feeling lonely and nostalgic, I'd look at my dog, but instead of seeing him I'd see a black wolf covered in blood. He named himself Run. When Run came to me I calmed down and felt connected to things I hadn't seen in ages, like Europe. It felt like I was in India but he was over in Europe, and so I felt like I was there too, somehow. Run terrified me, but he only came in flashes in those days. Back then I never told anyone about my visions.

My mom got really bitchy in India. She didn't do any

housework except for cooking. She'd say things like, "frikkin' this" and "fukkin' that." The slightest thing would get her ranting about her unhappiness, and that would get her ranting about her marriage to my dad, and his marriage to his job, and how she should never have married him. My dad was always working late or going on business trips to provide for the life that my mom complained about. He tried not to argue with my mom, like *his* parents never argued with each other. But my mom believed it was good for children to hear their parents arguing—like *her* parents always argued—so if they broke up their children would understand why. She argued with my dad, like, *all* the time, so he spent more time alone in his study.

My mom argued more and more with us, too. One day my sister was drying the cutlery, and my mom told her to stop making such a clatter on the marble counter. My mom's face went puffy and red as she ranted at my sister, who struggled to keep herself from shouting back. When my mom turned away, my sister locked herself in the bathroom, so my mom ranted at her for leaving when she wasn't finished ranting. Then she ranted at me for not washing the dishes. The next day she was calm—until the next time!

My mom started arguing with the housekeeper and demanded my dad fire her, even though she was the only servant working in the house who spoke English. After that our driver had to interpret everything. He interpreted through his cellphone because he drove for five hours every day. He drove us to school, my dad to work, my mom wherever she wanted to go, us home from school, us to extracurriculars, and my dad home from work. Kumar was so wonderful that he is the only person honored by name in this book.

When I was younger I thought moving around the world

was good, but now I began to think it stank because every time I moved I lost friends and I got more homework. My mom blamed moving on my dad, so I blamed homework on my dad. Fortunately for my homework, we all shared one slow dial-up internet connection, so we couldn't spend much time online and couldn't watch videos.

Most of my grade was Korean. The Koreans and the non-Koreans left each other alone. Only four non-Korean girls were in my grade, so we four were special and we stuck together. But there were only two non-Korean girls in my sister's grade, and she didn't like either of them. With no friends, she became miserable when her periods started, especially listening to my mom bitching. She was going in and out of depression and complaining about our school. She would find places to hide during recess, and she would draw murderers holding knives dripping with blood.

I was still a bully. I bullied an American boy until I ruined his life, just because I liked him. It was as if something inside me drove me to be an immature, selfish, insulting, vain, crude, sarcastic, annoying, naughty, and evil little bitch. And I was proud of it.

We went on a driving holiday around Sri Lanka. We stayed in a beach resort on the coast. Ten days after we stayed there, the resort was wiped off the face of the earth by the tsunami. Every human and animal was killed. I thought about the elephant I rode there; he was dead, so I felt sad. Then I thought about the guy I bought bananas from, to feed the elephant; he was dead, so I burst out laughing. Yet if our trip had been ten days later, I'd be dead too.

Even though the company planned for us to stay in India for two years, everything changed when my sister brought home a poor international test score despite having received top marks at our school. My dad wanted my sister and me to attend good schools, and this school didn't measure up. But his assignment was for another year. We would have been happy to go back to our school in Europe, but student visas there were only for boarding schools, and our old school wasn't a boarding school. Then we thought we might go to Britain, but it would take my mom months to get a visa. My grandparents were delighted that we might go "home" to where we had never lived, but the government schools there were probably no better than our international school in India.

In Singapore, though, if you were accepted by an international school, you automatically got a student visa and one parent got a support visa. So we applied to two Singapore international private schools: Plan A was one of the world's best selective schools, with a waiting list of over a thousand students. Plan B was a non-selective school with no waiting list. My sister and I were accepted by both. Our high grades, our extracurriculars such as music and art, our gifted children participation, and our high intelligence psychologist reports must have taken us to the front of the Plan A queue.

My dad asked his company to relocate my mom, my sister, me, and our dog to Singapore and to pay for accommodation in two countries while he gave up the mansion and moved into a flat. Meanwhile, my sister, who was holidaying at the time, sent my dad this message from Europe:

"I've been so happy in Europe the past days, and soon I have
to go home. I hate stinking India. I hate India!"

Now my parents were even more convinced they were doing the right thing, even though it would mean another separation.

My dad's company approved the special arrangement, and then my sister sent my dad this message from India:

"I like this house and our wonderful garden. I have been hard on you, complaining about the school. I know how hard you are working for Lina and me. I will strive to do my best at school. I would rather not split up the family. India is okay. Don't send us to Singapore!"

Talk about mood swings: my sister's total change of mind was just nine days after her first message!

We had our third family separation, and at the time we didn't know how long it would last. It would turn out to be eight months, totaling eighteen months of living without my dad over a four-year period, and that didn't include his endless business trips. It must have been harder on my dad than it was on us.

My dad took three weeks' holiday to settle us in, with his cellphone glued to his ear most of the time. We video called every weekend, and he flew back and forth every month to spend a few days with us and fix our computers. We didn't have servants and a garden in Singapore, but we had an apartment next to the subway and shopping, with private bathrooms for everyone, and a pool, gym, jacuzzi, sauna, and tennis courts. My mom had a membership in her best gym ever and took two different art classes every week. She wasn't as crabby and my sister wasn't as depressed ... at first.

I liked Singapore. It was a huge improvement on India. It was so safe we could take taxis and go anywhere on our own. I had liked the mansion and servants in India, but my friends there were such a bad influence on me that I didn't consider them friends after I left, the school was crap, the shops had nothing, and strange men stared at me everywhere I went.

For my twelfth birthday I asked for another robot kit like the Moon Walker I'd assembled in Europe. My dad couldn't find any robot kits in Singapore except for the $400 Lego Mindstorms kit, so he bought that for me. I built my first robot a week later, and my second robot four months after that. I realized I liked putting things together, not designing and programming them, so I only used the Lego kit twice. A year later my dad sold it and gave me the money.

But I falsely remembered that I asked my dad for *wood, nails, a hammer, and a saw* to build houses for my toys, even though we already had those things in the house and we lived next door to a hobby shop and a hardware store. I believed I asked him to buy me a *robot from the hardware store* and instead he got one from the Lego store, even though hardware stores don't sell robots. I remembered *I used it only once*, even though I have videos of me making two robots. And I remembered that, for years, whenever we asked for something that we might not use, he reminded me about my unused robot kit—but he was justified.

I started middle school, grade seven. My sister started high school, grade nine. Our school in Singapore was better than the one in India. It was ten times larger, and I made friends from all over the world. A former classmate from when we lived in America was going there now, and we reunited. The school had orchestras and drama theaters with amazing costumes and lighting. We had great music teachers. Everyone spoke English. My sister loved our school and she was happy.

I should have been as happy as her, but my self-esteem was starting to plunge. Before long, everyone at the school seemed to be mean, so I became mean to everyone. And I couldn't feel at home because I didn't know how long I would stay. My dad couldn't get a visa to live in Singapore unless he had a job there, and there was almost no chance of that.

My mom was raising us now. Before, my mom never said no to us, only to my dad. She always said, "Go ask your father!" when she wanted to say no, but now she had to say no herself. Having my mom telling me what to do was even more annoying than having my dad telling me what to do. Gradually I started hating my mom, but not all the time and not as much as I hated my dad. She yelled at my sister and me every day, like she had a schedule or something.

I was still studying violin and guitar, but I started talking about quitting all my lessons. I realized I was only studying music to spite people, not to be a musician. I had started violin lessons five years ago, in America, to make myself better than my class, and started guitar lessons two years ago, in Europe, to beat a girl in my grade. My whole family, especially my sister, talked me out of quitting music. In primary school, and later on in high school and adulthood, I enjoyed playing music, but during my middle school years I began to hate it. And then my mom talked me into taking voice lessons, maybe to impress her friends.

I started taking voice lessons to beat a girl in my class. I soon hated them and emailed my dad that I wanted to quit. He phoned my mom and asked her if I was practicing. She told him she didn't know, because she never heard me singing exercises like scales. During my dad's next visit he asked me to practice singing in the music room where everyone could hear me. I refused, so we argued about him spending a hundred dollars a week on voice lessons and me not practicing voice like I practiced my instruments. I ended up crying under my desk while he and my mom argued. My mom wanted me to continue taking voice lessons. My dad would pay for lessons only if I practiced. Finally they agreed I could practice when no one was home. I continued taking voice lessons, but I never practiced the complicated pieces. My parents and sister wouldn't hear me sing an arpeggio until I was sixteen, and then it was on TV.

In my twenties my voice lessons at thirteen became a false memory. I remembered *my dad enrolled me*, even though my mom enrolled me while he was living in India. I remembered *I enjoyed voice lessons*, even though I'd told my sister that I hated them and was only taking them to keep our mom happy, and I'd emailed my dad asking to quit. I remembered I was *happy to practice singing every day*, even though I refused to practice when anyone was home, so almost never. I remembered my dad asking me for a goodnight kiss that night and *shoving his tongue into my mouth*, even though I'd written to my Indian friend a year later, at fourteen, "my dad has never even *tried* to do that sick pedophile shit some dads do to their daughters" and my mom was lying beside me in my child-size bed; if molestation ever happened neither of us would have been silent. And I remembered that night as a *fearmongering power play* to force me to live according to my dad's family master plan, even though it was just my parents' wish to hear me practice the lessons they were paying for. Who wouldn't want to hear their daughter sing? Perhaps my memory distortion ten years later had grown from the seed my mom had sown when she warned my young sister and me to be wary of our own dad.

My mom would watch *Desperate Housewives* on school nights and ask my sister to watch it with her and study during the commercials. My sister tried to do it to keep her happy, but my mom would interrupt her homework so my sister would get pissed and go back to her room to study. Then my mom would yell at her and make her depressed. But if my sister yelled back, my mom would scream back. We could never see things the same way as our mom. She drove us crazy, and we did the same right back to her.

My mom would say something she thought was really witty but was common knowledge, and the rest of us would groan. Sometimes she'd come out with a howler and we'd burst out laughing. My mom couldn't understand the way my dad and my sister and I thought about anything. Many people have trouble understanding those who are smarter and better educated; they don't see any mismatch, or they see it as arrogance—especially from their kids. We loved our mom, but as we got older the way she talked in chat-speak made it impossible for us to take her seriously.

By the time we were in middle school, our education had surpassed her third world education, and it was harder for her to follow our conversations. As we started losing respect for her and demanding our teenage rights, things got nasty. Because my mom always blamed everything that wasn't perfect in her life on my dad, she blamed the way my sister and I sometimes treated her like shit on him too. But nobody trained anybody to be mean; we were four inflexible people with different ideas.

Four months after we started school in Singapore, the orchestra leader told us to bring our concert clothes to school and wear them to rehearsal because the yearbook photographer would be there. I purposefully didn't bring mine, so I couldn't attend the rehearsal and I got to go home early—a double win, as I saw it. I started to lose things, even my glasses. I knew my parents would buy me new ones and I could get a new style. I was the only one in the family ever to lose a cellphone, and I lost three of them.

Hearing my mom and sister bickering every day depressed me. I started hanging out on the internet, calling myself a goth, and shopping for black clothes online. No one in Singapore wore anything like it, and I had to be different. I changed my online name to *Super Damn Pissed At Everybody*. My dad saw it and complained about it, from India, so I changed it to *My Life Is A Fucked Up Blob*.

In my journal I wrote:

"I hate my life. Life is a shitty piece of crap. It is utterly useless. I need a drummer and a lead guitar. I need a band, that's the one thing in my life that I need. Holy shitty crappy fuck. I'm fucking twelve and *people think I'm ten!* Do not call me cute!"

My sister didn't have my self-esteem problem: I wrote in my journal "I hate" *seven times* more often than I wrote "I love," while in my sister's journal, the words were about equal.

Despite all this, I was still doing my homework. My first term was great: three A+'s, five A's, and two Cs in maths and PE. My dad was happy, except for maths because he could have helped me with my maths if we lived together. While my dad was still in India I emailed "I love you" to him for what would be the last time.

My dad's company transferred him to Singapore, to everyone's surprise. My dad and sister were delighted to be reunited. My mom and I were like, "... Meh." I preferred it while he lived in a different country, except that now he could walk the dog. I hated him because he cared for me and he treated me like the immature kid I actually was, which made me want to kill something.

My dad got us Permanent Resident visas so we could stay in

Singapore for as long as we wanted, even if he left his company. But my mom complained that she wanted us to be permanent residents of *Europe*. Permanent residency was probably the best gift my dad ever gave my mom, other than money and my sister and me: she still lives in Singapore today.

My mom was sour all the time, almost as bad as in India. Because my mom was always complaining, my sister was always sarcastic. My sister was wavering in and out of dark moods and would release her stress by pounding away at the piano, drawing gory cartoons, and laughing at me.

My emotions were all over the place. My childhood bully reemerged in a new form: I released my stress and comforted my self-esteem by pissing off everyone in my life. Even when my parents were being nice to me, I'd be like, "Fuck you" to them. I was an asshole to everybody, no exception. I got pissed off at my mom three times in one afternoon. If there was one thing I would change about my life, I would have made an asshole exception for my mom.

My dad often helped my sister and me with our maths. My sister appreciated his help but I hated maths, science, English, and geography, even though I still got A+ in all of them except for maths. In primary school I got A's without any studying. But that didn't work in a selective middle school that was full of smart kids.

My dad read on a website about a family bonding game called *Ask Me a Question*. He wanted to play it one night when he tucked me in:

"Ask me a question," he said.

"Why do I have to ask you a question?"

That shut him down.

I swore, complained, and felt depressed. I was so jealous of my big sister that it made me feel like shit. I wished I could draw like she could, even though I'm a good artist. I envied her intelligence, even though I'm as smart as she is. I wished I were slim. I hated the world. I hated myself. My mood swings worsened, especially now that my tall, slim, smart, artist sister was dressing goth on weekends.

I *hated* being compared with her, so I adopted an emo look, that punk stance with straight hair, long bangs, studded belts, wristbands, eyeliner, and painted fingernails—everything in fuck-my-life black to show the world how I felt. My sister laughed and told me I'd grow out of being emo because there are no adult emos.

I started sitting at the back of the class. I didn't speak, take notes, or study. It would make my dad happy if I paid attention and did my homework, so I couldn't do it no matter how much it might have made *me* happy. Something inside me had made me want to disappoint my dad ever since I was small; that feeling was becoming overwhelming. Pissing him off boosted my self-esteem and helped me to make decisions, but I made many of my critical life decisions just to disappoint my dad, and they became own goals.

My mom was way more fun than my dad, and she didn't try to control me like he did. I loved my mom, but she drove me crazy. She was like, "Your sister always tells me everything! Are you a lesbian? You never tell me!" She always set the timer on the VCR to record her favorite show when she went out. Once when I came home and watched TV, I left it on my channel so the recorder videotaped the wrong show. When my mom saw that she missed thirty minutes of her four-hour cooking show, she called me a *punyeta*, which means bitch or asshole, and she beat me with the remote control.

At least my mom had redeeming qualities, which is more than I felt about my dad. Most of our sleepovers were at my house because my mom cooked good food. My place also had the biggest swimming pool and a huge TV. I didn't give my dad any credit for the lifestyle and opportunities he gave us all. Because all the kids at my school had dads with good jobs, it was hard for me to see that luxury wasn't automatic and someone had to work for it, like my dad, or marry for it, like my mom.

I finished grade seven without a single day absent and with an A- average, the same as my sister. My final report said:

"Lina deserves to be congratulated for this outstanding report. These are wonderful marks. She has a *wonderful attitude* toward her studies and I am sure with determination she can further improve in mathematics. She is well on her way to *earning top marks in all classes*. Lina is a *delightful young lady* and I look forward to seeing her grow in confidence."

MY SISTER SPENT THE SUMMER DRAWING a fifty-page comic book about gay lovers. My dad printed copies and she sold them at our school fairs to raise money for charity. I was so jealous. When my dad mailed a copy to my aunt, she said the story was vulgar and she refused to show it to my cousins.

My dad bought me a $4,000 adult violin for my thirteenth birthday. The concertmaster of the Singapore Symphony Orchestra helped us choose it. It was European, more than a century old. It sounded and looked amazing.

My family went to Club Med in Indonesia for our summer holiday, where my sister and I went scuba diving. That was cool! It lifted me out of depression. I realized I had good friends, I liked living in Singapore, and I had my own desk, computer, bathroom, queen-sized poofy animal-printed bed, and poster-covered walls. I wanted to stay in my school until I graduated with my International Baccalaureate (the Swiss diploma that is recognized worldwide and gets advanced placement into the second year at many universities). Then I wanted to go to college and go scuba diving in the Great Barrier Reef. I headed into adolescence with good grades, lots of new friends, no nightmares, and no bullying.

But soon my emotions were all over the place, and I fell in and out of depression like my sister did at my age. My sister laughed at me, my mom yelled at me, and my dad helped me with my maths. I looked all right on the surface, but I didn't feel loved and I hated my life. I wrote a song called "Fuck You". "Fuck You" was the chorus.

Teenage Emo

GRADE EIGHT BROUGHT MORE HOMEWORK than ever before. My friends would message me on MSN Messenger, then *they* would go offline and do homework. But I couldn't focus on my homework. I'd spend two hours on a geography assignment and not bother to finish it. Then it would be bedtime, so I'd skip maths and English and be online the whole night talking to friends in other time zones. When my parents asked me to turn off the computer and do my homework, I told them I needed the internet for research.

My life revolved around music, art, drama (to be around friends), friends, and school. My sister and I performed piano-violin duets at school and at our teachers' recitals. We enjoyed performing and we sounded good together. My dad recorded every performance and put them on our annual CDs.

That year, the family went wakeboarding at a country club. After an hour of effort my sister was able to surf for two whole minutes, but I couldn't stand up without falling into the water. She had fun and wanted to go again, but when my dad offered a second session I refused. I hated when my sister was better than me, and I was not going to give her that satisfaction. If I couldn't be sure of being the best at something then I didn't want to do it at all. My refusal to go wakeboarding again was because of my self-esteem.

For years, whenever my parents dragged me to a boring adult gathering, I would walk around the house and draw floorplans, and then I would go home and recreate people's already-built houses using *The Sims* software. I told my dad I was considering becoming an architect. He was so happy. Later on, when my dad took my sister and me to a book festival, he found a copy of *Brøderbund Home Architect* software in the discount bin and bought it for me. It was for the old version of Windows, so it was cheap. But it was tough to learn, so I kept using *The Sims*, which is for kids.

When we made elective choices for grades nine and ten, I wanted to sign up for drama, music, and art, but I was only allowed to take two. I wanted to drop art, but my parents wanted me to drop drama. My dad supported my wish to take all three, by writing to the school and using my interest in architecture to ask for an exception. He argued that should my interest in architecture continue, art would be important and I shouldn't drop it. The school refused to make an exception, so my parents convinced me to drop drama and audition for challenging roles in the school productions instead.

The architecture episode became another false memory. I remembered that my dad concluded *I would become an architect*, even though no parent trusts a thirteen-year-old's career choices. I remembered my dad *arranged meetings with my teachers* to ensure I was taking the courses I would need for architecture, even though no meetings took place other than the twice-a-year parent-teacher meetings, and even though maths and science are the only prerequisites and I had to take those anyway. I remembered *my dad didn't support my hobby*, despite the fact he bought me *Home Architect*. I remembered it was *expensive*, even though it was cheap. I remembered that when I told him I didn't want to be an architect anymore, he became livid because *he hated who I was* and I cried, even though he was justly annoyed because he had pleaded to the school for me to take three electives, using my interest in architecture as the justification, and I'd already changed my mind.

I begged my dad for a bass guitar, and he bought me a good one: solid mahogany, five strings, a thousand dollars. I had a violin teacher, a singing teacher, and a guitar teacher who also helped me with my bass, but mainly I learned bass riffs on my own.

But a bass guitar isn't a solo instrument. I wanted to play bass in a rock band, but nobody in my grade was interested in playing with me and I couldn't bring myself to join their bands. My school had a huge music department, multiple theaters, and plenty of ensembles. It was loaded with seriously talented musicians, because if you weren't in creative extracurriculars when you applied to my school, you wouldn't be accepted, no matter how high your grades were. But I can't partner with talented people and survive being in their groups.

I began to lose my connection with my talented friends who were good for me but who could be critical and sometimes judge me negatively. I avoided hanging out with people who were better than me, so I avoided almost everyone at my uber-talented school and spent more time hanging out online. My new friends were followers who looked up to me and made me feel good about myself.

My guitar teacher arranged an audition for me as a voice-over actress for dubbing Japanese cartoons. The studio was amazing, and so were the cartoons. I would have made heaps of money. But I failed the audition because I sounded like I was reading the script.

Meanwhile my sister's drawings were so good that our

school referred her to a private club that was looking for an artist. She earned $3,500 at fifteen for drawing seven posters. I was so jealous of my sister. My emo self-esteem was killing me.

My sister took all the homework help she could get, but when my dad tried to help me with my homework I took it as harassment. I thought his attempts to support me through school were useless, and I just wanted him to fuck off.

I wrote in my journal:

"I can escape home at school. I hate homework more than school, and I can do homework at home."

That made sense to me at the time. I was no longer responding to a normal teenage situation—doing homework—in a normal way, but everyone thought I was just being stubborn and passing through a phase.

Our school organized field trips to other countries. On the way to Thailand a friend and I took our airplane headphones, tuned them to Cantopop music, and turned the volume all the way up. We did the same with the headphones in the seats around us, and people got so annoyed! Then we took our packs of sugar, salt, pepper, and creamer and mixed them all together. And we thought we were cool.

My English grade dropped from A+ to B. It was depressing to drop so much in one term, and my dad's concern about it was even more depressing.

At Christmas we went on holiday to Britain to see my cousins and grandparents. Snow is awesome when you live at the equator! But my sister and I couldn't relate to our nerdy cousins like we could when we were little kids, so we hardly spoke to them. My sister and I got really moody.

I wrote this story while I was there:

"I am twenty-six and I work as a DJ. I didn't go to college. I didn't even finish twelfth grade. I was useless at everything and had no talent at all. The only thing I was good at was DJing, and you won't get nowhere like that in a stuck-up private school. All my parents cared about were my grades. They loved my sister, an A student. I loved her too. She was the only family I had left when I moved out at nineteen. I got a career at the little club in the city near my apartment and she went off to college."

It was supposed to be fiction, but much became prophecy.

I auditioned for a non-speaking role in a school play. I asked my dad to videotape it and make DVDs so I could give copies to the cast. He did it, but then I didn't give copies to anyone. I hadn't made it into the "in crowd" because I didn't have a speaking role.

I quit the school orchestra. I hated ensembles, but solos and duets were fine so I continued taking violin lessons. My homeroom teacher hated me because I said I wasn't interested in playing in the jazz band, and my dad hated me for quitting the orchestra.

We had a homework diary in middle school. The parents had to sign it every week or the teachers would email the parents. Sometimes I'd leave mine at school or "lose" it when I got behind. When my teachers emailed my dad about it, he became even more obsessed with my homework.

I opened accounts on Bebo, DeviantArt, IMVU, Myspace, Facebook, and Buzznet. I already had MSN Messenger, like everyone else. I put photos of my friends on Facebook—social stuff—but Myspace and Bebo were pure vanity about *me*. I loved posing, and I became a "camwhore." I loved social media.

My mom discovered an amazing TV show called *Miami Ink*.

My dad complained to my mom about her watching a show about tattoos with me. We called it body art, but he called it body graffiti. I planned to get an antichrist symbol tattooed on my wrist and get thirteen piercings: a snakebite (two on the lower lips), left eyebrow, right nostril, navel, and ears; in my left ear I wanted two on the bottom and two on the top; and on my right ear I wanted three on the bottom and one on the top. I planned to do them while I went to college so my parents couldn't stop me.

My sister teased me by calling me a scene kid when I went out in my skirt, black top, striped socks, and chains. But I was *emo*, not scene. I hated it when other people dressed emo. Nobody in my family understood what emo was; they thought I was only making a fashion statement. I had nobody I could talk to about my problems, so I kept them all inside and nobody understood me or had any idea who I was. I felt very, very emo.

I used to love my school and Singapore. Now I called them hellholes. I was seething with hatred. I wanted to rip my maths teacher's intestines out and paint the walls with her blood. I didn't think of myself as depressed, but I hated my whole family. I knew I didn't have any *reason* to hate them, but I just hated them so much, especially my dad. Every night when he came home he would be like, "What's the homework situation? Anything I can help you with? May I do the honors?" As in, sign my homework diary.

My parents kept bothering me about failing school. I felt pressured to live up to my sister by being a wonderful student, but I was nothing like her. She studied every night; I couldn't. I told myself that someday I'd be rich and famous and I'd laugh at my family, or else I'd commit suicide. I nearly slit my wrists, but then I didn't.

I was still taking lessons in violin, voice, acoustic guitar, electric guitar, and bass guitar. I wanted to quit violin, but I wasn't allowed to because my parents had spent so much money on lessons and violins. I wanted to smash my violin into a wall. I wanted to be a bassist in a kickass emo-screamo band, but it wasn't going to happen. I never practiced the hard pieces my teacher assigned, so I had no guitar repertoire. And because I hadn't bothered to re-learn the bass clef after I quit piano lessons, I couldn't read bass guitar music except by counting up from the bottom G.

My mood could go up and down several times in a day. It didn't help that my mom was acting more immaturely. Like, she'd buy Maltesers. I'd open a pack and eat three. The next day the pack would be empty, and she'd complain that I ate them all! Blaming my dad for her miserable life was ridiculous, but blaming us for eating the chocolates was immature. My sister and I wondered if our mom was going backward, or she'd always played the victim, only now we could see it because we were growing up.

When I had a mood swing, it took effort to inhale and I felt like I had no breath left. I had my first emotional breakdown at my sister's concert when the orchestra that I'd quit started playing. I couldn't breathe! At bedtime I spent two hours in my bathroom, where no one could hear me, tearing my fingernails down my body and crying. Then I stood there, looking in the mirror. I had scratches all over me. I felt relief when one of them bled. The sight of my blood eased my pain.

We wore uniforms at school, but I wore black everywhere else. My black emo thing let me be myself and gave me comfort. It let me stand out, and it warned others to leave me alone. My rebel appearance gave me the privacy I needed. I didn't show physical signs of stress; they were trapped inside and only emerged when I had an emotional breakdown. Then I ripped myself up.

I overreacted to everything. If someone called me fat, I wouldn't eat for days. I was full of secrets that weren't important individually, but they added up and sent me into depression. I couldn't think of anything happy in my future. My mind only thought unhappy thoughts, like going to college or getting a job. When I got depressed I got aches and pains.

I took an online depression test. It said:

"You answered 9 out of 10 items with Yes. More than 5 indicates that you may be suffering from clinical depression. This test cannot substitute for a visit to a mental health professional."

My only "No" was because that question asked: "Have others noticed your lack of energy?" and I answered, "No, nobody cares."

I felt like I'd been acting my whole life, trying to appear normal, while inside I said, "Nobody understands me and I want to die." I thought about suicide way too often. I attempted drowning, throwing myself off a balcony, and hitting my head on a metal pole. I wanted to die young with happy memories. Now I was waiting for the man of my dreams. Then we'd carve each other's name into our arms, hug tightly, and shoot ourselves while videoing it.

I felt like I had a terrible family. I wanted to be an orphan. My parents didn't beat me, like my friends' parents beat them, but they didn't care about anything except my grades and music. My mom compared me to my sister, who was a momma's girl. Yet while I was falling apart, my sister was going in and out of depression. She did fine at school and had loads of friends, but for the next year and a half she would sometimes take a knife and slit her ankle or arm in places where she could hide the scabs. When I cried, my sister would be like, "Shut up, scene bitch. Go to school and stop complaining!" And I would feel like stabbing her. Our adolescent miseries turned us into adversaries for more than a year.

The more my parents tried to get to know me, the more I didn't tell them anything and the more I pushed them away. My dad cared about school, so my mom wanted me to do homework because she still cared about what *he* thought. Sometimes she tried to understand me, but I didn't let her because I didn't want her to know my secrets. My mom was like her mom, who was so random she scared me. My mom told me she thought I had cancer and screamed at me for the smallest of things, like when I left my swimsuit in the shower.

There were times when I wanted to kill my parents, but most of the time I wanted to kill myself. Then I'd cry in the bathroom for hours while I scratched myself up, leaving big red scars where no one could see them.

I'D ALWAYS BEEN THE BULLY, but now others bullied me. I had friends but I secretly hated most of them. I was famous in my school for being "the emo." From other middle school kids I got comments like, "What the fuck is wrong with you? Emo is a style of music. Go slit your wrists, bitch." From primary kids, I got comments like, "Whoa! Look! It's the emo!" And from upper school kids, looking down their noses at me, comments like, "Oh my God, you're wearing black! I can't talk to you!"

Half my class hated me. The other half teased me and

shoved rulers down my pants. People I didn't know kept phoning and texting me to harass me. During science I was listening to music while kids wrote emophobic death poems on the whiteboard.

One guy was like, "Ooh, look who's emo today!"

"Fuck off."

"Calm down! When you get to know me it'll all be okay."

"Fuck *off!*"

I wasn't proud of being emo—being majorly depressed isn't something to gloat about—but I didn't care what others thought. I didn't want to go out. I started to miss friends I hadn't seen for years. I couldn't get through a week without crying.

I was mentally disturbed when it came to straitjackets, pain, padded cells, and clowns. An audiobook of *Animal Farm* terrified me. I couldn't stand being in a room with a stranger in case I had another breakdown. When my dad said goodnight to me through the door, it would terrify me. I had such a phobia of being sexually abused, especially by taxi drivers, that I couldn't hug my dad or my grandpa—how sad is that? My dad never tried to do that sick pedophile shit some dads do to their daughters, but ever since my mom warned my sister and me to be wary of him I'd been paranoid about it, which was probably why I was so distant from my dad.

I'd have scratch-myself-up sessions and then be unable to remember them. Later I'd look in the mirror while showering and be surprised to see scratches all over my neck, collarbone, and back. My brain was fucked and I didn't know why. I told my friends and my sister, but no adults because I hated doctors.

I thought that if I asked my parents for a counselor, my dad would be like, "What mental problems? You never mentioned anything like this before!" And my mom would be like, "Why can't you tell *me* about your problems?" Then they would find me a male counselor and I'd have another breathing attack when I was alone with him.

When I felt really emo, I'd riff Bon Jovi on bass by ear and feel better. I wrote a protest song to rhyme with "It's My Life":

"My head's crashed on the desk
Don't give a shit about this test
Don't wanna grow up to be a college prick
The thought makes me fucking sick
Who wants to live the life you're living
All the shit that no one's giving
I just want to be me
I just want to be free
Don't wanna be a school professor
With a fancy PhD.
Just wanna live my life so wild
I'm just a crazy little child
Don't restrict me, can't you see
I just want to be free
You say you just need more potential
I wanna stab you with my pencil
Take your heart out, claw your eyes out
Make you see I don't want to be you."

I sent hundreds of messages a day while I was supposed to be doing my homework. I was only happy when my friends were online. I shared my problems with others who said they had similar issues and could understand me.

Meanwhile, my mom opened accounts on DeviantArt, Friendster, Myspace, and Facebook. She loved to upload photos of herself, but my dad asked us not to upload photos of him because he valued his privacy. So sometimes my mom's uploads included my sister and me and sometimes they included her friends, but they never included my dad. Online, my mom looked like a single mom. Guys started hitting on her, and at first she ignored them.

I'd always loved singing, but when I sang solo in a school concert I began to hate it. I wanted to meet my online friends and live in their countries, but my sister was happy living in Singapore, and it seemed to me that keeping my sister happy was all that mattered to my parents. My sister was so much better at art that she lowered my self-esteem and I wanted to kill her. I hated my whole family and lied to them so often that nobody trusted me. I began pushing my parents away.

I hated babies; they cry and laugh for no reason and they're ugly and useless. I hated toddlers and little kids. On Hug Day a kid walked up to me and hugged me, and I was like, "Get off!" and shoved it away. It looked really hurt, so I smiled. In the school cafeteria a little kid walked in front of me, and I was like, "Move!" and I shoved it away. It fell over, and I laughed.

I never paid attention in class because I was always thinking about too many things at once and my brain felt like it was about to explode. I nearly stabbed myself with rusty scissors—I froze right before they hit my stomach. My parents breathed down my neck and checked my homework diary every night. One night, as my mom walked into my room, I turned to face her and I crumpled my homework in her face. She got all "*Aaah!*" I uncrumpled it and said it was a joke. She believed me.

Maths homework gave me migraines. My dad would come into my room to make sure I wasn't doodling without realizing it. Sometimes I'd get determined to finish my homework and I'd be like, "Lina, do this simple question!" And then I'd start playing with a hairclip. I'd phase out, hear voices, turn around, and find my bedroom was completely empty.

To my caregivers it seemed that I *wouldn't* do what I needed to do, when actually it was that I *couldn't* do those things. Now I realize that my behavior was symptomatic of poor mental health, and I was doing my best with the mind that I had.

My family went to see *Phantom of the Opera*. It was special to my sister and me because we had been playing and singing Andrew Lloyd Webber's music for years. The expensive show was awesome. When we came out of the theater we were all really happy, like we were floating on air, so my dad invited us to a restaurant for dinner. My mom threw a tantrum right there in the foyer, shouting that because *we* didn't want to go to church with her the next day, Mother's Day, she didn't want to go to dinner with us tonight. She turned an invitation into a fight about going to church, even though we only went to church for Easter and Christmas.

"We are going to *church!*"

"We are *not* going to church!"

"You *are* going to church!"

My mom was acting like a fucking idiot. My dad and a hundred bystanders stared at her. We took a taxi home in silence and ate leftovers. My dad had wanted a nice evening for all of us, but my mom spoiled it. For my dad, my life was all about school, and for my mom, life was all about nothing.

I had to be right and know everything before everyone else. Because I always had to be the best, I criticized others. When someone told me something new, I would say, "I *know*" and then be pissy about it because I *hadn't* known. My friends told me I was slim, but I thought I was fat, and fat people bothered me. I wanted a corset, to make me skinny. I was a bitch because I had no self-esteem.

Anything could trigger another mood swing. When my best friend kept talking, I punched her. I punched another friend in the stomach so hard she couldn't breathe, and I ran away. I punched her because someone else was pissing me off and she happened to be the closest person. When my mom asked me if she could get my instrument for me to practice, I got pissed. When my dad greeted me, I got pissed. I felt like the whole world was out to get me.

My room was a pigsty. My mom had given up on me. I wanted my dad to give up on me, but he never did. When we got our reports, he'd read through them with me and I'd get a goddamn lecture. The only things he cared about were grades, homework, practicing music every day, and going to bed on school nights. He'd be like, "It's ten o'clock, and we all need our bedtimes!" I wished he'd stop trying. I wanted him to die and burn in hell.

I scribbled out a teacher's note in my homework diary, so my dad emailed her to find out what it said, so she emailed the head of grade, so he called me in and gave me a lecture, so when I came home I got another lecture from my dad. And then I had to walk the dog, play violin and guitar, eat dinner, and do homework. I felt like killing someone, but I took out my anger on myself and had another scratch-myself-up spree to make me feel better.

I couldn't concentrate in most subjects, but if I liked the subject, like history, then I could pay attention. In other classes I would think about the art and novels I wanted to create. Sometimes I'd think about something completely random and get so immersed that I wouldn't even know what was going on around me. I didn't want to learn French; I was never going to live in France! During French I drew on myself and doodled vampires all over my books. I spent a maths class drawing tattoos on my arm, so I didn't know how to do the homework. That night I got so frustrated when I tried to do it that I snapped my pencil in half.

I didn't tell anyone how I felt, so it all boiled up inside me until I went crazy, locked myself in my bathroom, and cried and tore at my skin for hours. I felt like I was dying! I told myself that if I wasn't so emotional, I could get on with life. I told myself that if I could just concentrate, I would do better at school. I could see I had a problem, but I didn't know there were treatments that could have lifted me out of my despair. My parents did their best with the information they had, but they didn't have the right information. So as a child I was never diagnosed and treated, only as an adult after I wasted my "gifted" opportunities for an outstanding life.

I despised almost everyone in my grade. I made friends quickly and dropped them as I pleased. Everyone eventually pissed me off, or they'd get pissed off at me because I kept changing. My teachers thought I was just a slacker, except my homeroom teacher. He was like, "You're going through hard times, but you're not alone! You can talk to people!" The last thing I wanted was a counselor, but my homeroom teacher would be proven right.

I had to live up to my sister, and it sucked because she still got top grades. I'd have so much homework, and she'd taunt me with: "Just wait until *high school!*"

Two friends and I sang three-part harmony in a school concert while my sister accompanied us on the piano. It was cool, but my parents killed me when we got home and they discovered my maths grade was almost a fail. I felt like shit. At thirteen I wrote, "I will drop out of school and become a tattoo artist."

My sister designed a lovely gown for grade ten Formal Night, and my mom hired a dressmaker to sew it. She looked so elegant in her gown that the dressmaker asked her to model some dresses for her in a fashion show, for a hundred dollars. She was happy and told her friends all about it. I was jealous because I wasn't tall enough to be a professional catwalk model, and my sister was. But my sister discovered she hated standing around in high heels for two hours, and she begged my parents to let her quit. They refused to let her quit, because now the dressmaker was depending on her for the show.

When my sister came home from the last rehearsal, she had a nervous breakdown. She lost it completely, and she screamed, "*I QUIT!*" And she burst into tears. My role model was gone. My parents were in shock. I felt like the stuffing had been kicked out of me. The next morning my sister asked me to chop her long flowing hair down to a butch tomboy cut, and I was delighted to do it. She started wearing black makeup and black androgynous clothing, and she never again tried to look attractive and feminine. My dad tried to be philosophical and said it would keep her safe from the boys.

My sister's modeling meltdown changed everything.

My sister played her last school jazz band concert, quit the band, and quit piano after ten years of lessons. My dad looked depressed, but my mom said it was up to her. Every day my sister swore and bitched, but she never stopped studying, because she knew education was good for her. She resumed her piano lessons a few months later because she got extracurricular credit for them.

I told my parents I wasn't going to be a mathematician, scientist, or *femme française* when I grew up, so I was going to stop studying maths, science, and French. If my sister could quit, so could I! Before her breakdown, my sister had been the perfect child and everyone had looked up to her. Now, while my emotions and grades were crashing, my big sister became a buddy who I could count on to take my side, even when I wanted to fail.

My home depressed me. My depression made the people around me depressed, except for my dad and my teachers. I wrote a song about myself called *Bitch*. As soon as my scratches healed I tore at myself again. I loved to give myself pain, but I hated it when someone else hurt me or I had an accident.

My dad brought home brochures for summer holidays: the pyramids in Egypt, wildlife safaris in Africa, and liveaboard diving cruises in the Great Barrier Reef. My dad enjoyed those places when he was young, and he wanted us to see them. But the thing is, during every family holiday my mom would get in a bad mood that would last for days. Then she'd be good for a few days, but something would happen and she'd be back in her bad mood, with my dad bitching about her spoiling the holiday for the rest of us and my mom bitching that she had every right to spoil it.

My sister and I had had enough of their holiday bickering, and now that we were older we could do something about it: we refused family holidays. My friends' mothers insisted on family holidays every summer for relaxing and family bonding, even when my friends didn't want to go. But my mom said if we didn't want to go on holidays then she didn't want to go either, and of course my dad didn't want to go if no one else wanted to go. So we never took another holiday as a family. By refusing exotic holidays, potentially great ones, I made everyone's stress even worse. We stayed home for the next year and a half as the family fell apart.

I finished middle school, grade eight, with three A+'s, two A's, and some Cs, for an average of B+. My final report said:

> "This is a very good set of reports. Lina is clearly an *industrious student* and is making good progress across a wide range of subjects. I look forward to monitoring her progress next year. Well done!"

My sister's middle school average had been the same as mine, but she had studied all the time to get the same grades I achieved with much less effort. But this would be my last good report.

I look angry in my fourteenth birthday dinner photo, and my sister looks grumpy. I'm dressed emo down to my black lace fingerless gloves, and my sister is dressed as a goth. Neither of us is wearing a speck of color. We felt as grim as we look in that photo. My dad is smiling but he looks tired. My mom has the big smile she automatically adopts whenever she sees a camera.

While our friends left Singapore for the summer, we stayed home, making us even more depressed. Tourists took videos of me in my emo clothes and makeup when I walked down Orchard Road. My sister hung around in my bedroom, and we became closer. We avoided our parents because they invaded our privacy. We agreed that our dad was a strict pain in the ass and our mom was stupid but trying to be smart. She would yell at me about my bed being messy and we'd get in fights. My friends' moms hit them, but my mom would make me bleed. We thought our mom was losing her sanity.

My sister was the most famous artist in our school. She got

another referral from the school, to illustrate a children's book for a thousand dollars. I was so jealous. But after she finished all twenty drawings, she had a breakdown and quit the project because the publisher told her they were too small and he asked her to redraw all of them with more pixels. My dad rescued her money by Photoshopping every drawing to make it larger and sending them directly to the publisher. So the book was published, but her name wasn't on the cover, only inside in a tiny font, and she didn't receive any more referrals from the school. My sister's emotions had ruined her reputation at the school and my dad could not rescue it.

My sister and I went to Malaysia for the underwater part of the scuba course my dad gave us for Christmas. Scuba was something I'd wanted to do ever since Indonesia. I lost interest when I found out the theory would be taught in a classroom, but I took the course anyway because my dad had already paid for it. At first I was scared to be where there could be jellyfish, but when I saw a sea turtle, a cuttlefish, a sea snake, and a moray eel, it was all cool.

At the end of the summer, instead of feeling refreshed, I blamed Singapore for not blessing me with an emo boyfriend. I was already psyching myself up about how much I hated the teachers, the students, the subjects, and the homework. I thought I wouldn't be able to cope because I overreacted to everything. If one itty-bitty thing went wrong, I wouldn't be able to deal with it.

Grade nine was bad from the start. I had no friends in any class except music, and there were people I loathed in all my classes. I drew centaurs instead of participating in lessons. The first night, I couldn't be bothered to do homework, so I drew graffiti and tattoos in my book and daydreamed about Europe.

I missed Europe even though I knew that nobody in Europe missed me.

I tried to study on the second night, but I didn't know how to start my French homework because I'd cheated in French in grade eight. I couldn't do the homework the other kids did even though I knew I was probably smarter than most of them.

I panicked just *thinking* of future exams. I assumed I would fail French, English, science, maths, and history and only pass art and music. I slept in English and drew tribal tattoos on the cover of my book. In maths I read a story under the desk and got in trouble when my teacher saw it.

I wrote this English essay but didn't hand it in:

"Go fuck a goat. Death death death. Essays suck balls. Why the fuck do we have to do all that essay shit? It's not like the teachers enjoy reading them, it's not like the students enjoy writing them, so why? Because life sucks. Let's have an example: this essay is about turning a book into a movie. Nobody fucking cares, but my teacher wanted me to do this anyways. AAAH! AAAH! No fear destination darkness. Behind my nose lies a world of darkness. Sniff my butt hairs and realize what it's like in hell. Ooooh, touch my banana. Why don't you push a tree? Aah, life. My house looks like a house. Ding dong. Spanish fly and his nachos eat shit. Fish and eggs. Fuck maths sucks balls."

That was the state of my mental health when I was fourteen. No joke.

Sometimes my sister would tell me to stop bitching, get off the internet, and pull myself together, but other times she'd tease me that my grade nine was so much easier than her grade eleven, rattle off all the assignments she had to do, and whine that she was going to fail. The thing is, if we hadn't gone to America, where she skipped a grade, she would have been the oldest student in grade ten instead of the youngest student in grade eleven. She wouldn't have been going through the most difficult time of her life, starting her International Baccalaureate, *at the same time* I was going through the most difficult time of my life, starting middle school in horrible mental health. She might have been able to support me like a big sister instead of being a crybaby.

My mom blamed my sister for making the family miserable, which was true, but that made my sister even more miserable. Then my sister would miss her friends in Europe and cry even more. And then my mom would tell my sister to see a counselor for her depression, which she refused to do, and that would make my sister feel even worse. She felt better when my dad and I organized a surprise Sweet Sixteen birthday party for her at Hard Rock Cafe. I wanted a big party like that when my turn came. At least I no longer hated my sister like I did in seventh grade. We hated our parents together and tried to block them out.

I was a scene kid with attitude. A couple of weeks after school started, I carved "SHIT" into the top of my desk. I thought my dad would kill me, so I changed it to "SHITAKE." When he saw it, he bitched that my furniture cost thousands of dollars, and then he banned me from using my computer until I repaired it. He rented a sanding machine, taught me how to repair furniture, and told me how to spell *shiitake*. My dad mostly did it because the machine was so heavy, but I had to stand there and watch.

Everything my dad did annoyed me. When I asked him to copy a music CD into my computer, the software automatically capitalized the first letter of each word in the song titles, so I thought he was an idiot.

I quit violin a month into grade nine, after seven years of lessons. I was being prepped for the Trinity College London Grade Eight Violin exam—the highest level—but I had a mental breakdown in front of my high school music teacher, who convinced my dad to let me quit for a while. I never took another violin lesson. I hated all my instrument teachers. No matter how much I first liked a teacher, eventually I hated them all. I continued voice and guitar sessions for a while longer.

I developed many false memories of music lessons. I remembered my dad *stripped my love* for the piano from me, even though I was the one who asked to quit piano lessons after I started learning guitar because three instruments were too many to practice. I remembered I loved playing jigs and reels but my dad *forced me to play classical* music, even though I performed many jigs and reels in recitals and school concerts, both solo and in duets with my violin teacher and sister, along with classical and popular music. And my dad loved jigs and reels; he brought the family to fiddle fests, where he introduced me to Tania Elizabeth and Liz Doherty and we bought their CDs. But my core lessons followed the Trinity syllabus, and its repertoire is entirely classical.

I remembered my dad used *the violin as a weapon against my mental health*, stripping my love for the violin from me, even though what he said to my sister *and* me was that if we took lessons, then we had to practice. I remembered *nothing was allowed to be a hobby*; if you wanted to learn an instrument, you had to join ensembles, orchestras, and bands. In fact, the school expected all students to be in extracurriculars and you needed extracurriculars in the International Baccalaureate program. My parents had only been trying to help us enjoy our instruments while developing our social skills and making new friends.

Instead of doing homework, I was doing "homesick." My head was full of nostalgia for Europe, for a primary school world where I hardly had homework and I'd been a bully. I traveled back there on Google Earth. I listened to the music I'd listened to there, stared at my old photos, and wanted to learn the language I once mocked. I was so miserable, I couldn't do anything, not even draw. I changed my online name to *Singapore Sucks.*

My sister studied like crazy and got good marks even though she dressed like the grim reaper. Sometimes, when her mood was up, she'd try to be a big sister by explaining to me that because I complained about homework and my classmates didn't, it meant I didn't know how to manage my time. But her mood was mostly down and she released her stress by bitching about school. And that made me dread the four years of school that lay ahead of me.

My Indian friend advised me:

"It's not easy but you don't have any choice: either you work a bit hard and do something you hate and get good marks, or you fail. You are smarter than me. I know it and you do too. Last year I studied and you didn't even look at your books and did way better than me. Either way, Lina, whether you like it or not, you don't really have a choice. If you study just a tiny, tiny bit you might do really well."

She gave me good advice, but I couldn't follow it. There were many things I wanted to do, but when I had the time, I didn't do them. Then I hated myself for not grabbing the time and using it wisely. Tiny things irritated me, especially anything my family did.

I didn't want to go to school. I hated it when people were better than me, so if I couldn't beat them at something I just didn't want to do it at all, even if it was good for me, even school. Just *thinking* about school filled me with turmoil, and then I couldn't concentrate. I'd get nostalgic for being a little kid when life was easy, telling myself that a non-existent utopia was still my home and I was in exile. I was too busy hating Singapore to enjoy it. I would cry twice in an afternoon, unable to do homework, unable even to think. I'd crush the sheet up and throw my book against the wall. I changed my online name to *Fuck Homework*.

My friend issues were all over the place. I tired of friends easily. I didn't want ugly friends because it was hard to talk to someone if I couldn't stand her face. It never occurred to me that others would feel that way about me after I started wearing black and spikes and I started piercing and tattooing my skin and stretching my earlobes.

I couldn't stay with a group of friends for long, and our split-up was always my fault because, after a while, I always saw their bad side. No matter how much I didn't want to leave them in the beginning, after a while I'd flip. I'd make friends, manipulate them one by one, then ruin someone's life by prying my way into her friendships by being deceitful and manipulative. Then I'd move on to another group of friends.

I had no mercy. I liked it when others suffered, because when anyone else felt bad, it increased my self-esteem. I liked it when others had bad hair days. When a woman helped a kid onto the bus and stepped into a puddle, I burst out laughing.

When a woman tripped, skinned her knee, and started bleeding, I laughed my ass off. When a man spilled coffee on himself and it burned him like shit, I cried out with laughter.

I felt the world piling down on me, blowing up in my face, and paralyzing my mind. I'd lock myself in my bathroom and tear at my skin with my fingernails. I still have the scars on my arms where I tore too hard. I felt like I was in more than one place, full of torture, burning, blood, and pain. I hated myself, but I couldn't talk to anyone about how I felt; I could only snap at them. I knew I was sick and out of control but I thought my problems had no explanation.

Now and then, when I was depressed and I closed my eyes, my huge black dog appeared. Run returned to me. I used to think he was a wolf, but he was a feral dog who looked like a wolf. One time when I slashed my face, a symbol appeared: my symbol for Run. Once, when I was tired and closed my eyes, I saw a guy in my mind who was so real, so perfect. He was Run in human form.

I was vain and trying to look evil. I'd walk through the school canteen and get teased for being emo. Teachers would yell at me for wearing too much eyeliner. Someone started a rumor that I kept razors in my pencil case. And when I walked down the street dressed like a goth lolita, people were like, "Holy shit! What the fuck is that?"

I hated being compared. If someone else wanted the same thing as me, I had to get it before she did. As soon as one of my friends did something I did first, it was a big deal for me. If another girl dyed stripes in her hair, I wanted to murder her. I could barely keep a friend. Mostly my friendships lasted for only one year. My friends hated me because I hated a few of them.

My emotions were pouring out of my eyeballs. When a singing rehearsal reminded me of my school in Europe, I nearly collapsed. It was like I died for a second, but nobody helped me because it was all inside my messed up, screwed up brain. I missed Europe, but going back would make things worse. I was so nostalgic I could hardly concentrate in class, and I'd break out crying. Sometimes I left my books at home. We spent hours at school learning, and then they gave us homework! What was the point of going to school, only to get more homework? I felt lost and confused.

I was addicted to Myspace and I met my first boyfriend on the site. We became best friends after talking three times and he told me how long his dick was. He was my best, best friend for about a year, but we never met in person. Then I found out his photos were fake, and I cut him out. When I got depressed I'd go on Myspace. Getting new comments on my photos made me slightly happier. But then my dad would stroll into my room.

He'd be like, "Are you done with homework?"

"I don't have any due tomorrow so for once I'm going to have a relaxing evening."

"You said your French test was shit. So you should study."

And then he'd go on a rant about education and totally ruin my evening. Ever since I was small I thought my dad didn't deserve to have my mom as his wife, and now I thought he didn't deserve to have me as his daughter.

But my mom could also be a fucking annoying cunt:

"Want me to get your guitar for you?"

"No."

"You get it then."

"No."

"Then I'll get it for you."

Sometimes my mom would pounce on me for not doing my homework, in the weird not-making-sense way she talked. Then she'd go out, even though she didn't trust me to keep doing my homework. She used to say she won the lottery when she married my dad. Now she ranted to my sister and me about writing a book about her miserable life and childhood. I mean, I never even saw my mom *reading* a book. When my dad asked my mom to supervise my homework while he was on business trips, which meant she'd need to stay home most evenings, she'd complain:

"Can't I have my own life?"

He'd say, "Not yet."

And she'd get so pissed.

My dad went on a rant about my messaging while I did homework, and he threatened to take away my internet if I didn't improve.

I was like, "I hardly ever go on MSN when I'm doing homework!"

"Then why should it matter if the internet is turned off during homework hours?"

"You don't understand, do you? I hate my school! I hate Singapore! I get to do things I love on the internet! How the fuck do you expect me to be happy and to have my effort grades go up if you take that away?"

I felt like fucking slapping the shit out of him. I hated him so much because he was in control and had the power to take away everything I loved. He was just encouraging my sister and me to do well at school because it was in *our* best interest, not his, but I couldn't see that and so I thought my parents were shit parents.

My emotions were blowing up: the stress of school, the pressure I felt to be more like my sister, my friend problems, the feeling that I still had homework to do, and the fact that I had to go back to the hell called school. I was never happy with anything and I couldn't do anything about it. I wanted someone to understand me and love me.

From A- in grade seven and B+ in grade eight, my first-half average dropped to B- in grade nine. I used to have so many A's. Now I had none, and I didn't care. My life was falling apart.

I didn't think my life would ever get better, and I thought it was all my fault. But it *wasn't* "all my fault." In my teens, I blamed myself. Ten years later, I blamed everyone *except* myself. It would take me another ten years to see things in a better way and to stop blaming anyone. I shouldn't have suffered so much for so long, but my disorder made me unable to tell my caregivers how I felt. My disorder protected itself, with a mind of its own, like a selfish gene.

Mental Collapse

MY MOM YELLED AT ME for not doing homework. My body ached. I couldn't stand anything anymore. I sat in my bathroom, crying. I cut myself with a knife for the first time, just deep enough to see my blood. I enjoyed watching my blood come out of my leg. It made me feel slightly happier. I loved it when my bodily fluids ran down my skin—not piss or sweat, but tears and blood.

My first self-cutting was six months after my sister first cut herself. I cut myself a few times over the next few months, then I went back to scratching with my fingernails. Death seemed sweet because after you die, there's nothing. I felt like killing myself, but I would never kill myself without saying goodbye. I wanted to die, but first I wanted to write a book, and my ideas and characters were so great that I wasn't about to kill myself first.

Studying depressed me, so I never studied. Because I never studied, I was screwed in every subject besides art and music—and I still had four years to go! I was surviving by never getting anything done. To cheer me up, my dad arranged for me to visit Europe, to stay with his colleague's family over Christmas. I was happy for a while and I stopped cutting myself, but I still didn't do my homework. I knew that even if I didn't do my homework, my dad would let me go anyway.

I became jealous of Avril Lavigne. She got famous, signed a contract, and then dropped out. I made a plan: start a band, drop out of school, and then get famous. School was hard, boring, and a waste of time. I didn't want to go to college. I hated how I never had enough time to write music or draw, but that was *because of me*. I hated how I got low grades, but that was *because of me*. I hated cleaning my room and running out of ice cream. Everything I hated, I hated *because of me*. Mental illness had taken over my life. My disorder was me.

My eye doctor said that special contact lenses might help my amblyopic eye, so my dad bought them right away. I never wore them. My dad supported me with stuff like contact lenses and teeth braces, but not with dropping out. Because he didn't love me the way I wanted to be loved, I thought he didn't love me at all.

Even though I hated how my friendships never lasted, I'd wanted to hurt my friends ever since I was small. It gave me pleasure to hurt them. Sometimes I warned potential friends to *expect* me to hurt them. Half of me loved hurting people; the other half hated it. Half of me was power hungry and evil; the other half was caring and nice. The nice half was harder to see. Instead of real friends, I started collecting "friends" on Facebook by the hundreds, then by the thousands.

I was an over-the-top emo scene kid with no control over my mind. My mind would go blank and I'd stare at the page when I had to read an English short story. Even with things I liked, like art and guitar, I'd blank out. How I could be so stupid when I was intelligent? I felt like emailing my teachers, but what was I supposed to say? I drafted this message to my French teacher:

"Hello, I'm writing about the homework. At home I tried doing it, but I didn't understand any of it. I listened during class when you explained everything, but I completely forgot everything. I tried reading the sheet multiple times but I still didn't understand. I am sorry for the inconvenience, I just thought I would let you know in advance that I couldn't do the homework."

I never sent it. I needed a psychiatrist to figure out what was wrong with me, like my homeroom teacher suggested seven months ago. I expected my friends to give me the solutions to my problems. But most were too happy with their own lives to care about mine. Or their lives were even worse than mine, so they thought my problems were nothing.

My Indian friend gave me more advice:

"Go offline. Clear your desk and concentrate. Listen to me: do it! Make space, move the damn books, clean your room, and shut your computer off. Throw it away. This is your problem. Do what I'm saying, and just concentrate. Stop thinking about other things. I'm just trying to get rid of your distractions. Go over your notes. Show initiative. Ask the teacher tomorrow. Email her now; she'll be like, 'Yeah, she's trying.' Work hard. You don't suck; stop saying that! I know, as your friend, that you are not stupid. And believe me, I'm not just saying that to make you feel better. You're *not* stupid. You may not be great at all subjects, but everyone is like that. Don't be so hard on yourself. You love Europe and your parents are letting you go—you should be fucking thankful—my parents would never do that."

I wanted to follow her advice, but I couldn't. And whenever I asked my mom for solutions, she'd deny my problems, scold me for complaining, then rattle off *her* problems and rant about writing her miserable life book. I told my sister that if our mom died, the only reason I'd miss her is that I'd be stuck living with my dad.

I stopped thinking my problems were because of me and doubled down on blaming my parents: it was *their* fault that I was the fucked-up girl my fucked-up parents raised me to be. But they controlled my life. I couldn't have fun because as soon as I did something I wanted to do, they would take away my computer, and my computer was my doorway to everything I loved.

I was never happy with anything, even going to Europe. I was going crazy. I felt like dying; living was pointless. I didn't matter to anyone. I could never make myself pretty enough. I hated all the songs I wrote. I felt like burning down the school and going back in time and blowing up the asshole who created homework. It seemed to me that everyone else knew what they wanted from their lives and I didn't know anything. I wanted a gun so I could pull the trigger. I knew I wouldn't die. I wasn't important enough even to die.

When I was depressed I drew people being happy, which made me even more depressed. I'd start crying, and Run, the big black dog, would come to me through my own dog. My real dog would wake up and come to me. He'd put his head on my arm, whimper, and stare at me. I knew he was Run. We'd hug and he'd lie down next to me, his tail wrapped around my foot, until my problem was solved.

There were three voices now: Run, Seek, and Hide. Seek was a small pack of at least three white wolves, but I refer to her as one wolf. She was all about me being nice to others and how I treated other people. She told me how much I needed my friends. After Seek came Hide, the gray wolf. He was the evil one, the most complicated; the opposite of Seek. There are many different types of evil and deadly sins, like vanity, so Hide was a huge pack of wolves. He was always fighting with Seek.

He was very much a part of me. And, like me, he was vain. Sometimes one would be victorious, but one little thing and my mood could flip. I didn't choose how they looked or what their names were. They just *were*.

I saw every bad part of me as the gray wolf, Hide, and every good part of me as the white wolf, Seek. Hide and Seek were always fighting, tearing each other to shreds. When I was ruining the lives of people who pissed me off, Seek would try to help me stop. But Hide would get pissed, come and take me, and help me release my inner bitch. Seek and Hide were my moods, and they fought with each other constantly, which is why I was so emotionally unstable. I had limited control over myself, but I began to gain a bit of control once I started visualizing my voices. Eventually I reached a point where I could control how the wolves acted.

MY TRIP TO EUROPE WAS AWESOME but I came back even more depressed and confused. My sister said that while I was in Europe she got along fine with my parents and she was happy, and then when I returned under my storm clouds of doom and gloom and started criticizing our parents, I depressed her. My best friend was an imaginary dog and my life revolved around adding friends on Myspace, two thousand so far. My dad called me his dark angel.

I was having mood swings, breaking down, and hurting myself. I knew I was deteriorating. I'd lose concentration when people spoke to me because my thoughts would spiral out of control. I wore my hair in front of my face and spent hours in front of the mirror doing makeup and hair to show the world my pain. I thought about death and killing people. My family thought I was being a bitch because of the influence of the people I talked to online, but I knew something was wrong with me and I wanted to know what it was. I didn't ask my parents to take me to a psychiatrist because I thought my dad would think it was another excuse for doing badly in school.

So I took internet quizzes, which said I had major depressive disorder, anger management problems, and attention deficit disorder. I knew it wasn't attention deficit disorder, because if I had that I could still have concentrated on the subjects I liked, like history. I was convinced my parents thought I *wanted* to be emo, *wanted* to fail school, and *wanted* to be angry all the time. Nobody in my family realized that I wanted them *to understand me*, but that's because I didn't want them to know. No one understood that my grades and clothing were acute symptoms of a chronic problem.

I wanted to drink my mom's laxatives that she took to stay skinny. I nearly stabbed my stomach. I thought of myself as short, fat, ugly, and unphotogenic. I thought I had bad breath, yellow teeth, a fat chin, square face, flat nose, uneven eyes, and too much body hair. I hated my hands, fingers, feet, legs, arms, breasts, stomach, hips, ribs, neck, shoulders, lips, eyebrows, and mustache. I'd wanted body modifications for years because I'd never been happy with my disgusting, ugly naked body, so I planned to get thirty piercings on my ears, belly button, lips, septum, eyebrows, hip, tongue, and back.

When I look at my old pictures today, I see I was too hard on myself. I wasn't ugly! The thing is, my mom was chubby when she was young and she got bullied for it, and she didn't want us to have to experience that. So she monitored what my sister and I ate to protect us from becoming fat, and that is how she destroyed our body confidence. My immersion into the distorted, filtered world of social media made my negative feelings about myself worse.

I dreamed of being famous. I told all my friends I wanted to be famous. I would *kill* myself if I didn't become famous. Because many celebrities had dropped out, I seriously considered dropping out of school, as if dropping out would make me famous. I put off dropping out because I didn't want to lose my friends, computer, cellphone, and music player. My friends told me I would regret dropping out because I would never get rich without an education. They wanted to be famous for being rich, but I wanted to be rich for being famous.

When I was feeling miserable I'd draw pictures of Run guarding the souls of dead girls. When I tried to drown myself and was out of breath and my mind was blank, Run flashed through my mind and scared me so much I shot out of the water. When I tried to suffocate myself and was almost dead, Run flashed through my mind and scared me so much that I took a huge breath and didn't die.

Whenever I locked myself in the bathroom and dug my fingernails into my body, Run came to me and kept me company. Before, he couldn't come to me because he was a part of me. But as soon as I opened my body with my nails, he could escape from me. Instead of just flashing through my mind, he could be with me. After that, when I needed Run, I'd lock myself in the bathroom and scratch myself until he arrived. Then I'd stop, and he'd make it all better.

Run began possessing my dog after I started cutting myself. The first time I was bleeding, my dog shoved open the bathroom door and came to me even though the door was locked. He lay down next to me and curled himself around me like Run used to do, but this time, Run used my dog as a solid form so I could touch him. The second time, when I argued with a friend and became suicidal, my dog jumped up from sleeping, lay down at my feet, and curled his tail around them. Soon everything with my friend was perfect. The third time, when I felt lost and alone and I was crying, my dog was lying on the bed beside me. I had a picture of Run beside my bed, and I said, "I miss Run" to my dog. My dog looked at the picture. Then he moved closer, snuggled in, and curled his tail around my hand.

My dog was my connection between my inner turmoil and the netherworld; he knew when I was experiencing too much, and he would come to me and stay with me until it was over. He was the only one who could comfort me when Hide and Seek fought. Whenever things got too tough and my inner war overwhelmed me, I'd disappear into him, run through the forest, and escape. Even at the time, I remember feeling crazy envisioning these possessions.

For my school art project I drew a dramatic mandala poster of depression and emotional misery. Through my artwork I was screaming for help, but no one could see what it meant. Even though I wanted help, I also didn't want anyone to know I wanted help. So when I had to stand up in class and talk about my mandala, I hardly told them anything. My dad had it framed. He was so naïve.

I cheated in French, but at least I memorized some words while cheating. My best sentence in French was, *"Jai voudrais une cigarette,"* and even that was wrong. I started writing a fantasy novel instead of doing homework. I'd been thinking about the story and characters for about a year, and I'd invented a secret alphabet for it. Whenever I worked on it, it looked like I was doing my homework.

My sister and I would hate each other, then get along, then hate each other again. When she was depressed she'd put me down, and we'd call each other a bitch. She was going in and out of depression, but she studied for hours every night because she knew it was something she had to do, and, unlike me, it was something that she *could* do despite her emotional state. But she *complained* about it, like, *all* the time. When she played the piano I felt like screaming at her.

When I was depressed I'd yell at my mom and my friends for no reason. I got so pissed at school that I destroyed a metronome in the music room. I nearly trashed my bedroom when a piece of paper fell on the floor; just a piece of paper. I hated my dad for favoring my sister, expecting too much from me, and hating everything I did. My dad went away on more business trips, which helped me to feel a bit less depressed. My mom didn't come home until eight most evenings, and when she was home she didn't supervise my homework.

I started smoking. It soothed my ego because in Singapore smoking was even more restricted than drinking and I risked huge fines. On Facebook my mom saw pictures of me smoking and was pissed that I didn't tell her about it. She wasn't pissed about my actual *smoking*, only my not *telling* her about it.

The voices in my head made things so hard. I'd hear people saying my name when I got tired, and my nightmares came back. I recorded this nightmare in my journal:

"It was snowing. The town was deserted and I was trying to escape from something. There were a few people with me and we were standing by a bus stop.

This guy was like, 'You have to escape from under the train tracks!'

No trains were going, so he jumped between the tracks

and I followed him. There was water underneath them and I had to swim to the other side to escape. Then the guy got out. Trains started to go over the tracks and I couldn't find an exit, so I would either drown or get run over.

Suddenly I was in a huge building with kids from my grade and a guy was trying to kill us. We needed to escape, so we had to find the keys. My friend read this riddle and she was like, 'I know where the key is!' and she found it. She tried unlocking the door but it wouldn't work and the killer guy was coming.

This girl was like, 'Oh my God, give me the gun!'

I was like, 'We don't have a gun!'

So we ran away. I found this door leading underground and it was full of pipes and all weird. We ran in there. It turned into a car park where we all met up and I became the leader. I was like, 'OK! We're fifty stories off the ground in a building with a mass murderer trying to kill us!'

Everyone panicked. I found an elevator with strippers standing inside it and I was like, 'OK, people, get in!' I clicked to go to the first floor and then the elevator went down two stories and the doors opened.

Two girls were going to get out, and I was like, 'No! It's not the first floor! Don't get out!'

And then they got out and they were like, 'It *is* the first floor!' and I could see the open ground. I was like, 'Everyone get out!' And then we died."

My whole dream was about paranoia, murder, and escape.

I started planning what to do when I got out of school by graduating or dropping out. I ruled out careers that required education. I wanted to drop out and become a tattoo artist or piercer, perform my songs in bars, or work in a fetish store selling corsets to fat women. But if I said that to my parents, they'd freak out. Half the reason I *didn't* care about school, started smoking, craved piercings and tattoos, and wanted to drop out and get famous was that my parents and sister *did* care about school, and I naturally wanted to do things that people didn't want me to do.

I felt ugly and fat and disgusting, but then I went straight to McDonald's, ate a cheeseburger in their bathroom, and I cried—in a public bathroom! I went home and yelled at my dog. I yelled at a woman who telephoned to ask for my mom. I lost control and trashed half of my room and broke my table mirror. When I saw my reflection in my bathroom mirror, I flipped. I threw my glass at the mirror, and there was blood and glass everywhere.

I felt like nothing would ever go right for me. I was the bad child and my sister was the dream child. My parents were going to kill me because of my grades. I felt like I wanted to die because there's no point to life: you're born, you go to school, you go to college, you get a job. By the time you're ready to retire and enjoy life, you're old and you die.

My dad complained that my mom and I didn't walk the dog with him anymore. Only my sister still did, every weekend. One night I surprised him by walking the dog with him. On the walk I told him I wanted to drop out to be a tattoo artist, piercer, hairstylist, or makeup artist, and so I didn't need school. He told me not to drop out and to keep those jobs in mind for side jobs while I went to college.

A few days later he downloaded a survey that showed that tattooists earned less than hairstylists, waitresses, truck drivers, and stable boys. He told me I would need a higher salary than these jobs if I wanted to maintain my standard of living and live independently, but I just thought he was putting me down.

I complained to my mom that his "support" for my future only made me want more piercings. My mom and I told my dad, together, that he had to support my career choice, not his. I wanted to become a really good tattoo artist, earn loads of money, become a millionaire, and spit in his face and be like, "Fuck you, Daddy!"

While my parents watched TV with my beautiful, all knowing, perfect sister, I wanted to kill myself. It gave me comfort to go through my stuff and figure out which of my things were poisonous. I sorted out my poisons and the ways they could kill me. Every time I told my mom I was miserable, she ranted on about how nobody asked *her* how *she* felt about her horrible and tragic life.

I thought about becoming a prostitute, but not an ordinary prostitute: I'd charge customers $300, offer them wine laced with sleeping pills, and run away with their money. I'd steal their transit cards because I could use them in McDonald's. I'd get rich and disappear to London with millions of pounds and buy Camden Market so I could wear whatever I wanted.

The only booster I had left in the school was my wonderful music teacher:

"I will cheer you up! You have to let it ride over you. You have three more years to survive. Have you told your dad that all he cares about is school? Ask him to take you out for dinner, have some sweet chatty stuff, and tell him in a caring way that you love him. Then say, 'Dad, we need to get through this school thing in a healthy way. I want to do well, not just for you and Mum but for myself. You need to give me encouragement along the way. But at the moment I am prone to rebel against you, which I really do not want to do.' Lina, do what I suggest. Develop the self-confidence to let whatever he says wash off you. Don't change for him; change for yourself. It isn't easy being a parent. Parents only have experience with their own kids, so they don't get the full picture like teachers do. We deal with students as part of our job. Maybe you can't change your parents' behavior, but they will be your parents for life.

Don't be like me and skive school, get to the mailbox in time to tear up letters from school, and fail everything even though you were top of the school until grade nine. I spent the next four years feeling sorry for my miserable teenage years and my shitty parents and used this excuse for failing everything. I ran away to escape my family, went from one punk party to another, got pregnant, and wasted a lot of time. It took me years to stop blaming my parents for everything. Your life is in *your* hands! *Embrace your parents*. Listen to them. Practice mindfulness: listen to your mind's voices, recognize the negative ones, and then try to dismiss them. Mindfulness will give you insight into what is really bothering you."

I wasn't able to follow any of her advice because the more she talked, the more she sounded like my parents. She came closest to understanding me, but she thought I could turn my life around on my own; even my music teacher couldn't see how fundamental my problem was. Later, I left as much spit on some gum as I could, stuck it on the back of the doorknob in her music department, then watched her students touching the gum and being like, "Argh!"

My dad kept saying I was smart, only making no effort, so he made me study an hour of maths every day until the exam so I wouldn't turn into a hobo. I concluded his purpose in life was to make me a miserable, whining bitch. I decided that no matter how much maths my dad made me study, that *even if I understood it*, I was going to fail the exam on purpose, to spite him. I thought of asking him for a shrink just so I could ask her to tell him to fuck off.

My problems were all inside me; nothing in my environment had changed. I started searching the internet for job offers so I could drop out, but they were all serious job offers; jobs in Africa, no shit. I missed being young and innocent and happy, even though I was never innocent and happy; I was always disturbed. Sometimes I blamed my parents for screwing me up. Other times I blamed the voices in my head because my mood swings came from them.

There was a fourth voice now, Let, a bear. I wanted to be Let. She was purple, turquoise, brown, and white, the colors of my dreamcatcher. She wasn't really a voice, but my sixth sense. Let could stop the wolves from fighting. She could control them. Sometimes she would tell the other voices to shut up. She controlled my dreams. If my day was miserable, then I'd get a good dream. If I spent the whole day being mean to people, then I'd get a bad dream that punished me for it.

I was fourteen and my body looked normal, but I still had never had a period. My dad took me to the family doctor for a checkup. When she asked me questions, alone, about school and family, I started crying, so she referred me to a gynecologist for my amenorrhea and to a psychologist for my unhappiness. The gynecologist scanned and tested me. My hormones were normal, except they never cycled, as if I were in menopause. My thyroid was normal. Twice a year she retested me and gave me hormones to induce a period to preserve my uterus. No one has ever found the reason I don't have natural periods.

I wanted to sleep in the snow and stare at the night sky, watching the snow fall. So I started running my air conditioner on maximum and wearing winter clothes in my bedroom. After a few days water started pouring down from my ceiling and damaging the walls. Repairmen came and hacked out chunks of ice. I thought it was funny, but my dad was pissed at the expense. Behavior like this caused my family so much distress and made me look irresponsible.

I was sending and receiving a thousand messages a day. To help me focus on my homework, my dad programmed the router to turn off my internet during study hours, but that didn't work because my sister-buddy let me use her internet when he wasn't home. I would soon be away on a tall ship cruise in Australia, and I'd promised my dad I would study before and after the trip so that he'd approve it. But I still didn't study, and I hated him even more for cutting off my internet in the evening. I teased him about failing:

"What would you do if I failed?"

"You won't fail."

"What if I do?"

"You won't."

"But what if I do?"

"You won't!"

"Just imagine I fail the exam!"

"You *won't!*"

I couldn't wait to fail the maths exam, on purpose.

Everything I wanted was expensive, like branded eyeliner and Häagen-Dazs. To get more money than my allowance, I stole from my mom. The principal ordered me to stop wearing so much eyeliner to school. He was like, "Lina, are you a *working girl*?"

My dad kept nagging me to study for the upcoming exams, and now even my mom couldn't stop talking about them. They were just making it worse for themselves because I was never going to give them what they wanted. They were only making my life miserable. I couldn't get through a day without crying.

I shared my misery with my Indian friend:

"The fucking school counselor sent my dad a fucking studying timetable so my dad is even more fucking careless about my fucking mental state and how he's fucking ruining my life. I can't get through a day without crying because of him. He can't tell that I'm a fucking heap of lost and confused shit because of him. I need to fight back. And the school counselor made me a fucking study plan, and every hour is fucking planned out. 8: maths. 9: English. 10: history. 11: music practice. 12: lunch. 1: biology. 2: French. 3: fitness (what the fuck?). 4: friends. 5: maths. 6: dinner. 7: English. 8: computer, MSN. 9: reading. Let's kill our parents. I'm hoping to fail everything. Even music, I'm going to fail."

She replied:

"Lina, I hate this shit as much as you. I feel bad for you, but you are better than you think. I'm just saying that when you study properly, it helps, for everyone. Everyone hates studying. I'm sure if you study for every subject you'll do really well and your parents will not say anything ever again. Study this week and think of your Australia trip as your reward."

Her advice went in one ear and out the other. I thought I was this bad because the whole world wanted me to kill myself. I felt lost and confused. I broke down before the first psychologist appointment, and I cut myself again.

The first psychologist session was together with my parents. I wrote "Fuck you" and "I hate you" and "Fucking die" all over my legs and wore pants to hide it. I went to see her privately a dozen times. I went with my sister once, my parents went to see her once, and we went as a family once. Her specialty was counseling troubled teens, but I didn't like her so I never told her about my nightmares, depression, mood swings, and voices.

My Mexican friend and I walked into Häagen-Dazs looking like trashy goths and bought vanilla ice cream. We poured chocolate sauce on it and melted it with our cigarette lighters. We added condiments and water and shouted, "Oh my God—penis!" We kept on giggling and changing tables. We left a note for the waitress: "Thanks, bitch. We love ya." My Mexican friend told me she had started seeing a psychiatrist and was taking Prozac.

My tall ship cruise was the best trip I have ever been on. I missed it so much that I didn't want my sea legs ever to go away. I climbed a seven-story mast, saw dolphins, and did freezing night watches. I threw up over the bow on my first night watch, like, twenty times. I threw up all over the deck, then I ran to the side and kept throwing up, even out of my nose. I had wanted to get a rose tattoo under my underwear, but now I wanted to get a tall ship tattoo. I was the happiest I'd ever been!

Meanwhile my sister was so stressed out by her grade eleven exams that she slid back into depression. One night she cried so loudly while she was cutting herself that she woke up my mom, but my mom couldn't stop her because my sister locked herself in her bathroom all night.

When I returned from the cruise, I felt alone. I locked myself in my room and didn't come out all night. I lay on my bed, singing to myself and crying. My parents had cleaned and organized my room while I was away, and I was furious at them. I couldn't wait to move away from my whole family.

The next morning, Saturday, I was in my bedroom crying when my dad came in.

"Lina, shall we do a maths paper now? Your exam is in three days."

"I just got back from Leeuwin! I miss the ship so much. Do I have to study?"

"Of course. You didn't study at all on the ship."

"I'm *not* going to study right now."

Even though I'd promised to study before and after the trip because it was in the middle of study leave, there was no way I could touch a schoolbook now. So I went to the kitchen and started making a pie from scratch, to stall for time. My dad came in and told me to make the pie after maths, but I said no and he left me alone. My sister came in and we bitched about him for an hour.

My dad came back when the pie was baking and asked me to do maths. He said he was sure that just a few hours of maths practice would be enough for me to pass. He tried to encourage me by talking about the joy of knowledge and the value of a career needing an education. I thought he was a retard who thought he knew everything, so that got him nowhere. Finally he tried to hold me to the studying promise I'd made before going on the trip.

I was like, "I'm *not* doing maths. You made me study the whole first week of the holiday because you said I didn't have to study this week. I have two days before school starts and I die. I am *not* doing fucking maths!"

"You have to do some maths. I'm not going to let you go to bed until you do maths."

"Maths isn't the only thing in the world!"

My sister stood up. "All you care about is fucking maths!"

"You need maths to get through life. I'm doing this for you because I love you."

"You *never* support me! I want to be a tattoo artist, and you printed a hundred-page piece of shit to prove that being a tattoo artist would kill me!"

My sister shouted, "Any other father would be better than you! You're the worst father ever!"

"It hurts me to hear you saying these things, but you need to do some maths."

My sister and I flipped. We screamed in his face so loudly that the neighbors could hear us. "*We hate you!*"

My dad stayed calm, but then, when we started to walk away, he grabbed my arm to shove me into the kitchen chair to do maths. "You must!" he shouted. He looked like he was about to kill me.

I started crying, so my mom got up from watching TV and told him to leave us alone. My sister and I ran from the kitchen and locked ourselves in her bedroom. I wanted to go back for the pie, but I was afraid of running into my dad and being told to study.

I decided to fail everything to spit in his face. I decided to write nonsense answers on my maths exam and then write "Thank you, Daddy. This is for you!" on the last page. My sister was behind me all the way. We packed to run away, but I fell asleep while my parents were still up and my sister was cutting her wrists and taping blood-spattered nightmare sketches on her wall.

In the morning the house was quiet. My dad was cheerful, as if we could forgive him overnight. I wanted my mom to divorce my dad, but I worried that if she divorced him we'd be poor and computer-less. For my 3,000 Myspace friends I changed my banner to *Lina Is Not Studying For Exams*. My dad left us alone.

My sister and I talked about everything. We talked about how we sometimes broke down and cried for hours without any idea why we were crying. We talked about our self-harming. We talked about how I'd tried to have a good relationship with her, but I always thought she put me down. We talked about how we couldn't stand people who were even slightly like our dad and how we couldn't get along with studious people because they reminded us of him. We talked about how headstrong he was about studying, and how that proved he valued grades more than our happiness.

We wished our dad would die.

We decided we'd had enough of school and we needed a break from it, even for a few hours. We wouldn't have cared if we were hungry on the streets for a week. We might get thinner; *that* would make us happy. We were bonding, but not in a healthy way.

MY DAD LEFT FOR A BUSINESS TRIP that Monday morning. My sister and I left the apartment in our school uniforms, hid in the swimming pool bathrooms until our school bus came and went, changed out of our uniforms, left our school bags there, and ran away.

We bummed around malls and spent the day eating ice cream and getting piercings. When my mom, freaking out, called my dad at the airport, he told her to keep calm and not to worry, because we would turn up. He wasn't always so uncaring, but he didn't realize that it was shit to our teenage self-esteem when he was.

The secretary, principal, and teachers searched for us. The school counselor asked our friends about our whereabouts, so they all discovered we were skiving. They were worried, and my sister's friend thought she'd committed suicide.

My mom sent us frantic texts like, "Don't run away! I can't live without you!"

We didn't return any calls, except one from my mom later in the day, begging us to come home.

We came home because my mom was going crazy. She was bawling, mental, and really scary to look at. We hugged for ages. We were the ones running away, but *we* had to comfort *her!* She blamed herself. My sister and I blamed our dad. We felt bad about putting our mom through all that worry just because we were rebellious teenagers, especially while he was away. She promised he would leave us alone because she wasn't going to support our dad anymore. She asked us whether she should stay home to give us more attention, or live her own life and give us more space, which would mean eating leftovers. We told her to have a life.

My mom took away my sister's knives.

After that, it was like we lost a mother and gained a sister with credit cards. She ordered me a $500 corset just for asking. She was forty-two and didn't enjoy her life as a teenager, so she was doing it now.

Our mom shifted responsibility for being grown-up to my dad, who became like a single father of three teenage girls who ignored him.

BEING AWAKE WAS HORRIBLE. Just being alone freaked me out, even with my dog. But even when I was happy, the things that made me sad were always there, and eventually they took over again so I could never escape my misery. My dreams were getting worse. My mind wandered to bad things and horrible places while I slept, so I needed someone to sleep nearby or watch over me when I fell asleep.

I wanted to fall asleep and never wake up; not to die, but for Let to take over my mind and body. Without my reflection I felt lost, but my reflection made me miserable. My reflection was Hide. Hide scolded me a lot. He took over my body, and although it was me in the mirror, it was the Hide in me. I wanted to forget about school and forget about my dad. All I wanted was to draw and write stories. Then I could die.

My dad returned two weeks after my breakdown, and we went to the psychologist as a family. It was supposed to be the four of them supporting me, but my sister supported me by turning against our parents and my mom supported my sister and me by turning against my dad. My mom sat down next to my sister and me on one sofa, my dad sat on another sofa, and the psychologist sat on a chair.

The psychologist started the session:

"I've spoken to each of you separately, and now we get to speak together. I want to establish what you want to get out of this today."

My dad leaned forward. "I love my children more than anything else in the world. That's why I'm doing my best to help them set themselves up for the years ahead. That means giving them choices, opportunities, a good income, everything they need to be happy and stress-free as *adults*. The catch is that that is not always what you need to be happy and stress-free as *teenagers*. So there's a gap. As they become adults the gap will disappear, but right now it's causing problems. Help us deal with the gap so we can get the happiness, the connection, and the love back again."

"I just want the children to tell us what they really wanted," said my mom, leaning back, her arms crossed.

"We want space and to be left alone and stuff," I said. "Dad isn't helping with the whole control freak thing."

"Not only the computer," said my mom, meaning the internet. "They know the computer."

My sister scowled. "After we argue with him, everything is the same as it was before. Dad acts like nothing happened. That's *not* the right way to go about it!"

"What's the effect on you?" the psychologist asked.

My sister said, "It *pisses* me off!"

"What does it do for your sense of connection?"

"Makes it worse," I said.

"How do you understand how you got to this place?"

"I'm stuck in the middle," my sister said. "Too much effort is required. It was all gradually building up until I *cut* myself, but you wouldn't *get* that." Then she started crying.

The psychologist handed my sister a tissue from the box on her desk, and I realized the room was padded and plush to muffle crying.

"It's getting worse because we're fighting back now," I said.

"Lina changed after we moved to Singapore," said my mom. "I don't see why—as a mother, right?—Lina does some of the things she does that she continues. It's only what I do is what I want her to do, and that's what I want her to do, as a mom."

Baffled by my mom's English, the psychologist asked, "What is it you hope for, as a mom?"

"Being loved and try to give them what they want—at least we can afford, right? But, at the same time, trying to tell them what is life, actually. I'm torn between the living in the house and my children, sometimes in the middle now. They're big and I cannot do anything anyway. I wish I can do something as a parent, as a mom, as a dad, whatever you call it. It's too late now, but I'm thinking, ah well, might as well do something, or else too late."

"You are very different from one another. How have you found a way to work together in your uniqueness?"

"They're still young going through that, like you cannot really, so just leave them alone. He will come home and be in his study in front of his computer. This is the only time I can have my time, like, oh my God, I need to have *stuff*. You're the one earning money, so I might as well listen and then I will give my suggestion. He's the one with money and we live like this because of him and he's working hard for it, so *we* have to understand *him*. We're fighting behind my back. I really wanted to stay in America or Europe, but because of his work we have to go, and my problem is my passport. We're dependent. The lifestyle really ruined—everything! It's the *moving*. And we cannot say, 'Oh please, can I just stay in Europe because of my children are happy here and teenager?' That's what I kept on telling him: *Just leave me here and the kids!*"

My sister said, "Actually, the lifestyle is good because we get to see the world. It's annoying, though."

"I wanted it to be in one place, but because of his job, every time we move, it's hard. I explained to them that I tried and *I argued with Daddy* and *you heard Daddy and me fighting*. Every time we moved, I tried to argue to ask your company where you're working for twenty years, but we cannot do anything. That's why they're doing this: because I told them I missed a lot of stuff growing up when I was a teenager, lack of money and everything. So if we can afford it, I wanted them to have everything, like free as a teenager. But they're overdoing it!"

"How did the girls come to be so different?"

"Because he and I are so different. I became flexible because we had tight control growing up. And for him, being a westerner, very loose. I wanted it not too tight, not too loose. I don't know what happened, actually."

"Do you think the situation happened because of your influence?"

"My God! If it is *my* influence, I will be conservative and not let the kids do this."

My sister said, "There is a point when children distance themselves from their parents. But the older we get, the more they treat us like little kids."

The psychologist asked, "If you parents could respond to your daughters' frustration, what would you ask of them?"

My dad replied, "I'd like to get our communication back. I'd like them to be happier."

"Do you want us to be happy for *ourselves* or happy for *you*?" said my sister.

"Happy for yourselves."

"*Happy* seems to mean 'study your whole life and be miserable as *shit*, so after you graduate, you'll be able to do a sum that only math teachers can do, and you'll thank me.' That's not happy for *me*, that's happy for *you* because that's what *you* want to see. I have a basic idea of what I'm doing so I'm working toward that, but that's not what you want."

"I want you to be happy for the rest of your life. That's the *only* thing I want."

"But forcing us to study winds up with us screaming at you and running away!"

"That is why we are here with a psychologist, to get help for all of us. It's not a competition."

"It's a competition when Lina and I stay up late, doing everything you don't want us to do. And there's the *cutting*, to show you what we mean."

"I've been away the last two weeks, and when I returned you weren't any happier. To be happy we have to talk and to understand each other."

"That is not going to work when you pretend that nothing happened after we've talked. 'Good morning' in the morning, small talk at dinner."

"That's why I liked to go for walks once or twice a week."

"Dog walks that only *I* went on because Lina hated you. I was trying to be the buffer zone—the medium for you and Lina to talk because she wasn't talking to you directly."

The psychologist said, "You sound like you've got some ideas about what your dad could do differently."

"He's like, 'If you don't go to college, then you'll have a miserable life.' We're like, '*Open your eyes* because that's not how life works anymore.' And my mom's been talking to my friends' parents. They know jack shit, and yet she's getting all these ideas from them."

My mom said, "I kept telling him because he listens to them whatever they wanted. I cannot say anything. Like, whatever they wanted, now just listen, and then this is now but before. They wanted, don't complain about money. He always complains about money."

"I try to pay for everything, so I don't have to use your money," said my sister, "because I don't want to rely on either of you."

"Yeah, but what my point is, like, it's just that every time we spend, like, especially if it is more than gift amount, I will do it for them. For example, we say for Lina, but I will do a sermon first: *naman*, this is a big amount! I am not looking, but then you know, there's always try for her to understand that I will do anything for you. I will give it to you, but please consider one for your dad earning the money, because you know, like, money is not that easy to get. But still, I'm not working, so I always make sure they know I will give it, but—remember Daddy."

"How does that help your children bridge the gap?"

"By giving them this sermon about money and study and future. He didn't know that he's a bad guy between these two. The children also know the reason why they don't want to talk to me anymore. It's because they hear the same thing."

My dad said, "Maybe we should increase their allowance and then say, 'What you don't spend, you can save.'"

"Would that work? Your dad saying this amount is what you are responsible for?"

I said, "I know people who get a small allowance and I also know people who get five hundred. Giving me more money but *still expecting me to do maths* wouldn't make it better."

"If you were getting average grades, would you talk about maths?"

My sister said, "The problem is that I'm getting A's and Bs while she's getting Cs, so it's assumed that she's not studying as much."

"The more you talk about the International Baccalaureate, the more I want to fail."

"Lina, what do you think you need to do to get your dad off your back?"

"That's only going to happen if my grades go up, and that's *not* going to happen!"

My dad said, "The principal said your problem is your *effort*, not your grades."

"Your dad expresses a lot of care. How can he show you better that he cares?"

My sister said sarcastically, "What do you mean by 'care?'"

"Is the best way to give care to step away from your space?"

"Yes. When you reach a certain age, you can't say everything to your parents. I don't know if that was the right answer."

"Take what your dad said at face value: he has concern for your happiness. How can you let him know what will make you happy?"

I said, "He wanted me to go on a dog walk, and for once I was like, 'OK, I'll go and let him know how I feel.' I told him about my friends on the internet and how one of them is going to get a tattoo without telling her mom. Everything I said, he put me down."

"I didn't realize I was doing that."

The psychologist said, "Let's wrap this up. How you deal with the internet is up to you."

"It's on all the time except Monday to Thursday evenings, study time," my dad said. "There was a note from the teacher that Lina didn't hand in a big assignment this Monday. I'll turn the internet on all the time as soon I see more effort."

"If you want my effort to get *higher*, it will probably get *lower*. Restricting the internet won't help."

My sister said, "Even my mom's telling him not to restrict the internet."

My mom said, "Like I wanted, there's no point in removing it now. They're in a level thing and they have this fashion where there's internet and everything. You have to do that when they were little, not now that they're teenagers where they're into it. That's why I told your daddy that, you know, like, if he's in the situation from the very beginning then it works for you to control it now. It's no point of, you know, the internet now."

My exasperated dad cried, "Then what *will* help?"

"Nothing!" I shouted back. "When I told my friends I'm seeing a psychologist, we laughed our asses off."

The psychologist stood up to end the session after ninety minutes and three hundred dollars. She was almost in tears.

Listening to that recording today, it bothers me that nobody was alarmed by my sister's self-cutting, *even the psychologist*. My mom was trying to score Brownie points with my sister and me, and my dad was too focused on my education. From my dad's memoir I learned that, after my last session, the psychologist had said to him, "With a wife like yours, you need to lower your expectations for the children."

If my dad had followed her advice he would have saved himself a lot of trouble. My parents' lack of teamwork made it impossible for me to work around my mental disorders or even discover I had them. I was trapped between their incompatible values and expectations. Things might have been different if my parents were knowledgeable enough to realize why I was totally unresponsive to psychology: I needed *psychiatry*. Our doctor made the wrong referral, the psychologist was not about to send me upstairs to a psychiatrist and lose her patient, and my parents and teachers didn't know what to do for me while my education gurgled down the drain.

I sometimes wonder if it would have made any difference if my mom and sister had been able to bottle up their problems for a while, take me by the arm, and coach me like my music teacher and my old friends were all doing, instead of adding to my drama by sharing their own mental health issues.

One day I had a fight with my friend. She told me that I looked confused after it was over, and I'd said to her, "What happened?" She thought I was completely not myself. It was scary hearing her talk about it. I wondered if I'd been perfectly normal in a past life, but this life was the opposite. I started twitching so badly that I wanted someone to hit me with a baseball bat.

Hide, Seek, Run and Let started to annoy me. I began to think I might have schizophrenia, especially when Hide was in me.

Academic Collapse

ON THE EXAMS, WHICH I HADN'T STUDIED FOR, I failed history and literature and I got a C- average. I drew gay guys kissing on my French test just to piss off my teacher. My final report said:

> "It saddens me to read this report as it is not representative of Lina's talent and abilities. There are no A's, not even in her forte subject, music. Lina comes across as disaffected at times. She needs to help herself. Teenage music, fashion, and lifestyle are transitory. Academic qualifications are important and permanent. The summer offers time to reflect on a disappointing grade nine."

Whenever I reflected, I saw Hide! Compare the principal's delight in my grade seven and eight with his disappointment in my grade nine. It was such a crash, in the most critical years of my life, that today I can hardly believe I was never sent to a psychiatrist for evaluation. I needed a lot more than "time to reflect." I needed medical care! Maybe I would have received the attention I needed if I'd threatened to act upon some of my violent thoughts.

My mom was often careless and left her email logged in, so one day I read all the emails between her and my dad and my teachers. It looked like a conspiracy, and I got pissed. The school counselor had written to my dad that he was concerned that I had only two friends left at school and they both had a negative attitude, and he thought I urgently needed a mentor or a psychologist to "guide me out of my self-destructive rut." I used to like school more than home because my dad wasn't there, but now the counselor took his place so I liked home more than school.

Sometimes I'd manage to do some homework, then my brain would wander off and I couldn't even do the things I *wanted* to do. I couldn't focus on homework long enough to finish any of it. I got distracted by completely random things. Every assignment gave me a headache.

I wanted to do well in history, so I revised for the exam. I thought I did well, but I got an E, which was even worse than a D. My history teacher lectured me about how I didn't listen in class. I used to be good at history, but now I felt like I couldn't get any information into my brain. I'd wake up and say to myself, *I must do history!* Then I'd feel like screaming at myself and splitting into two because I couldn't turn thought into action. Doing homework made my eyes sting, my brain throb, and my legs shake. I just couldn't do it. So I drew tattoo designs.

My school sent home a warning letter:

"Lina appears to be disillusioned and disaffected, and her outcomes reveal limited achievement. Lina has the ability and that is a fact. Her progress in grade ten will be critical. Should her minimum effort grades continue, Lina will not be considered for the International Baccalaureate and will need to leave the school at the end of grade ten. The decision rests with her."

I didn't care what school I went to. All I needed was a certificate from anywhere saying I graduated. I was going to fail at life anyway. I didn't want to do the International Baccalaureate and be a martyr like my sister. Plus if I got kicked out of my school then no other good school would take me, so there'd be no reason to stay in Singapore and we'd go home to Britain. There my sister would go to college while I went to a lazy ass government school.

All my relationships were unstable. I would love people one day and hate them the next. Whenever I liked someone and somebody else liked that person, I'd try to get that somebody else to like me just to spite the person I liked. Whenever I liked someone, I became obsessed with trying to make that person like me. If it was a guy, even if I didn't want to date him, I wanted him to bow down to me like a slave. I couldn't get along with guys who were studious, controlling, and clingy, because they reminded me of my dad.

Wass came to me for the first time. He was part of Hide, and he was dangerous. Let held Wass back, and Seek decided that Wass wouldn't make me do something stupid. Wass and Semb were partners; they were similar and both part of Hide. If I were in a burning building with a bunch of people, Wass would be like, "Kill them all! Save yourself and the hottest guy! Kill the rest! Slimy scum!" Semb, with an evil grin, would be like, "Dude, save the day. Make them worship you." It wasn't funny. I *needed* Let.

My Mexican friend and I planned to travel the world and get jobs wherever we ran out of money. When I told my Chinese friend about our trip, she was like, "I'll be in college studying to be a doctor or a lawyer." I figured she'd been brainwashed by her mother, so she would end up as a brainwashing mother too and her kids would hate her. If I had kids, I wouldn't pressure them to do well in school. They'd grow up happy, and they would love me like my mom loved me. Yet I also thought I would never get anywhere, and my life was over.

I wrote on my maths book cover, *It's okay to be gay, let's rejoice with the boys in the gay way.* The teacher reported it to the principal, who told me it was juvenile and flippant and ordered me to remove it.

I had a dream about my dad:

"My dad asked if he could see the homework I was supposed to do. I yelled at him, and he stayed calm like he always does. And then I called him a cunt and he punched me and I fell to the ground. I ran to my room, locked the door, packed my bag, broke my bathroom window, climbed down, and ran to a party with all my friends. I had so much fun. When it was over, I went with my friend to her home. She went through the front door while I climbed up to her room from the outside. I lived with her, but I had this huge bruise on my face. Her mom came in and was like, 'Oh my God!' and reported my dad for child abuse and he was arrested. I visited him in jail. He was like, 'Aw, you're visiting me!' I was like, 'Only to say this and not be hit for it: I hate you, and you deserve to be here.' And then I walked away, and all his jail mates were like, 'Oh, burn.'"

That was a nice dream, except for my dad being in it. My dad was trying to get on my good side, but he always seemed to do it the wrong way and annoy me.

On Friday nights he'd be like, "Will you walk the dog with me tonight?"

"No, thanks."

"Aw, but it's nice." Then he'd stand by my bedroom door for ages, staring at me.

On weekends he'd be like, "Lina, would you like me to order you McDonald's for lunch?"

"What?"

"Would you like me to order you McDonald's for lunch?"

"Why?"

"You need to eat."

"No, thank you."

"No?"

"No."

"Would you like me to make you a sandwich?"

Then, pissed off at him, I'd trash my bathroom.

He'd come back into my bedroom and be like, "Lina? I'm going to the hardware store. Have you started on your maths?"

"No."

"You have seven pages; you better get started. I'll check it when I get back."

"Would you mind ordering me McDonald's?"

My dad gave me love and support in ways like that. But I was unable to feel his love, and could only see him as a resource.

The principal pulled me out of class in the last week of the school year and walked me to his office. My parents were there, all dressed up. It was their wedding anniversary! I sat in the armchair in the corner, my parents sat on the two-seater sofa with my dad next to me, and the principal sat in the armchair at the other end. The walls were decorated with child artwork, certificates, and photographs.

The principal began: "Lina, I'm sorry to have taken you out of class, but this is a very important time. This meeting is at my instigation in light of your reports. This is the most important meeting you will have in your educational life. Do I make myself clear?"

"Yes."

"Is there anything you would like to say before we start?"

"No."

"This meeting is to work out how we're going to move forward, or not. You are bright. You have ability in certain subject areas. Your music, English, and art have great potential. But your exam grades were disgraceful. For a person of your ability, they were shocking and embarrassing. I had to read them *three times* to believe it. The situation can be redeemed, but it's going to come down to one person, Lina: you. In six weeks, when you come back for grade ten, you must decide either to work hard and go for the International Baccalaureate starting in grade eleven or make other arrangements for your education. What did you find difficult in grade nine?"

"I don't want to do the International Baccalaureate."

"What are you going to do in grade eleven?"

"A levels."

"Where?"

I shrugged. "At another school."

"Wouldn't you find it challenging to start over in a new environment? You could stay here and have your existing friends. Are you ready to change schools?"

"Yes."

"Do you think the academic provisions there would be as good as here?"

"Lower."

"Are you happy to settle for second best when you don't have to?"

"Yes."

"That is *really* alarming, Lina. Let's think about this. You could do art, music, and English. You could do psychology, and that I think is a subject that should appeal to you. You could do math studies, which would be a breeze. And ecosystems: user friendly science in the real world. I can see an International Baccalaureate for you, but you can't see it for yourself because you don't want it."

I sulked in silence.

"Lina, I'm looking for any glimmer here to try to fight for you. You could have a great three years here. But you're giving me nothing back! Name something positive that happened in grade nine."

"Music and art."

"So a third of your diploma could be two passions of yours that you really enjoy! But you are prepared to walk away from that. You've got two subjects you adore, and are real interests of yours, but that's not enough for you."

I refused to be drawn into the discussion.

"Honestly, Lina, you are making it very difficult. How are we not providing what you need? Why are you in the bottom five percent in terms of effort?"

"I'm not happy."

"Why? Is it fear of failure?"

Maybe fear of failure *was* crippling me. I said nothing.

"Are you envious of your older sister?"

"No," I lied. "I want to be a tattoo artist."

"If being a tattoo artist doesn't float your boat later on, what's your fallback?"

"I'd still want to be a tattoo artist."

"But you are limiting your options, aren't you? It would be foolish to go down this one line of work with no alternative. The whole idea of education is to widen the field in which you can work. Do you feel disaffected, alienated from the school's culture, sports, and academic achievements? Do you find all that a bit square?"

"Not really."

"So I don't understand why you are unhappy and you want to leave."

"I don't want to leave, but I don't mind."

"Do you classify yourself as an emo?"

"No."

"Look, Lina, if you enter the government school system, you'll find like-minded people—and there's nothing wrong with those people, they're perfectly decent—and you'll end up in the job market and you might be a tattoo artist. The problem is you are *bright*. Few job opportunities are going to stimulate your mind. You *need* to stay in education. I'd say you don't really want to be a tattoo artist, but you don't want to stand up to the educational challenges that face you at the age of fourteen. Would that be fair?"

"I don't mind being a tattoo artist."

"This *Miami Ink*—or whatever it's called—these are actors paid to be on TV."

My mom spoke up: "No, they really do tattoos."

"They take five hundred tattoo artists, interview them, and pick the most engaging tattoo artists for the show. The ones selected make real money, but the rest barely survive."

"I know. It is *real*," my mom replied.

"It's a *make believe world*."

"It's still *popular*," she said, defending our favorite show.

The principal looked back at me. "Lina, your parents are prepared to support your education. That's a tremendous commitment for them to make, and you should honor that. We don't want you to fall by the wayside. Yes, there are people who drop out and become millionaires, but they're a very small percentage. There are far more people who turn around after they get a dead-end job and say, 'If I'd stuck it out at school, I could have had a much better life.' This is your life, Lina. How will you feel in two years if your sister goes to university and she's having a ball, and she's traveling, while you're tattooing people's arms?"

"Bad, I guess."

"What if your old friends are getting their International Baccalaureates and you're not part of that because you made an early decision to be a tattoo artist? You won't have their options. How will you feel then? It takes *guts* to say you don't care."

"I won't mind."

"You might mind in a year's time. Is that possible?"

"Maybe."

"Yes, it's possible. Lina, you have to start helping me here. No one is making you do anything, but we've outlined some very serious obstacles to your future based on your current choices. But you seem to be refusing to take this on board. What could anyone do to help you?"

"Leave me alone."

"Be careful what you want, Lina, because you might just get it, and you can pick up the pieces from there. I'm severely worried now. Are you too cool for school? Do your tattoo aspirations mean that school is irrelevant to you?"

"Yes, school is irrelevant."

"Would you rather be a tattoo artist than go to university?"

"Yes."

I hated him. Most principals would have given up by now. The more my caregivers cared for me, the more I hated them. I was taking caregiver support for granted, as if it were due to me like the tribute due to a queen from a vassal.

"And how long are you going to be a tattoo artist?"

"It would kind of be, like, my life."

"I'm not saying you won't be able to live independently as a tattoo artist, but I don't see why you can't shelve that dream for three years while you get your International Baccalaureate. You have the potential to do it, and you can get to university. The scope for achievement, self-esteem, and confidence—we can give you all of that here. Do you really want to drop out? You said you don't want to go back to Britain. Do you prefer to live in Singapore?"

"Well, I've never lived in Britain."

My dad spoke up. "Another possibility is Europe for your International Baccalaureate. There are international boarding schools there, and you could get a student visa."

"That's a very generous offer from your father, Lina. We still have an opportunity, but a very short time frame. We have to eliminate *what's stopping you from doing well*. I would never want to be a teenager again. I realized that if I wanted to make the most of my existence, I had to do a bit of work. I didn't do it because my parents and teachers told me to do it; I did it because it was going to make my life easier."

My mom said, "Same thing for me. I don't want to stay like this. You have to study hard to grow up. It's my decision."

"So what are you going to do now?" said the principal.

"Study."

"That's the aim. But what's the *method*?"

"I'll just ... try harder."

He smiled. "Lina, in the next three days go to your teachers and tell them you are going to change. The school is proud to have people with different approaches as long as they do what is expected in the classroom. Teachers don't expect perfect behavior, but they do expect respect and not sneering, monosyllabic responses. Don't email 'Hey, it's Lina!' to your teachers and write to them all in lower case. Even your art teacher told you to write using proper grammar. You've got to come up with ways you will improve, not just saying you will try harder. Like limiting your internet. What are you going to put in place?"

"I'll ... spend more time with my homework."

"I'm looking for something *concrete*. Review past papers. Start getting ready for exams. Stop doodling in class and start participating. Remove yourself from antisocial situations. The bottom line is that it's really up to you. You have six weeks to think about it. But you have to let me know so I can help you find another school or write you a job reference for a tattoo parlor. You are bright, talented, and erudite, and the job market will have a *place* for you. Whether you reach your *potential* is the question. University will stretch your mind, give you the best social life, offer a sense of achievement, and give you experience. I can see a lot of benefits that you can't see right now. So what are we going to do?"

"I'll do the International Baccalaureate."

"You've got the power to change the course of your life. The only reason we are having this conversation is that I think you can do the International Baccalaureate and get to university. I think you have the ability to do well. If you were a lost cause, I'd have phoned your parents to make alternative arrangements."

"You can ask what you wanted to know, what you have to do, to make it easier for you," said my mom.

My dad said, "If you qualify for an International Baccalaureate program, you can do it in Singapore, Britain, or Europe; you have options. But if your effort remains so low that you have to leave here, then you might as well go to a government school in Britain. No options. All sorts of things become possible if you get just *normal* marks."

"Expats come and go, but even so, over ninety percent of our students stay for the International Baccalaureate. How do you feel now?"

I ignored the question. Asking for my private thoughts was too much.

"I know you want to be a tattoo artist, but something like textile design or interior design or architecture would give you the chance to express your abilities and give you a sense of achievement and a lifestyle that you will want, something more high powered and lucrative than a tattoo parlor. University is a great experience because you are with like-minded people and you'll have great fun. I know you have more important things in your life right now, but teenage life is transitory. Promise me one thing, Lina. You will never say to your parents, 'I wasn't aware of the situation.'"

"Yes."

"I've tried to state the case as clearly as I possibly can. I'll fight for you tooth and nail. The ball is in your court."

I went back to class. My parents talked to the principal for another hour and went out to dinner. They would have had a lot to talk about. Yet despite what I was putting them through, they are smiling in their anniversary dinner photo. It would be their last.

If a year of encouragement from my teachers, parents, friends, psychologist, principal, and counselor hadn't helped a "gifted" child with "ability and talent" to aspire to be all she could be, or at least to drag herself up from the bottom of her class, then there was no way that the bravura performance from the principal could make a difference. I'd fallen from the *top twenty percent* of my class to the *bottom ten percent* in one year, and my sister was cutting herself with a razor blade and hanging bloodstained posters on her wall, but my parents took our mental health for granted and looked for other causes for our behavior, such as adolescence. I'll never know if diagnosis and treatment at that critical time would have improved my outcome, but words could not change anything. I ignored all my caregivers, so instead of benefiting from their adult wisdom in my childhood, I am limited in my adulthood by my childhood behavior.

Sometimes my reflection talked to me. I'd hear random voices in my head: I'd be holding a muffin, and different parts of me would be like: "Eat it"; "Don't eat it: if you eat it, you'll get fat"; "Eat it, then work it off"; and "You don't have time to work it off, so don't eat it."

I finished grade nine with a C+ average, down from B+ in grade eight. It was a huge drop.

THE WEEK I GOT MY REPORT CARD, I had a dream where I had to stab a wolf to death. I woke up crying.

I had fourteen voices now—twelve official ones and two that weren't really voices. They were different animals that spoke to me. Everyone close to me had animal forms, including me. I was a raccoon. My friend was a white tiger. Once, I saw a spirit raccoon leap out of me and into my friend's body, then all my other friends' animal spirit forms came out of them and went into her body. When she was gone, I saw a spirit white tiger as if she was still there, so I didn't cry for her. When I first started seeing spirit animals I didn't know who they were, but after a day or two, it was like, "Bam! That's someone I know!" And it all made sense.

My dad told a publisher that his daughters were artists and asked him if he needed any books illustrated. He did: each page of his new book had an interesting question-and-answer about culture in Singapore and needed a cartoon to illustrate it. I would do fifty drawings and earn $9,000 during the summer holidays.

It was pretty cool, my first job as an illustrator. One page said: "Do Muslim babies read the Qur'an? No, they hear the Qur'an. The expectant mother should read the Qur'an to calm her during childbirth in order to have a healthy child. The father holds the newborn and whispers the *Azan* prayer call into his right ear and the *Iqamat* recitation into his left ear; in this way, the first words he hears are the call to God."

I drew a Muslima holding a baby next to a Muslim reading the holy book. Then I gave up. I didn't even show it to my dad. My God, the *money!* It was more than my sister earned in her entire life. I wanted to do it more than I'd ever wanted to do anything. But I needed ideas on what to draw and I refused to ask anyone for help. My disappointed dad offered the work to my sister, but she was having her own issues and didn't want to take over my project. I thought of tattooing LOSER across my forehead.

My sister changed her mind about family holidays and wanted to go to Egypt to see the pyramids and go diving in the Red Sea, but I vetoed it. We stayed home for another summer while our friends left Singapore for their family holidays.

I went to the mall with my sister, lied about my age, and got my tongue pierced. It got so swollen I talked like a retard.

My mom noticed, crying, "Aaah! You talk like a stupid person!"

"Eeths cuth off the thwelling."

"*Aaah!*"

She was worried I would talk like that for the rest of my life, but she didn't tell my dad about it. He ignored it when he discovered it.

My mom would walk into my room in a G-string, talk to me, wiggle her ass like a whore, and walk out. She was cool in her special way, nice but dumb.

She caught me with shoplifted goods, and she was like, "You might get caught. I'll give you more money next time!"

My mom didn't care about the *stealing*; she only cared that I might get *caught*. She agreed I could get a small tattoo in a hidden place, without telling my dad.

My music teacher kept trying to mentor me, sending me emails like this one:

"Are you going to pull things together this coming year or are you still determined not to do the International Baccalaureate? Your teachers have a low expectation of you, so when you turn it around, they will be blown away. You just need to understand the psychology of teachers. All you have to do is be punctual with deadlines, even if you do not do your absolute best. Just be on time and smile a lot and say 'hi' and 'goodbye' and 'thanks' at the end of lessons. Easy-peasy. You are in a win-win situation now. Impress your teachers quietly, then your folks will be happy. You'll get a bit of slack. Exams are a piece of piss. I can help you with your maths. Just do your best and be pleasant."

I couldn't even follow my music teacher's simple coaching. Instead I whinged to my Korean friend:

"I can't bring myself to give a shit about grades anymore. I'll get kicked out of school, have to go to another school, fail there, and get nowhere in life. My sister is emo because of the International Baccalaureate, and I'm stupider than she is. I'd kill myself two seconds into the program! I got an E in my history exam! When I was doing the exam, I thought I was doing so well. I was proud of myself. I thought I would get an A, and then I got an E. What the fuck? English, history, biology, French, and maths are all the same: me being stupid and complete shit, and my teachers hating every piece of me."

"Lina, the school hates nothing more than low effort. I was getting low grades but high effort because I always went to the teacher's desk, put my hand up, asked questions, and stayed behind every now and then. When I handed in my homework, I said things like, 'I tried on this bit here, but got stuck there.' Effort is what matters. The teachers don't hate you, take it from me. They may think you're a difficult student. If you walk into a class and think, 'Fuck this!' your body language will show it. I understand where you're coming from, and it's not realistic to expect you to walk around loving school and everyone, but if you go in with an attitude of 'I'll try,' or at least look like you're trying, the teacher will react more positively."

"I'll try, but then my teachers are going to be like, 'What the fuck?'"

"This is the perfect time, after the holiday. You come back fresh and ready to go. They will realize that and appreciate it. They are human, and if you give off positive vibes they will respond in kind. More importantly, your mood will be better, and you will enjoy the lesson and learn."

"My face is going to be tired from being held in a positive expression. But it's not that simple. I never ask questions or anything—I really have no idea how to."

"OK, repeat the last thing they say. For example, maths. If the teacher says, 'All angles in a triangle add up to 180 degrees.' You say, 'Is that for all triangles at all times? Is that a rule or does it sometimes not work?' Something general, but it shows them you're engaged."

"Or deaf."

"Lina, you can't fake your way through all of school. You have to give a shit to a certain degree because you have to do the work."

"I need to know that there will be a reward in the end."

"The reward is having an International Baccalaureate, which puts you miles ahead of 99% of the world. You don't care now, but at some point you have to get a job. You can fuck around for 75 years once you leave school. Just stick with it for three more years."

"When you're retired you're too old to do anything."

"You are not too old when you retire! And your job can be something you love doing. Even if you wanted to get an apprenticeship as a tattoo artist, if you have an International Baccalaureate showing your independence and your creative work ethic, you will be chosen over the person that doesn't. The International Baccalaureate will, however, be a golden ticket to 80% of universities, if you should choose to go to university. You will have that option."

I thought about my dad's job and how hard he worked. I couldn't see that he liked—and he chose—his job that also gave us a great life and let him retire ten years early.

I was an attention whore; I hated it when other people got

more attention than me, unless I really liked them. I got bitchy and moody when I didn't get noticed. I acted retarded when I wasn't with my friends, especially around people I didn't know, and the people I did know didn't particularly like me. Attention whoring soothed my self-esteem, especially on the internet where my social ineptitude didn't matter.

My mom usually went out at six, so she cooked dinner at about five. Her cooking was getting to be crap, like pasta, rice with disgusting tofu dumplings with overly salty vegetables, make-your-own sushi, salmon with pesto, or burritos—the same thing every day. When she was home she snacked all day so she mostly didn't eat with us. Neither did my dad, who usually got home from work after my mom went out. When my mom sat down to eat with us, she'd sit at the end of the table, eating kimchi out of a can.

So I baked. Then my dad would piss me off. Every time I baked, he came into the kitchen.

"Lina? Can I have a slice of your cake? It's good!"

"Just fucking eat it."

I was rude and sarcastic to my dad, especially whenever he tried to be nice.

I asked my dad for a tattoo gun for my fifteenth birthday, but instead he gave me a digital music recorder. He took the family out and took photos throughout my birthday dinner. It was fucking annoying. He was like "Smile! Smile!" I hated him. I thought he was doing everything he could so I wouldn't become a tattoo artist.

The week before school resumed, while my dad was away on a business trip, my sister had a nervous breakdown. She was crying and babbling, "I can't go back. I can't go back," over and over, like she'd completely lost her mind. She told me the only reason she was doing the International Baccalaureate was that my mom was happy living in Singapore, and if we failed, we'd move to Britain. She wanted to cut herself again, but my mom had hidden the razor.

More and more, my sister escaped to the fantasy world of Ryzom, an online role-playing game. Before, whenever I was baking, she would keep me company in the kitchen and draw and we'd talk because I hated doing things alone. Now, when I asked her if she wanted to draw in the kitchen with me, she'd shout, "No! I'm about to finish this quest! I need the *ranger armor!*"

GRADE TEN STARTED. I WANTED SCHOOL for social purposes so I could feel special, but I didn't want to go back for any other reason. It would have made my dad happy if I paid attention in school, so no matter how much I'd have liked to do it for myself, I couldn't because it would have satisfied my dad and I was not going to give him satisfaction. I made up my mind to hate school.

I'd be sitting quietly, then start screaming at people. Then I'd burst out crying and apologizing, then hit them and yell at them again. I felt confused, frustrated, complicated, and alone.

I didn't know what I should do or who I should be. I wanted someone to tell my problems to, even though I talked about my problems to anyone who would listen, and everyone gave me advice which I ignored. The thing is, most people know who they are, but I was so many me's that I didn't know how to be anyone.

I didn't know how to be nice. I was never good enough for myself. While my friends were gorgeous, I felt ugly. They were skinny and pale. They didn't feel *they* weren't good enough for themselves. They didn't let other people change *them*. I wanted to change my body: dye my hair, get a corset, get more piercings, and get tattoos.

I felt like people hated me. I felt like everyone was watching me, but if they *weren't* watching me I got pissed off. I missed being worshipped by 10,000 friends on Myspace, Bebo, and Facebook. Before, I felt like my photos had been worshipped and everyone was like, "Whoa!" Now, even though the world hadn't changed a bit, I felt like I was going to explode. I hated dressing like a normal person. I needed to be different. I decided I wanted to be a famous actress-model-singer-author-artist-tattoo artist-baker.

Hide was killing himself because he wasn't getting enough attention, and Wass and Semb were about to murder someone.

My mom started using my dad's computer on DeviantArt and she'd often cry. She was like, "I'm so sad for no reason ...." She ran to the TV and watched a cooking show and kept crying. I hugged her and asked her to help me bake, so she cheered up. She told me she liked my dad sometimes, but the reason she was sticking with him was because she couldn't get a job, and if they divorced she would have to repatriate to the Philippines because of her passport.

The whole house was depressed, except for my dad. He had his globe-trotting job to keep him busy. He thought everything would turn out fine after I passed through my emo phase.

My sister found her razor and cut herself again. She posted a photo of her bleeding arm on DeviantArt, where she knew my mom would see it but my dad wouldn't. I felt like slapping my sister when she cried, because she used to abuse me whenever I walked around looking depressed after I cut myself.

She would say to me, "You don't even do slitting right!" But she cut herself the wimp way in her photo, across and not deep, and then she tensed her arm to get more blood to come out. What a hypocrite!

When my mom saw my sister's bleeding photo, she offered to send her to a psychiatrist. My sister refused, telling her that a psychiatrist would be no better than our psychologist. Looking back, my mom shouldn't have *offered* psychiatric help to a child who was so disturbed she was cutting herself: she should have told my dad what my sister was doing, and, together, they should have *demanded* it. My parents should have *forced* my sister and me into psychiatry to get to the root of our problems. But there wasn't much awareness about mental health issues in those days, and especially not about the peculiar symptoms that we presented.

THREE WEEKS INTO GRADE TEN I was still where I'd been at the end of grade nine: frustrated, angry, and exhausted, with teachers pounding down on me. My effort grades were low because I couldn't bring myself to try. None of the voices in my head told me to do well in school.

My friends came over and we were going to go clubbing with our fake IDs. But my dad was like, "Fifteen years old is too young for nightclubs. May I offer you some wine? Vodka? How about Tequila?"

What the fuck? We wanted to go out! My friends agreed that dads sucked. Moms sucked too, but mostly it was our dads who sucked.

During maths, my mind flew away and I started writing a script about a retarded gay man who talked about how boobs disturbed him. My maths teacher was standing behind me, which I didn't notice because my mind wasn't even in the classroom. I nearly cried when she caught me. She was like, "Lina, you're an excellent student and you can do better. I've heard that you like maths."

What the fuck? I had to write an apology letter to my teacher.

A few days later, my dad walked into my bedroom and asked to see my homework diary. Notes in homework diaries meant that parents were supposed to contact the teachers. There were two notes from my history teacher saying I didn't focus in class.

My dad read the notes, and I broke down and cried.

"Why don't you focus in class?" my dad asked.

"I don't know."

"You must know. Do you want me to sit next to you in class to see what your problem is?"

"It won't make a difference."

"This is an issue, Lina! You need to focus in class."

"I can't."

"Why not?" My dad looked at my homework diary. "Erase what you drew on the cover."

"Why?"

"It's offensive and unprofessional."

"Everyone does it."

"Erase it!"

"It's *ink*."

"I'll get the solvent."

I felt like drawing my middle finger on the cover and throwing the book at him.

My dad still assumed my sister and I would pass through

our teenage angst. Then he'd retire early, we'd move to Britain together, my mom would get the passport she wanted and stop bitching, my sister and I would go to super universities and have super careers, and life would be glorious for everyone. He was working and enduring long separations to give his beautiful wife and talented daughters the finest life he could give, but I hated him for expecting performance from *us* in return for performance from *him*.

I decided that I was never going to be able to live one hundred percent for myself until my dad was dead. Part of me became dedicated to spiting my dad *even if it meant ruining my own life*. Now that my dad's out of my life, I realize I'm no freer to live my life than I was before. My mental state had made me squander my opportunities and compromise my life to spite my dad, for nothing.

My emotions were all over the place. When my mood swings were up, I'd be happy that I finally worked myself out, and I'd be like, "Life is amazing. You've only got one life, so live it!" But then I'd feel like my life was over and I'd cry in the bathroom for hours.

My mom attacked me about school, and I broke down again. I wished the hospital had connected my brain to a giant computer when I was born and programmed me so I already knew everything, and then I could spend my life clubbing. Even my hair pissed me off.

And then my dad walked in. "You're going to review half an hour of maths with me every day," he said.

"I would kill myself."

"Because it's me helping you?"

"Yes!" I wanted to add, "Yes, you idiot," but I couldn't say that out loud.

My music teacher even offered to tutor my *maths*—no shit—and I refused her help too.

My Korean friend kept trying to help me:

"What do you want me to say? Do you want me to give you a lecture? It's not lost. It's 100% up to you now. You can blame the teacher; you can blame the subject; you can blame other people; you say you can't concentrate. This may all be true, but they don't care. There will always be a problem with something—always and everywhere—and either you can blame something for it, or you can just do your best. As in, you go to them and say the following in teacher language: 'I've had a fucked up time, difficulties at home, etc., but I want to do well, and I want to do the International Baccalaureate.' I'm going to sound like a dickhead, but your effort grades are low for a reason! They don't give you low effort grades because they are psycho bitches. That's why I'm saying it's up to you. If you want to do the International Baccalaureate and stay in the school with us, you will try. If you don't want to, you'll keep doing what you do."

I kept doing what I was doing, so the principal called me into his office and harassed me about my low effort. He tried to force me to tell him about my personal life. He was like, "You can't choose your family, Lina, but you can choose your friends. Choose wisely."

I wanted to say, "Fuck off. My friends are the only thing that's right in my life." He was trying to help me by taking time to try to understand my problems, but all he achieved was to give me a fear of ugly fat people.

When most teachers harassed me, I *didn't* want to study for the International Baccalaureate because of the work and stress.

Then when other teachers encouraged me, I *did* want to do it. Sometimes I wanted to go to a different school because it looked interesting. Then I didn't want to go because I hated moving countries and I wanted to graduate with my friends. I thought about going to college for film studies. Then I didn't want to take film studies because film was only a hobby for my spare time.

The principal sent home my final warning just one month into grade ten:

"We had a lengthy conversation with Lina outlining her need to make a positive start to grade ten. Last week there were three instances where this proved not to be the case. First, Lina spent a considerable part of a maths lesson writing a puerile script for a play. Second, Lina failed to attend the meeting scheduled to catch up with the maths she missed. Third, and most serious, is that Lina chose not to attend the next maths lesson and excused herself without permission. Lina has been aloof and ambivalent about her education, and this is very disappointing. As there is limited time left, I would encourage her to reflect on her actions and take the necessary steps to realize her potential."

I quit voice lessons because my teacher wouldn't teach a student with a tongue stud and I refused to remove it. I felt fat, ugly, unwanted, stressed, and stupid. I couldn't finish my art piece so I snapped my pen in half. I had a mood swing and nearly yelled at a friend because she was sitting in the middle of a bench and nearly yelled at another friend because her pigtails bothered me.

Two months into the term, after my lowest grades ever, I panicked at the thought of losing my friends. I asked my dad for tutors in maths, biology, history, French, and English. For five months I spent hours every day with tutors and in taxis rushing to them, and my dad spent a fortune. But I'd never learned how to study. I expected my tutors to be my secret weapon, to do my studying for me. And now I did even less homework because I spent so much time with my tutors. I couldn't catch up and keep up at the same time, so I couldn't participate in class and my grades hardly budged. Sometimes I got so frustrated that I skipped tutor sessions, even though my dad had to pay for them anyway. I felt like a retard who saw a problem, tried to avoid it, and then crashed into it. Whenever I got depressed, I fought with my friends, locked myself in my bathroom, and cried.

One night I was writing a song and crying, and I turned around and Run was sitting on my bed as my dog. I could tell he was Run because his eyes were different. As soon as I saw him I started crying and he smothered me in licks and affection. The next morning he was lying on my bed looking at me, and then I looked at him and saw Hide was in him. His eyes were greenish-blue and he winked at me and turned away, and then when he turned back his eyes were back to those of my normal dog.

When Hide took over and I looked in the mirror, it wasn't me, and I had fights with my own reflection. Seek was stronger than Wass and Semb. Night wanted people to understand me. My dreams all meant something, and I understood them. I had a dream where Khaos joined me, and I killed her and woke up crying. Rubchen was the fragile part of me that nobody could take care of and only I could protect. Rubchen died, and I woke up depressed. My dreams were controlled by Let. The voices that came to me in my dreams were always sad.

My mom started staying up late on the internet while my dad was on business trips, typing like a crazy woman until four in the morning. I'd been stealing from my mom, because my dad never left his wallet where I could find it, but she started noticing fifties were missing and rampaging through the house checking our wallets, so I had to steal less often. I used to feel bad for stealing from my mom, but then I told myself that I was actually stealing from my dad, so I felt good again. When I asked my mom if I could borrow money to buy Christmas gifts, she gave me $300 and told my dad she only loaned me $200, so I saved a hundred dollars.

My dad returned from a business trip. He was standing by the door and talking to my mom about problems at his company. She wasn't paying attention, and she started singing and typing on DeviantArt. My dad was like, "Are you listening?"

She kept singing and typing, ignoring my dad.

He walked away, rolling his suitcase behind him, and I felt sorry for him that time. My mom was naturally mean to him.

I started watching *America's Next Top Model*, like, nonstop. I wanted people to discover me and ask me to be a model or actress, even though I was too short to be a model, but nobody did. Now I *did* want to do the International Baccalaureate, so I could go to America for college; then, when I got there, I would audition to become a famous scriptwriter, actress, singer, model, or director. I didn't need maths to work out that "Ahmad had a larger ratio of potatoes to apples." Part of me knew I wouldn't get into the International Baccalaureate, so there was no point in working. And part of me knew I *would* get in if just did my homework and spoke up in class.

Parts of me wanted different things, and I'd try for them all at once and get nowhere. Then I'd skip my homework, watch

Desperate Housewives, and gain weight from all the Doritos.

When my moods were up, I wanted to make Singapore good and create some amazing memories. I was sure I'd gone from being depressed, crying, whining, and cutting myself in grades eight and nine to being mature. I was sure everything was going to be fine. But when I had exams, my mind would wander and I'd start doodling. Something inside me would shout, "Hey, you! Finish the question!" and I'd be like, "Oh, good idea!" This would repeat a thousand times in one exam.

I dropped out of the singing ensemble that I'd been in for years, just after my mom bought me a new jacket for our annual concert in The Esplanade. She was so pissed. My homeroom teacher was like, "Oh my God, why do you have commitment issues with stuff like this, Lina?"

I spent my Christmas holiday rushing from tutor to tutor. One minute I was sure I was going to be admitted into the International Baccalaureate program, and the next minute I was sure I was going to be kicked out of the school. My parents were so desperate, I could haggle with them:

"If I get in, can I get a cat?"

"Okay!"

"If I get in, can I have dad's office?"

"Okay!"

"If I get in, can I go to Boston next Christmas?"

"Okay!"

"Wow, you really don't think I'm going to get in, do you?"

The principal called my parents to a meeting. When they came home, they walked into my room and my dad gave me the news:

"The principal said that you have to leave the school at the end of grade ten. Your effort is insufficient. You failed exams in five subjects. He has never seen such a catastrophic decline in a bright student in the absence of psychological problems. You have the third-worst effort grade out of the 260 students in grade ten, and the next worst student has major psychological issues and is on medication. You are immature, disengaged, and unconcerned. He thought your sister might be holding you back by whining about the International Baccalaureate, so he asked her to stop it, but she refused and asked for both of you to be left alone. He said your outcome is a crying shame because you are in danger of wasting your life. He said there is no reason to spend tens of thousands of dollars a year on your school fees and recommended you go to a government school."

My mom's face went blank. I turned and stared at my computer. Tears rolled down my cheeks. My parents were ashamed of me. After they left my bedroom I broke down and cried like a baby, with a red and puffy face. Then something in me was like, "Shut up, Lina! Pick yourself up, get yourself together, and stop moaning and making everyone depressed."

A false memory about my expulsion soon replaced reality. I remembered I was kicked out, not because my minimum effort grades had continued, as the principal had warned in writing, but because *my dad called the school every day* to force my teachers to pay attention to me until they realized that I hated the school, hated the work, and hated everything and everyone. In reality, I'd given my teachers plenty of reasons to pay attention: I ignored them, skipped homework, failed exams, lost my books, drew in my diary, never raised my hand, drew on my arm, wrote scripts, fell asleep, listened to music, and wrote songs about death. They were so worried about me, they had been calling my dad.

I had effort grades in the bottom one percent despite an IQ in the top two percent, but everyone thought I was still going through my emo phase! Even my Mexican friend, no "gifted child," made the effort, but the pressure to conform and perform really did me in. The principal had come close to diagnosing major psychiatric disorders, but my parents didn't think I was that bad. My caregivers didn't understand what was wrong with me any more than I did, so they did the best they could with what they knew. But there are no do-overs in life.

Now I expected my family to move to Britain and stick me in a government school, and my mom would blame her misery on me. I could have a new start and dye my hair pink, because government schools don't have uniforms, but I'd miss everyone in Singapore and be depressed. I hated being the new kid. I didn't want to move to Britain. I thought I'd die. I was angry at myself, and I was angry at my family because I never felt my family showed their support in a way that could help me.

My music teacher bade me farewell:

"I will miss you! I did my best, believe me. So did your homeroom teacher. You need to get a decent high school certificate, so you will have to play other people's games for two years. It's unavoidable. All that shit about getting one chance is true. You can make it easier on yourself if you try to at least pass everything. High school sucks, but things get way better after. Choose your friends carefully; don't go with the anti-establishment as you might find people are a bit shallow. Be true to yourself always. Never compromise. You should write, and write now, while you feel and think the way you do and the way you see stuff. Capture it now: parents, school, everything."

As always, my music teacher gave me good advice. I've been writing ever since.

Family Collapse

MY MOM WAS BEGINNING TO FAVOR ME and tell me things she wasn't telling anyone else. She was like, "Lina, I need to have a very secret conversation with you without anyone listening." She had shifty eyes. "I don't think I love your father."

She told me she might divorce my dad, but she didn't know what to do because our lifestyle would be gone if she divorced him and she didn't know whether my sister would still like her or not. So she was staying with my dad for the lifestyle and my sister and me, and she'd given up on my education.

Even though I loved my mom and hated my dad, the way my mom turned my sister and me against our dad did nothing for anyone. The way she undermined the goals he was working for and spurned the values he stood for only added to my stress. Sometimes I envied my friends with parents who were well matched and raised their kids as a team.

Only my mom supported me with whatever I wanted to do with my life, maybe because her own college education hadn't done her much good except for impressing my dad when they met. I knew my dad would pay for anything for my education, but I kept telling him I would never need an education after I graduated. The way I saw it, my dad was refusing to accept me for being *me*.

I wanted to drop out to earn my own money by doing what I loved: writing music, making videos, acting, and singing my songs and hearing that people liked them. I decided to stay in my room, record songs, and send them off to record companies until something happened.

My Korean friend thought I was out of my mind that I'd even *consider* dropping out and that I thought I could become famous by recording my own material in my bedroom:

"Hey, want to hear my plans? I failed, so I'm moving to Britain. I'm sending my shit off to record companies, and I'll just keep composing and living my life till I get a reply."

"Lina, you're not going to bother with school at all? Why not enroll in some composition and music courses? I don't want to sound like a meanie, but are you the perfect composer already?"

"Because I hate music composition courses; they're ugly and technical. I don't care about all that shit. It just has to sound good."

"What makes you different from the other 200,000 girls who do what they like? Why does a record company pick you?"

"I'm amazing. No particular reason. It's just that this is the only thing I can do."

"That's not true! I understand you might be stinging from not getting into the International Baccalaureate, and good God I'm all for someone pursuing what she wants to do, but you have to understand that you need to cover other bases. Are you going at it as a singer only, with a band, or as a singer-songwriter? You play a commercial type of music, which means you have to form some sort of angle—what is your target audience? Domestic market or international? I'm not trying to shut down your plans. I just don't want you to assume that the second you go to Britain you'll be a rich pop star."

"Singer-songwriter. I don't know about the band thing; I'll just go with the flow. I don't really mind how big I get. I just know that singing my songs and hearing that people like them is what I gotta do."

"Composition courses don't have to be technical and boring. At the very least keep up private music lessons, and for fuck's sake, Lina, music's a *full-time job*—you gotta work at this like hell! Some bands work nonstop for fifteen years before they make a penny out of it. Not many people can handle getting rejected for that long. If someone told you every single day for fifteen years that your music isn't good enough, then you might start to lose faith. I'm just trying to offer advice."

"Haha, yeah, I appreciate it."

I appreciated my Korean friend's advice all right; I just didn't follow it. Nor did I follow my Chinese friend's advice:

"Even if my parents didn't push me, I'd still be like, 'School! School!' Because I'm doing it for myself. I'm not doing school for my parents. I need this for *me*. If I had stupid parents I'd probably be stupid as well, so thank God my parents are intelligent. My mom and dad are a team when it comes to me and they're so united it's not even funny."

"Haha. My mom is always like, 'I'd be stricter if it weren't for your father and you wouldn't have ended up like this!' My dad is like, 'I would've been stricter if it weren't for your mother and you wouldn't have ended up like this!' My parents used to be a team, but then my mom realized it's hopeless. If your kid has been rebelling her whole damn life, by the time she is in her teens, she's pretty much a lost cause. I was born like this. I used to think that I was failing on purpose, but apparently I wasn't, after all that tutoring in December."

My mom also wasn't happy about moving to Britain, so we asked my dad to stay in Singapore for two more years and to put me in another private school. My dad wanted to give me a second chance at the International Baccalaureate, so I would have the same opportunities as my sister, so he agreed. He hoped I'd learned my lesson and would do well after a fresh start. Sometimes I thought my dad was all right. My mom could never help with anything complicated, so my dad had to find me another private school even though he was away on business trips for weeks at a time.

The first private school he checked out had a waiting list of four years. The second rejected me because of my grades. The third was the non-selective school we'd applied to before, as our Plan B when we lived in India. They never had a waiting list because they took everyone who could afford the fees, which were even higher than at my old school. My dad applied for me there on the condition I take their International Baccalaureate program. He said there was no point in staying in Singapore, one of the world's most expensive cities, and paying private school fees just to get an ordinary high school diploma. I agreed to take the International Baccalaureate because I wanted to stay in Singapore with my friends.

I kept getting the feeling that everyone hated me. Many people were nice to me, but I felt like they really didn't like me. When we passed one another, it was like, "Hey, what's up?" with a fake smile and nothing else. My mood swings were going crazy. I lost my cellphone and my wallet. Different mood swings, different times.

When I looked at anything, my thoughts and opinions about it were categorized into the voices in my head, suited to the thing itself. Like when I talked to Bum, Niko was like, "Oh my God."

Wass was like, "Dude, forget him; you don't need him."

Semb was like, "Use him, go and use him."

Seek was like, "Be nice, be friendly."
Selena was like, "He's just toying with your heart, girl."
Then Niko was like, "But he's so nice. I think he likes you."
I'm like, "Wait … no … Oh my God. No! What?"
My life was so confusing. I thought I had schizophrenia.

ONE DAY MY DAD CHOKED ON A PILL, but he didn't die because my all-knowing sister did the Heimlich maneuver on him, while my mom and I stood there and gawped. I thought it was a missed opportunity to have him out of my life. Not only had I wanted to ruin his life through spite, I had even wanted to end it.

As soon as I got home I'd sit in front of my computer and try to find something to do, wasting away my life. It was wrecked anyway because I failed school and was totally not trying now that I was being kicked out. My dad was away so much that I managed not to do any homework for two months. The maths department hated me. I'd messed up my life so badly. Everyone in Singapore knew about my fucked-up grade nine.

My mom bitched more and more about my dad. My sister was depressed all the time and bitched more and more about her International Baccalaureate. My whole world was crashing down on me. Now I didn't know if I should stay in Singapore and go to a private school to do the International Baccalaureate, or I should move to Britain and go to a government school to do a normal diploma.

I was going through family issues, school issues, trust issues, and friend issues. It was impossible for me to keep friends; I'd never been able to keep a friend. I had no best friend and I'd never been anybody's best friend. I couldn't keep friends no matter what I did. I always did something wrong no matter how hard I tried to make things right. No wonder I ended up friendless or estranged: everyone had a problem with me.

I liked my mom a lot, even though she was strict, because she was so dumb she believed anything. Once when she was cleaning my bathroom sink, there was some shaving cream in it:

"You don't want to touch that," I said.

"Why? *Is it sperm?*"

But no matter what I said to her, she thought I'd screwed every guy in my grade, even though I was still a virgin. She was like, "Don't wear that! It's too provocative! You look like a skank!" When I yelled back at her, she took away my new cellphone. The strange thing is, she got angry that I went out every day with my friends, while she was doing the exact same thing with her friends.

I got accepted by the Plan B school. I was happy for a while. Life would be peachy because I knew two people who went there and I could still hang out with friends from my old school. I had always had an expat life so I wouldn't have belonged in Britain in a neighborhood school.

My sister and I were approaching our final exams, grade twelve and grade ten. My dad was working in Japan for three weeks and my mom was crying all the time, like she was bipolar or something. I wasn't studying because I didn't know how to study, and I couldn't bring myself to care. I just did an hour of cramming before each exam like I did in primary school. But my sister's final exams were her International Baccalaureate exams, and she was acting like the world revolved around her.

My mom and my sister kept fighting and yelling at each other for the stupidest of reasons. No matter what my mom did, like asking my sister to brush the dog, she would reply in the most disrespectful way, and then a huge fight would start and everyone would end up crying and yelling. It would begin with nothing, then explode into everything.

My mom was yelling at me and crying. Everyone was yelling and crying. Sometimes I didn't even know the reason. I just wanted them to shut up!

My sister was the biggest bitch in the world when she had PMS, and I thought PMS was a stupid reason to make our mom decide on a divorce.

MY WHOLE LIFE I'D LOOKED FORWARD to having a Sweet Sixteen party. My sister's Sweet Sixteen party had been a surprise party. My dad booked her favorite place, Hard Rock Cafe, and I invited all her friends. After everyone else had arrived, my dad brought my sister in and everyone leaped out and surprised her. She had the best party ever. It was fun for me too because her friends were also my friends so I didn't get lonely. It was now a few months before my sixteenth birthday. My parents offered me a party like hers, except it wouldn't be a surprise. It would be held a month early, as my birthday parties usually were, because my birthday always falls during the school holidays.

I was like, "There must be booze."

My parents were like, "You are under eighteen. How about Hard Rock Cafe? Invite your friends and have a sleepover!"

I refused to have a party without booze, so I turned my parents down. A party with booze would have to be secret from my parents, which meant I would have to pay for it myself, but I had no money, so I had no party. If I couldn't be sure of being the best at something, like having booze in a restaurant, then I just didn't want to do it at all.

This became a false memory. I remembered that my parents and my sister *did jack shit* for my birthday, even though they'd tried to give me a party like my sister's and I'd *turned it down* several times because I insisted on alcohol. To make my actual birthday even worse, my sister was away and our parents were divorcing, so my Sweet Sixteen birthday was just dinner with my divorcing parents. I wrote a song blaming my dad for not offering the party I rejected.

My thoughts belonged to the voices inside my head. I had millions of opinions on the same thing and never knew what to do because so many different voices told me to do different things. It was weird, complicated. I used to keep track of their names, but by now there were so many voices I didn't bother anymore. My old friends thought I was just seeking attention by coming up with stories about the voices in my head.

ONE NIGHT I TOLD MY MOM I was going to my friend's brother's farewell, so I'd be home really late because his flight to London was at five in the morning. My mom gave me permission to go. When my dad came home from work and my mom told him my story, he checked the flight schedule and confirmed there were no flights to London at that hour. So he called my friend's mom and everyone had to come home from clubbing.

When I walked in the front door, my mom was snickering while my dad was like, "I've never felt so disappointed!" They grounded me for a month for lying.

My family received a letter offering all of us Singaporean

citizenship. My mom was overjoyed to renounce her Philippine passport, which she saw as the cause of her miserable life. But Singapore doesn't allow dual citizenship, and my dad, my sister, and I refused to give up our British citizenship. My mom tried to accept Singaporean citizenship but was turned away because it was an everybody-or-nobody offer, which it didn't say in the letter. My mom was furious at my dad for not giving up his British citizenship.

I didn't think about the consequences at the time, but if my dad hadn't stood up for us, my mom would have made me exchange my British citizenship for Singaporean. I would still be living on an island half the size of London. My mom and I couldn't live without each other, and I was blind to how selfish she could be.

My mom opened up even more and told my sister and me why she married our dad: "for a purpose." She wouldn't get another chance to get out of the Philippines; she didn't want to marry a Filipino drunk; and he seemed nice. She said she was naïve because she was young—twenty-four—and so my dad— thirty-five—had "forced" her to marry him.

She said he treated her like shit while we were growing up, but she put up with it until my sister and I started showing signs that we weren't happy, in adolescence. But those are the most difficult years for most children; that's when parents really need to do their best. But my mom was like, "Fuck, what am I doing wrong?" And she started using the internet, like, ten hours a day, and started making friends online. From these friends she got a lot smarter, she said, and she began realizing my dad was such a shit.

My sister was trying to fix things up, but she made things worse by telling my dad how my mom felt about him. So my house split: my mom and me versus my dad and my sister. If anyone crossed over to the other side, all hell broke loose. My sister complained to my mom that she was dividing the family, but my mom was like, "Stay out of this—it's my problem," and she stopped sharing secrets with my sister, only with me, which divided the house even more.

My mom and my sister fought whenever my dad was away. Everything my sister said became snappy and my mom wouldn't listen to her. My sister treated my mom like she was stupid. Because it takes a lot of effort to understand what my mom is saying, my sister would get pissed off. Then my mom would get pissed off. They shouted at each other all the time—screaming, crying, and slamming doors *right in the middle of my sister's International Baccalaureate final exams.*

My sister vented her frustration in an open letter to our mom on DeviantArt, while my dad was on a plane:

"This house is a battlefield, and we're choosing sides now. Lina's on your side. I'm trying to stay neutral. Both of you have forgotten what it was like when we actually acted like a family—which is the part I want to preserve so much. I hated Daddy that day Lina and I ran away, but I got over it. So what if he doesn't have the right approach to getting Lina to care about her future? At least he *cares*, and if it's really bothering you then for heaven's sake, talk about it!

You have our house on edge. Nobody's happy. I have my final exams, my mom won't listen to me, my sister's partying, and my dad has no clue and has all these plans to make things better. You know what he told me when we were walking the dog because no one else would go with him? He said that he hoped his retirement would mean he could spend more time with you. To see you push him away is driving me crazy because you're acting just like that bitch of a sister. The other day I gave Daddy a hug before going to bed because nobody else seems to. He appreciated it so much I cried in my room afterward. He was waiting for his hug the next night—don't you think he's missing something too? I can't believe you want to put your kids through this. DeviantArt and Skype are more important to you now than sleeping with your husband.

And I don't know what happened to Lina. Her attitude has gotten worse, like she lives to spite her teachers and father. She doesn't put any effort into studying for her exams. She lies about where she's going and laughs about it. Why wouldn't Daddy be concerned about Lina's future? You've changed, and so has Lina. I'm trying to keep the family together— what's left of it—because I remember how it used to be, and I'm trying to figure out where it went wrong."

My mom screamed at her to delete it. My sister locked herself in her bedroom and didn't talk to anyone unless it was to say something mean.

My mom told me she had a boyfriend online and wanted to visit him in Europe, but she would tell my dad that she was visiting her sister. I asked if I could come with her and stay in Europe, but she didn't know yet. She didn't tell my sister about her boyfriend, so only my mom and I knew how broken my family really was.

There hadn't been love in my family for years. When my mom didn't want to leave Europe for India, she told us she wanted a divorce, only not yet because we were too young. Now she wasn't even trying to make her marriage work, but she wasn't initiating a divorce because she was too lazy and unqualified to work and she didn't want to lose her lifestyle.

My dad loved my mom, but she treated him like shit because she thought he treated her like shit. When he phoned home, she'd be like, "Call back later—I'm watching *American Idol,*" and she'd hang up. My dad was trying to make the marriage work, but when he invited her to anything, even walking the dog, she'd invent stupid excuses not to go. Everything was just so fucked up.

My thoughts were all over the place. I started wondering if I should move to Britain after all.

Good: new start, nice clothes, easy school, close to record companies, I could go to *Britain's Next Top Model.*

Bad: not as safe, so I'd hardly be allowed out, I'd leave all my friends behind, it would be really hard for me to fit in at a government school full of local kids because I'd lived my whole life as an expat, and my relatives there would make me watch documentaries and play board games. On the other hand, I only had one friend left to leave behind, and she was leaving Singapore.

I talked to the voices in my head and I was like, "Help—send me a sign!"

Then, when I walked into the living room to talk to my mom, the television started showing scenes of Britain. My jaw dropped—thank you! I talked to my mom about it, and she emailed my dad on his business trip and asked for us to move to Britain. He replied that the Singapore housing and school were booked and it would take months for my mom to get a visa.

I got so pissed! I'd finally decided that I wanted to move to Britain and began getting excited, but now we had to stay in Singapore while I did the International Baccalaureate, which I knew I would fail. My mom started crying, and I got pissed at her for crying.

I was depressed for a while, but then I was happy to stay in Singapore because whatever career I was going to have, it wouldn't require academics. My old friends would get high paying jobs while I scavenged money to feed my hillbilly babies by tattooing bikers' asses.

My mom and I found an amazing gown for my grade ten Formal Night. It made me look slim and tall. My mom figured out a way to hide from my dad that it cost $700: she planned to pay half as a deposit in cash and tell my dad the gown cost only half, then get a friend to pay for the balance and, slowly, steal the other half from my dad to repay her friend. Then she figured out a better way: she paid half as deposit in cash and put the rest on the credit card and told my dad the gown only cost half of what it cost.

My nightmares continued, but now whenever anything bad happened to me in my dream, my point of view would switch so I'd be watching somebody else suffer. Then, when the suffering was over, my out-of-body point of view would switch back, like in this vivid dream:

"I was walking, and I passed all the ninth graders. They were all smoking, doing drugs, and drinking. I passed my friends from twelfth grade and I said 'Hi!' but they laughed at me and kept on going. Then this guy started talking to me. Suddenly it became night, and my point of view switched so I knew something bad would happen to the girl in my dream. She was in bed. The grim reaper appeared in the window by her bed with a massive knife, and she woke up and started screaming. He smashed through the window and started slicing her and stabbing her down to the bone. He picked her up by the neck and started smashing her face with a hammer. The knife cut deeper and deeper into her throat and her screams became blood-filled and quieter. He smashed her face in again, and it collapsed.

As he dragged her away, my point of view switched back. I woke up in a room that looked like a hospital room, except it was a normal bedroom with medical equipment. My face was covered in bandages, like when people are getting their faces reconstructed. Only my eyes were exposed. I couldn't move because I was in so much pain. Then the guy who spoke to me the day before came in and was like, 'Good morning, darling. I hope you aren't in too much pain—sometimes I get a bit carried away.'

I was so scared. He acted like there was nothing wrong. He said that I behaved exactly like his dead wife, so he was going to reconstruct my face to look like hers, but he wouldn't operate on me until I recovered. He said he had dressed up as the grim reaper for fun.

His mother came in, and she was like, 'Hello, dear!' Over several days they nursed me back to health. When they replaced the bandages, I saw that my face had imploded and my nose was gone. When I was strong enough to move around, the guy was like, 'I'm going to operate on your face tonight.'

I was like, 'No!'

His mom was like, 'Hold on now. Dear, why don't you go to the next room while I talk to my son?'

I went into the next room, and there was a window. I pushed it open, climbed out, and ran hard, but I felt I was moving in slow motion.

And then I remembered—in dreams, I can fly! So I ran faster, because that's how I get my momentum when I fly in my dreams, and I leaped into the air and flew. I saw a friend, so I landed and grabbed her. She screamed, so I dragged her into an alley and covered her mouth. I had no face, I was covered in bandages, and my voice was low and hoarse because my vocal cords had been cut.

I was like, 'I'm Lina.'

She started crying. She told me that my mom had gone to the police because she heard screaming in my bedroom, and by the time she ran in, I was gone and there was blood everywhere, so everyone knew I was dying. My friend took me home, where everyone was crying, but I knew whenever all the bad stuff happened, it wasn't happening to me."

My mom constantly told me she hated her life and didn't love my dad. She bitched to her friends all day and cried, then stayed up all night on the internet talking to men and giggling. But she'd lie that she was watching Oprah Winfrey—until, like, six in the morning! I hated it. And whenever my sister encouraged my mom to try to be closer to my dad, my mom accused her of "siding with him" and blamed her unhappiness on my sister, as if it were *her* fault she'd married my dad, which made no sense.

My sister's Graduation Night was held in the Shangri-La Ballroom. My dad was looking forward to seeing my sister in a gown, like the one she wore to Formal Night that started her modeling fiasco. But when he came home from work she was in Doc Martin's buckle-boots, a black miniskirt, striped stockings, corselet top, black eyeliner, and black lipstick. My dad was speechless. My mom was so disappointed. I remembered when my sister was so pretty that I used to be jealous. Now, we looked like the Addams family.

I loved the audience's faces when she went on stage: a goth zombie from another reality, looking completely out of place in the line of elegant graduates in their gorgeous formals.

My sister's reward to her parents and teachers for the best care they were able to give her was a giant "Fuck You!" It was a humiliation, but it was only seen by the school staff and the families of the graduating class, and only once. Her disrespect for her caregivers was nothing compared to the flood of scorn I would begin to release upon my family, especially my dad, on the internet.

My dad acted as if he didn't know what went wrong. Well, he had his head up his ass, pretending his wife and daughters were normal and assuming our lives would fall into place according to how he wanted things to go. My sister was the only one still spending any time with my dad, walking the dog, but that didn't stop her from wanting to disappoint him too.

The three of us women got closer and started talking again. When my mom reminded us that she didn't love my dad, I told her to stop crying and just leave him. She used to tell us about how her mom used to whine and bitch about her dad; now *my* mom had turned into *her* mom. I hoped to God I wasn't turning into mine.

Formal Night was a week later, the night that all girls love: everyone telling them how good they look, everyone obsessing over them, and professionals taking portraits of them. My dad was away on business. My mom ran out to a party, and she was like, "Have fun! Bye!" My friend said she'd text me when she left home, but she didn't so I was late. As I was leaving, my sister was like, "Mommy wanted me to take some pictures—smile!"

When I arrived at the party it was in full swing. My friends already had their portraits taken, the photographers were gone, and nobody even noticed I'd arrived. My expensive dress was useless, and I never wore it again. I had a mood swing and burst out crying. I was almost sixteen, and I couldn't organize getting to a party on time.

My dad's business trip got extended by a week. A few days later my mom went to the ATM and returned empty handed. She was livid and she emailed my dad. When he called back, she shouted, "Why are you taking the money? My friends tell me there is something wrong!" and she hung up on him. Then, although every store in Singapore takes credit cards, she stopped buying groceries until my dad came back and fixed the bank account problem.

My dad was trying to make it work with my mom. He gave her gifts and flowers with cards saying, "I'm still crazy about you after all these years" to display in the house like advertising slogans to show that he was the good guy. My mom never did things like that, and she was so set on it not working that she acted like a complete bitch. She was really pissy. Whenever my dad tried to hug her, she just pushed him away and came up with bullshit reasons not to talk to him. My mom wasn't doing anything positive, ever. She just complained, all the time.

Both our parents were being nice to us, as though they were trying to get us on their side. My dad always went to bed at a decent time, and when I went out my mom would be like, "I'll wait up for Lina." Then she'd sleep on the couch next to the computer because she wanted to use the internet and didn't want to fuck my dad. When I came home at four in the morning she'd let me in. I came home late one night, stomped through the house in my heels, tripped, and puked. My mom helped me clean up. I knew she wouldn't tell my dad.

I hadn't done homework in ages. I canceled my tutors. I left studying until a few hours before each exam, and then I slept. I walked into my literature exam without having read the books.

I finished the history exam in fifteen minutes, and I thought it had been soooo long. I looked at the clock, like, "Yay! We're finished!" Then I saw I had two hours left, so I sat with my feet on the table, and it sucked because I couldn't sleep. The examiners walked by, shaking their heads. I got Ds on the two final exams.

My sister did well on the International Baccalaureate final exams and flew to Europe for a holiday. After A and B+ in grades seven and eight, and C+ in grade nine after my disorder struck, I finished grade ten with C, my lowest average ever.

I felt like absolute shit.

I felt so uninspired, I went to bed at noon and ate dinner for breakfast. I was at the low point in my psychological wave pattern. Then I would get high on life and start to enjoy my holidays.

I STAYED UP ONE NIGHT PAINTING a T-shirt with fabric paint. My mom walked into my room the next morning, while it was drying, and was like, "What the fuck is that? Why is there *blood on your shirt?*" She made me go back to feeling like shit again.

My dad flew home for my parents' nineteenth anniversary. He sometimes missed being home for birthdays, but he never missed an anniversary. They took a taxi to the Fullerton Hotel for their romantic riverside evening. When they returned, my mom looked smug, and my dad seemed pensive.

After he flew back to Japan two days later, my mom told me their dinner had ended in an argument because she treated my dad like shit. That was because after my sister and I skived school a year ago, she'd compared herself to her two friends and, coached by them, she figured my dad was "blackmailing" her into being miserable because she was stuck with him for our lifestyle. Her friends advised her to end her misery by divorcing him, but she decided that instead of leaving the marriage or fixing it, she would stay for the lifestyle but treat him like shit so he would get so fed up *he* would throw *her* out. At their dinner my dad told her she wasn't a prisoner and she should love him or leave him but stop complaining—especially on their anniversary.

She got all dramatic, so my dad asked her if she was having an affair. She denied it. They skipped dessert and came home.

I advised my mom not to leave my dad until she had a job. The thing is, she never *tried* getting a job. She was as lazy as her dumb sister in Britain, who married a fat bum who never held a job, so they had eight kids so their family could live on the dole. My parents would have been so much better off if they divorced ages ago. I thought they weren't going to split up, but they weren't trying to fix any of it either. Sometimes parents are more immature than kids.

My dad came back from his long business trip, and a week later everything changed.

My parents walked out of their bedroom on Saturday morning and asked me to sit down with them. My mom looked annoyed. My dad calmly announced that my mom had been unfaithful since last year and he was going for a divorce. He said he never wanted a divorce, but her behavior left him no choice because he couldn't trust her again. He had discovered that she loved someone else, and we already knew it.

My mom mumbled something about being the guilty party so she had to accept divorce.

He was like, "Why did you treat me like shit on our wedding anniversary and make me look to see what you're up to?" He announced that instead of moving to a townhouse when our lease expired in two weeks, we would move to two apartments until I finished school, then we would leave Singapore. My dad asked me who I wanted to live with. I chose my mom.

My parents called my sister in Europe and broke the news. My sister chose to live with my dad, and she broke down and cried after the call was over. She was the only one to shed a tear for our family, and the news hit her hardest of all. She called me as soon as they hung up:

"So they're getting divorced."

"Yeah," I said. "I wasn't surprised about the divorce, only about the speed."

"She was having an online affair?"

"Yeah. And she was fucking with a webcam, which I had no idea about."

"I had no clue. That's disgusting."

"Yeah. Cybersex is sick," I said.

"Dad said the guy is thirty-five, unemployed, diabetic, and living at home. That's kind of an odd choice. She was flashing him her pussy and doing everything."

"She doesn't actually love him. She was playing around just for fun!"

"What! The shit! What the hell? It's her stupid decision, isn't it?"

"Yeah," I said. "She's a gold digger and doesn't even want to be with him. A very stupid mistake. Now she's all sad about the divorce, and I'm like, 'What the fuck is wrong with you? Make up your mind!'"

"What upsets me most is how much she hurt Daddy. He feels the secrets we had to keep for Mommy were affecting his relationships with us."

"Yeah. Trust and communication are number one."

"I kind of saw divorce coming but hoped it could be avoided. They've been arguing in front of us and bitching about each other our entire lives. That, we got used to. But Mommy degenerated into a whining teenager *this last year*, telling me she didn't love Daddy, I saw her as my enemy, and I was his little pet."

"And now she's like, 'He's gonna find someone else, and I'm gonna die alone!' The situation is better over here in Singapore, but it's also worse because they're moping, and I'm like, 'Well, if you're miserable about splitting, then why are you splitting?'"

"They should talk—but you know Mommy! Every time you tell her to talk to Daddy, she mopes about how she's the *victim* and he won't let her talk! Well, look what happens when you don't talk! She always has to be the victim and always needs pity. She should've seen divorce coming, after she did all that shit."

"Yeah," I said. "What she did was stupid. I don't think he'll forgive her for fingering her pussy on a webcam. The guy could've been taping it for all we know. If Dad had done it, she wouldn't forgive *him!* But she's like, 'I have a friend whose wife did this, and he forgave her!' And then she's like, 'He's such a kind man, been a great father and provider to us, but that's not all we want in life.' And then she mopes! She's so immature."

"It's her own stupid mistake. What did she expect from fooling around? For us to side with her all the time? Lina, I'm sorry you have to put up with their moping while I'm away. When I was there, I had to put up with Daddy asking what was wrong, and I had to bite my tongue."

"They both don't get it: Mom doesn't really get anything, and

Dad doesn't get that he's made her feel like shit throughout their whole marriage, but she never showed her feelings."

"The divorce is her decision and her fault for doing what she did, and it was her choice lumping it all on us. I can't even understand Mommy anymore. She's never wrong in an argument because you can never follow her damn points."

"Yeah," I said. "And she's never wrong because she can't connect her brain to her tongue that well and she always has to be right. 'You didn't do your homework!' 'I did it before I left.' 'No you didn't!' 'Yes I did, look.' 'No!' 'Yes!' 'No!' 'Yes!' Haha … yeah."

"Her changing the topic all the time doesn't help anyone understand her. Daddy and I talked on the dog walks, but I couldn't get through to Mommy, not anymore. With her, it's all me-Me-ME! She just didn't want to work things out or even attempt to make the marriage work."

"It's about time they did something about it. Mom just doesn't 'get' marriage. She's never, like, gotten it. What if we end up like her?" I groaned. "Oh my God!"

"Don't even think about it! At the psychologist's Daddy put in the effort, but Mommy was just sitting there with her arms crossed. She told me she didn't love Daddy anymore and I had to keep it from him, even when he sensed something was up and he asked me!"

My mom's mouth was bigger than the Atlantic Ocean, but she made us keep ours shut. She blamed me for telling my sister about her affair and she blamed my sister for then telling my dad, even though we'd both said nothing. I thought I wouldn't have to keep her secrets anymore, but I was wrong.

MY DAD SOON TOLD ME HIS SIDE of the story. My mom had started dinner by saying she wasn't sure they'd reach their twentieth anniversary. She was sitting there wearing solid gold bangles, diamonds, and a gold Rolex, carrying a Louis Vuitton handbag, and smiling with her new dental implants and laser-whitened teeth.

She drummed her manicured fingers on the table and snapped, "Why don't you pay me like a maid?"

He was so shocked, he couldn't eat. He suggested marriage counseling; she said it was too late. She'd never talked like that before. She denied having an affair, but the tone of her voice wasn't normal so he guessed she was lying.

So he started snooping. He found calls to a European cellphone in their phone bill. He took the computer backup disks to Japan and found some photos of a European man. He discovered my mom had been deleting her history files, which meant she was hiding something *and* someone had taught her how to do it. I mean, my mom didn't know what the Recycle Bin was! But she missed deleting one history file. My dad was shocked to read it: "I need to spank you baby, bend over and show me your white flesh. I love you baby." My mom had typed that, and more, at noon on New Year's Day, seven months ago while the whole family was home together.

After seeing that smoking gun my dad bought a recorder, and he set it up when he came home from Japan. It soon captured their white and brown flesh *in flagrante delicto*.

The announcement made me feel independent, reliable, and grown up-ish because I had to take care of two whiny adults. I needed to become a matchmaker, but where could I find people that were perfect for both my parents? My dad had the worst luck choosing wives, and he wasn't exactly appealing.

Now that I was the big sister at home, because my sister was away, I understood how my sister felt. Now I was the one cooking dinner, cleaning dishes, taking my mom shopping, and offering to pack my dad lunch. I felt good. I learned a lot, like trust no one.

My parents had switched places. My mom used to tell us she hated my dad, but now when *he* called for divorce, *she* told us that she realized she actually loved him. For almost twenty years she told herself she was miserable, and for almost ten years she told us she wanted a divorce, but now that my dad was giving her what she wanted, she realized she loved him. But he was like, "... No."

My mom even went for dog walks with him now, after turning down every request for three years. She had been so rude to my dad for so long, and suddenly she was so nice to him it was sickening. Except now she didn't use the internet when my dad was home, and she tried to make sure I didn't see her chatting with her boyfriend when I was home.

For my whole life, I thought my parents didn't share any real love. They didn't like the same things and they couldn't communicate without fighting, so I thought the divorce was going to be a good thing. But now all my mom did was whine and bitch and cry because they were getting divorced. She even accused *him* of having another woman, and he was like, "Even if I wanted another woman, I'm not the type women go for."

When my parents separated, it was like I'd passed through a phase or recovered from an illness: the voices and visions in my head disappeared. After two years of seeing and hearing them, Run, Let, Hide, Seek, Coon, Khaos, Semb, Wass, Selene, and the others no longer came to me. Sometimes I missed them all, but mostly I missed Run. Eventually my hallucinations became another false memory. I remembered *keeping my hallucinations secret*, even though I'd been describing them in detail to my friends as I was having them. There are dozens of colorful conversations about them in my archives.

Hollywood Dreams

I HAD A BRAIN MRI ON MY SIXTEENTH birthday to try to find out why I never had periods. The scan showed my pituitary was slightly small but not small enough to explain anything. I looked feminine and my baseline hormones were normal. My parents took me to a Korean restaurant for my birthday dinner.

Three days later my mom and I moved into a three-bedroom apartment near my school, with the dog and the piano. My dad moved into a nearby two-bedroom apartment, with my sister's furniture. My parents saw each other daily for the first few weeks, when my dad wasn't on business trips, and then every weekend.

My old school charged my dad $500 for not returning my textbooks, and he made me pay for them from my allowance. So much for feeling grown up! I returned them, and then he gave me my allowance back.

I decided I didn't want to be a tattoo artist after all. Now I wanted auditions: acting, singing, and songwriting in Hollywood. I would take a gap year there after high school and be discovered! If nothing happened, then I'd go to college. Maybe I'd go to acting school in Hollywood while I got an agent and auditioned, because acting school would look good on my resume. I wanted paparazzi chasing me. I wanted to hear scandals about me. I wanted to be on the cover of magazines. I wanted to be all over YouTube and Twitter. I wanted followers. My friends thought I *wanted* to be famous because I was self-centered, but it was something I *needed*. If I died before I was successful, my spirit would return as a ghost. Because I wanted to be famous, I started talking to myself as though I was in an interview. It became a habit.

The first day at my new school was horrible. I hated being the new kid. The school had no uniform, so I turned up in a black tank top, baggy cargo pants, and buckle combat boots, not to mention bright red hair. People were, like, judge-judge, and nobody spoke to me. Every student was an expatriate, like at my old school.

The homeroom teacher smiled at me and said, "What do you miss most about home?"

I shrugged. "I don't have a home." I wasn't smiling.

I wanted to hide in a corner and cry when I didn't know anyone. I hated being shy and introverted. Then, when I finally did know people, I never spoke up because I didn't want to be wrong, thanks to my self-esteem issues. I cried when I got home.

The second day I made some friends. It was easier to make friends there than at my old school. My old school was like, "How many people got A? Yay!" My new school was like, "How many people even passed? Yay!"

The third day I wanted to drop subjects because I'd hardly learned anything in grades nine and ten. Like, how do you simplify square roots without solving them? English homework was hard. I had to read, annotate for language and literary features, look up new vocabulary, and prepare a presentation. I didn't know how to annotate and I didn't know about literary features. When I was nine, my vocabulary tested in the 99.6th percentile, the best out of 250 kids. But at sixteen, I had to read a sentence over and over before I realized I was reading it, and then read it over and over before I understood it. I hadn't read a book in years.

I lost most of my textbooks during the first week, before I'd written my name in them, but I managed to do my homework on the day I got it.

During the second week I felt exhausted. I had French homework, but I was already so far behind from grade ten that I couldn't even understand the *instructions* because they were in French. I had to do the International Baccalaureate so I could stay in Singapore until I graduated, and I needed intermediate French for the International Baccalaureate because Spanish was full and Chinese or Japanese would have been even harder. I wanted to drop the International Baccalaureate without having to move back to Britain, where I couldn't go clubbing and probably wouldn't be able to visit Singapore again. But my dad said if I was just going to do a normal high school diploma, I should do it in Britain for free.

One night when my dad was over, I said as a joke, "I have a boyfriend."

My mom cried out, "God, no! Don't lose your virginity!"

My dad smiled. "Don't get AIDS."

Thank God I never saw my parents tipsy. My mom would have freaked out and my dad would probably have recited mathematical laws.

Now that I was under the care of my mom, I liked my dad—in small doses. My mom was way cooler than my dad, but she was emotionally unstable and had massive mood swings, hardly more together than her children. Sometimes she hugged and kissed me. Other times she ignored me or yelled at me. Sometimes when I came home she'd be crying, and I had to comfort her for hours. Whenever she came home she'd bitch about her friends. But nobody cared about being friends with my mom; it was *her* that wanted to be friends with *them*. Nobody really respected my mom.

At dinner one night, she bawled, "I'm a horrible mother! Oh my God, your dad is right! I haven't been doing my job as a mother for years! I've just been a friend! Now I'm going to be a mother. Go do your homework, and don't go out!"

"Calm down. I would've been like this no matter what you did, no matter what anyone did, whether it was to support me or not. I've been like this my whole life."

My emotions were all over the place. I ended up crying in a cab because I spent ten dollars on a taxi to go to the wrong address, so I had to get another taxi and spend another ten dollars to get to the right address, and I ended up late. I lost my cellphone for the third time and my dad bought me the shittiest new cellphone ever. I was pissed at everything. I did a school art piece where I drew myself tearing my chest open. The skin that was being torn formed into a dreamcatcher, and there were eyes inside looking out.

I wanted to start selling my music in Singapore and then start expanding, so I asked my dad to help me set up my recording studio, which used to be his studio back when he made our family CDs.

I told my mom I wanted to be a tattoo artist if I couldn't get anywhere with my music or acting. She was like, "You can be a tattoo artist as long as you don't end up like those tattoo artists who are covered in tattoos." My mom could never see where things were going.

She was on the internet whenever she was home, video talking to cyber boy. She always tried to hide his face on the screen from me, as though she didn't trust me not to tell my dad, but she asked me to take some pictures of her on the bed in her red nightgown.

My mom used to spend hours massaging me before we moved. Now she didn't massage me anymore. I realized that massaging me had been an excuse for not going to bed at the same time as my dad.

I dropped French during the third week, and along with it the requirements of the International Baccalaureate program. I replaced French with development studies. It was too late to move to Britain, so my dad had to accept my broken promise.

I went to his apartment, and we cooked steak with vegetables and baked an apple pie. While the pie was in the oven, we rode bicycles to buy ice cream. After dinner I organized the stuffed toys in the cupboards in my sister's room (she was still in Europe). When I gave my dad a hug and a kiss as I was getting into the taxi, he said it was my first hug for as long as he could remember. The divorce had wiped away my mom's secrets and everyone was trying to make a fresh start, but nothing could wipe away my disorder. My hugs would not last long.

MY MOOD SWINGS WERE NOT AS BAD as they were before, but stories and movies about rape reduced me to an emotional wreck. I was scared that if any man came even slightly close to raping me, I'd end up in jail for manslaughter. I had many dreams where I smashed men's faces into walls until they were dead. I was scared to walk down a street alone. If I noticed the same man a few times and he was going the same way as me, I was terrified. If I stood in a lift with a man, I held my keys and got ready to gouge his eyeballs.

I became really anti-touch. When I dropped my glasses and

my friend reached out to pick them up for me, I ducked down and slapped her.

My Chinese friend gave me advice for the last time:

"The shittier I do, the more chance I have of being able to drop out. Stupid essay. I should probably try to concentrate. Why do we read literature? Because people make us."

"Lina, you mean don't read for fun?"

"Nope. It hurts my eyes. The contrast of black against white hurts."

"Maybe you should get a better light."

"I have to read in dim lighting otherwise it's too stark, so it damages my eyesight and everything falls to shit so I stay away from books. Plus, it takes me at least five tries for the words to sink into my brain. I'm trying to get out, so wouldn't it be best if my work was absolute shit?"

"But don't you read stuff online? It's the same thing, isn't it?"

"I don't read, apart from MSN Messenger."

"Oh, I see. I couldn't live without reading. If I had to choose between the computer and books, I'd pick books. Yes, I'm a nerd."

"I write stories, draw, watch videos, hang out, sleep, play guitar, sing, write songs, and complain about how bored I am."

"You don't study?"

"Nope, haha!"

"Lina, studying is my job."

"You're good at it and you don't seem to mind it."

"Because I'm a student! Of course I mind it! Who would prefer to stay home and do homework instead of going clubbing? I'm not a complete idiot; studying is something that I just have to do. I want to do well, so I do well. It's simple as that."

"I want to live for the moment. Everyone has different ideas of happiness, so we all do different things. You really want to be successful with, like, jobs and stuff, right? Business, money, brains. I just want to do what I love. What makes you shit your pants in happiness?"

"Getting good grades, but that's brainwashed into me; that's a part of my life. I want to make a difference. I don't want to be just some nobody who did nothing for the world and died a nobody."

"Oh, like the world peace changing-type difference? Or, like, a cure for AIDS?"

"Either, but I know that's not going to happen because I'm not the smartest at school, so there's no way I'm the smartest in the world. If I can't make myself happy, I'll settle for making my parents happy."

"That kind of sucks assballs. You need to find something that makes your heart pump, your blood rush."

"I've found that, but I know I won't achieve it. I really want to be a somebody."

"I want to be someone, but with my music and my acting and stuff."

"Oh, like a celebrity? That's a good dream, and achievable if you work hard."

"I have to get off my ass and start recording my stuff with botheredness."

My Chinese, Indian, and Korean friends gave me good advice for two years. I wish I could have followed even half of it.

When they graduated from my old school, my Chinese friend went to Wellesley College then MIT, my Indian friend went to LaSalle College of the Arts, and my Korean friend went to Johns Hopkins University then Harvard Medical School.

While I was tattooing bikers' asses, the first became a Wall Street vice president, the second a filmmaker, and the third a cancer researcher, no shit.

My dad had dreams like these for my sister and me, but after we became teenagers, we and my mom didn't share his values. My superstar Chinese, Indian, and Korean friends had all been good friends before my meltdown, but we were now worlds apart, and I lost touch with them. My non-superstar Mexican and American friends never gave me advice, and we are still in touch.

My dad cooked for my mom and me at his place. He made stew, so it was automatically bad. Even my dad was like, "This tastes like instant leftovers." But other than that, it was fun.

I baked an apple pie and overheard my parents talking. My mom blamed her infidelity on my dad's working hours when we lived in Japan, back when I was a toddler, because he didn't pay her enough attention. My dad said that moving to Japan was a shock to him too, going from European to Japanese hours, and he'd had no friends or hobbies for five years. But he was happy because he was saving for our education and his retirement, and she was enjoying a lifestyle with a cleaning lady, a car, a gym, and a social life in the Tokyo American Club with other Filipina wives. My mom had all that at twenty-nine. But she said other wives had the same things. He said that's because they had husbands who worked like he did.

I went into my sister's room and played with her toys while they quarreled. When I was a kid I thought my parents always gave my sister the best toys. But she didn't play with them very much, so they always ended up being mine.

My mom went online to cyber boy as soon as we got home.

Life was better now that I wasn't doing the International Baccalaureate. I loved my new school. My new friends were great.

Singapore was cool. I wasn't doing any homework. Whether or not I did anything in class depended on who I was sitting next to and if I had something to draw on the back of my book. My dad said if my grades improved, he'd go down to Zirca and shout a round of drinks for me and all my friends.

I kept going back to the academic advisor to ask about switching hard subjects for easy ones:

"You don't like working, do you?"

"No!"

I became nostalgic again, not for Europe, but for my childhood. I missed Europe, but only because of the weather and scenery. There are such cute childhood videos of me, like where I'm sitting alone on a hotel balcony singing, "Twinkle, Twinkle, Little Star" and I get the lyrics wrong. And where I'm sitting on a beach and shoveling sand into my diaper. I sit there like, YAY! Then I get bored and remove it all. And where I'm cooking sausages over a campfire with my sister. She tries to help me, so I scream, "Don't!" in a shrill voice. As I watched the family videos I became puzzled about how I could have been such a perfect little kid, and then become so insecure that I bullied and judged people all the time and thought I was better than everyone else.

When my parents were still together, my dad was strict and my mom would let me go out just to piss off my dad. But now that she was in charge she was obsessive and controlling. Sometimes she sounded like my dad, telling me I wouldn't go anywhere without an education and that my celebrity dreams had only a one-in-a-million chance.

One day my mom would ask my dad to reconcile, and the next day she would tell me he was full of shit. One day she would blame the divorce on my dad's long working hours, and the next day she would blame it on my sister and me for skiving school a year and a half ago.

My mom got her first job, changing diapers in a kindergarten. In the evening I would hear her watching *Are You Smarter Than a Fifth Grader?* in the living room and yelling out the answers. Half of them would be wrong. Once when I walked out of my bedroom I saw my mom cybersexing; her foot was still on her desk when she looked up at me. I swore I would never have cybersex because you can't actually hug and kiss.

My sister returned from Europe, and the family picked her up from the airport. We ate together at Five Star Chicken Rice and went home to my place. My parents were so nice to each other that my sister asked me if they were really divorcing!

When my dad took my sister home to his empty place, things were a lot clearer. My sister cried and was like, "How do you know Mommy did it? Do you have photos?"

My dad nodded and her tears stopped. They had been trying to hold the family together for years, and my sister was the last to see it was hopeless.

I would feel tired, then pissed, then calm. I would sing sad songs, then I'd start thinking random thoughts and begin crying. I'd fall asleep while mumbling because I was so tired and my brain was gone. I slept through English and fell asleep in theater class with my head on my arm, and when I woke up I had the pattern from my jacket indented on my forehead.

There were times when I thought I could do well and I worked my butt off. Then I would fail something and my motivation would disappear. It was depressing to hear my new teachers say the exact same thing as my old teachers: "Lina has the potential to be at the top of the class." I felt like screaming "Shut up!" I had no respect for any of them.

A teacher emailed my dad:

"Lina has not been bringing her textbook to class. She lost it or never got one at the start. She needs to get one immediately to bring to class. I've asked her several times and she keeps saying she will get it but still has not done so. Please make sure Lina takes care of this as soon as possible. Term exams are coming."

My mom never asked to see any textbooks, but now my dad demanded to see them all. I told him I left them at school because that's where I studied.

My dad emailed all my teachers and asked them to confirm I had the right books. He discovered I'd lost all my textbooks, I would have gone the whole year without any textbooks, and at the end of the school year he would have had to pay for them anyway. He was so pissed. He bought new textbooks and complained to my mom about her lack of supervision. My mom threatened me that if I didn't obey her instructions, I'd have to go live with my dad.

I liked Singapore a lot. I didn't want to spend Halloween with people from my new school, but all my old friends went to a party which I wasn't invited to. It was hard for me to make friends and keep them. My trust issues got in the way of getting close to new friends, especially because I couldn't talk about my problems without sounding like a psychotic bitch.

I TRIED TO DROP OUT IN GRADE ELEVEN, twice, and both times my mom helped me. The first time was when she took me to an audition in Singapore for a Filipino talent contest, a clone of *American Idol.* Segments of the show were broadcast daily across the Philippines. Weekly, for three months, some contestants were eliminated until one winner survived. It was my first audition outside of school after my voice acting audition at thirteen. If I survived past the first week, my mom and I would stay in Quezon City and I would drop out of school. We didn't tell my dad.

After having refused all his holiday offers for four years before they separated, my mom asked my dad for a family holiday! She asked him to take us to Boracay, the expensive resort island in the Philippines, and my dad made all the arrangements. It felt odd to have a family holiday with the family broken up, but I was happy to go for the beaches and white sand. I hoped my parents wouldn't fight.

I won the Singapore audition. My mom and I had to fly to Manila in four days, so we told my dad. He supported me and called my school to arrange a week's leave of absence for me.

Manila was fun. There were eight foreigners on the show, out of the twenty-eight contestants, but I was the only one who couldn't speak Tagalog. The director shoved me into a red *cheongsam*, and I had to wave at the camera on opening night and shout, "My name is Lina and I'm representing *Singapore!*"

We had workshops for singing, acting, dancing, modeling, poise, and makeup, and we partied every night. The director made the show as dramatic as possible and portrayed me as a bitch. The singing teacher played a scale and we each had to sing "ma-ma-ma" arpeggios. Then the teacher, who was also a talent judge, asked me about singers in Singapore:

Broadcast on Filipino television, I answered, "Where I live in Singapore there are amazing singers, so I was really surprised that a lot of the contestants couldn't keep up with the singing exercises."

Cut to the teacher: "Lina insulted you all! What do you think of her?"

Cut to second contestant: "Lina is so conceited!"

Cut to third contestant: "Lina is overconfident and I don't think she's good at anything else."

Cut to fourth contestant: "*Eew!*"

Cut to the teacher: "Lina's attitude!"

At the end of the first week I was eliminated, along with thirteen other contestants. I felt like shit. My attitude had protected my self-esteem by giving me an excuse in case I lost, but it also helped me to lose. My mom and I flew home. I wanted to spend the rest of my life in front of a camera and crew, but I'd missed six days of school and was failing my exams. I told everyone the show was shit and I'd lost because of my attitude, not because of my talent.

Looking back, I couldn't speak Tagalog, so even if I won the show I wasn't going to be offered product sponsorship contracts like past winners. I could only stay for a month, as a tourist with no right to work, because I had a foreign passport. And I was never going to live in that poor third world country from which my mom was so desperate to emigrate. I had made my mom proud, but she should never have signed me up.

My family spent Christmas week on Boracay, which has the world's most beautiful sunsets. Our room was a thatched bungalow with a banana leaf roof. My dad booked a two-day advanced scuba course for himself, my sister, and me as soon as we got there. My mom looked sexy in her string bikini, until she drank a tall Long Island iced tea and spent dinner puking in the bathroom.

She was acting like she wanted to reconcile. My dad treated her like a girlfriend, and they walked around holding hands.

I got seasick on the diving boat and threw up. But the diving was awesome! Reefs, lionfish, pufferfish, groupers, a wreck dive, and a night dive on Christmas Eve. There's a ghostly underwater photo of the three of us standing on the bow of a wreck that looked like the Titanic.

Diving became a false memory. I remembered that *I hated scuba diving* because the equipment is suffocating and the only reason I did it was that my dad *made me do it* because he liked it—as if my sister and I had to dive and triple his cost so he could dive. In fact, I'd raved on social media to my friends about how much I loved diving on Boracay, as did my sister, and one of the goals I wrote when I was twelve was to scuba dive the Great Barrier Reef.

The theme of all my false memories was victimhood, blame, and spite. I needed to convince myself I was miserable even when I was having fun.

On our last night on Boracay, my mom invited my dad for a walk along the beach. They weren't holding hands when they got back, and my mom looked really angry. She told me that she'd said to my dad that, because he gave his ex-wife a second chance when she cheated twenty-five years ago, he should give *her* a second chance too. But he said no.

Later, my dad told my sister that he'd been a fool twenty-five years ago but he was wiser now. He said my mom had never apologized for her cybersexing and had never said, "I love you." I couldn't tell my sister or my dad that my mom had never stopped cybersexing; I still had to keep my mom's secrets, even on the white sand of Boracay.

MY MOM AND I VISITED MY DAD AND SISTER'S place for New Year's Eve, then my sister went out with her friends. I left to join my friends while my mom stayed with my dad to drink champagne during the countdown, like they did every year for twenty years. When I got home, an hour after midnight, my mom was already home and was online with her cyber lover.

I just didn't want to get involved.

My sister flew to Britain to start college. At first she liked it, so I thought if college wasn't so bad, I would follow her in two years and have her there to guide me around. I didn't care about college for the education; it would just be an excuse for me to be in Britain so I could go to record companies.

I wanted to be an actress-singer-songwriter-director, but my dad was like, "Stay in school! Go to college!"

My mom accepted that I didn't want to go to college, but my dad refused to accept it. I planned to tell him I'm going on a gap year in Hollywood, so he'd pay for it, but then I planned not to return. If nothing happened in Hollywood, then I'd let him drag me off to college and spend thousands of dollars for me to just sit there and not learn anything. I'd take the tuition money and move out.

My mom seemed to become unhinged. While I was playing the piano she started crying in the kitchen, so I went to her and was like, "Are you crying because of my song?"

And she was like, "No, I'm chopping onions," and she kept on chopping *carrots*. She was like, "Aaah!" and "I hate him!" all the time.

I was like, "Well, that's why you're divorced!"

My mom was out partying night after night, and I hadn't gone out in three months. I'd been high on parties at the end of the tenth grade and the beginning of the eleventh, but now I ignored everyone and stayed home like a hermit, writing and drawing and making music.

I hated being part of the norm. I kept a photo album in my computer to track the changing colors of my hair. I had a mood swing and was crying while eating waffles and ice cream. Then I went shoe shopping with my mom, so she would pay for the shoes, and I felt better.

I dropped English and replaced it with media studies. My dad started getting emails from my new school like the emails he got from my old school. This one came from my art teacher, even though I *liked* art:

> "I am concerned that Lina is knowingly not meeting some of the assessment criteria. I spoke to her about her attitude and I have tried to encourage her to view art as an academic course as well as a passion. I will ask her to commit to spending an evening a week in the studio."

My mentality about school was so bad that I kept forgetting I had to go to school. I didn't feel like I even *had* school because I just didn't care about it. I left assignments to the last minute because I couldn't work otherwise, and then I couldn't be bothered to complete them. Maths made no sense to me. "Gino invested $20,000 in a term deposit for three years with interest of 3.8% p.a. compounded monthly while inflation over the period averaged 3.4% p.a." I just copied the answer from the back of the book.

Most people who don't like school don't like it because it's shit, but I hated it because it took up the time I could have spent recording my music, writing, scriptwriting, and filming. My fantasy novel was taking over my life and was already twice as long as *The Hobbit*. I couldn't concentrate in class. I'd be like, "Lina, listen!" Then I'd stare at the teacher and think about my novel.

I asked my dad if I could spend the summer in Hollywood so I could look around for acting roles. I was sure my looks and talent would get me discovered. I wasn't worried that I'd never had a speaking role. I didn't know that a non-resident foreigner couldn't even be hired. My dad said no, not alone at sixteen. He sent me information on summer acting courses in Singapore at Centrestage, Stint on Stage, NYU Tisch School of the Arts, and LaSalle College of the Arts. He sent me the contact for the dubbing studio where I'd auditioned three years before and asked me to try there again.

I ignored all of it. Because my dad wasn't sending me to Hollywood immediately, I believed he was doing everything he could to stop me from acting.

My school distributed some brochures for the summer Filmmakers' Program at the NYU Tisch School of the Arts. I pleaded to my dad to attend it. He said it looked good but I had to be passionate about it because it cost $10,000, as much as a year in college. But my parents approved it, and I wrote my application letter:

"I have been in many team experiences where I collaborated with other students, some of which were school plays and small films I made with my friends. In school plays I was an actress or singer but when I made small films I wrote the scripts, directed, filmed, and edited. I love working with other people and from a course like this, I feel I could learn a lot more about the subject of filmmaking that I am passionate about.

I was on a Philippine national television talent show, the only contender chosen from Singapore, and I learned a lot from the experience although I was only there for a week. I am used to intense work and when it comes to a subject I am passionate about, I always dedicate my full attention to the work, putting in as much effort as I can. I hope that from this experience I can become a lot more experienced in filmmaking, also learning about camera angles and lighting as I do not know much about them.

I feel the training and education is necessary for my future career, as my passion has always been with performing, acting—especially on camera—and singing/songwriting. Ever since I can remember, my dream has been to be an actress and a singer. I love directing and seeing everything happen, knowing that I can help to produce something great. I also read novels and I see everything happening like a movie, and it is one of my life goals to publish my works and turn them into films.

Upon hearing that Tisch School of the Arts was holding this course in Singapore, I was excited. I am currently taking Theater Arts at the International Baccalaureate level and I took a summer course in musical theater a few years ago. I hope I am granted a place in your program."

My dad checked my letter and paid the application fee, and I submitted my application. I was excited and told my friends. Next, I had to get two letters of reference and ask my academic advisor to send an official transcript. That's when I discovered that Tisch expected a B average; mine was C. I abandoned my application, wrote a song called "So What if I Fucked You in the Ass with a Dildo," and told my friends I didn't feel like doing Tisch filmmaking anymore because I wanted the summer to be a holiday: no work or education, so I could relax, write songs, make videos, draw art, and write stories.

School was ruining me. I felt like I didn't know anything. Teachers seemed to freak out at me for no reason. My new school was like my old school all over again, where the teachers picked on me. I was failing everything. I thought to myself, if only my teachers and parents cared! I gave myself a break and skived school for a day.

I thought about how it was always my fault our pets died. My mouse in America died because I didn't give her water. My chipmunk in India died because I crushed him in a doorway. I wanted to have his picture tattooed on my neck. Every time I thought about killing my pets, I broke down and cried. I'd promised myself that if God let my pets live, I'd believe in Him, but all of them died. I prayed for them to live before they died, and I used to pray for a happy childhood and happy parents. Then I became an atheist.

MY SISTER HATED HER COLLEGE. She didn't make a single friend there, and dressing goth and acting antisocial didn't help. She was bullied, spent her time hiding in her room playing Ryzom to avoid her classmates, who knocked on her door at all hours just to piss her off, and had a nervous breakdown.

My dad had advised her to study at the School of Visual Arts in New York, where she would study with super-artists like herself, probably some of them equally eccentric. But she refused to write the SAT that many American colleges require even if you have an International Baccalaureate, and she had chosen this British college herself. I told her to come back to Singapore and look at LaSalle College of the Arts. My dad said her choice was up to her. My sister dropped out of college two months after she started, and she returned to Singapore.

SCHOOL WAS HORRID, and I was sick of it. So many celebrities talked on the internet about how they dropped out. I felt that if I had to sit through another exam or parent-teacher conference I might shoot someone.

I secretly wrote to the producers of *Glee* and *Mildred Pierce* in Hollywood:

"I'm a sixteen-year-old British singer and songwriter. I have a YouTube account and I've aspired to be a successful singer and songwriter for as long as I can remember. I'm recording a demo CD, with multiple voice tracks and a full band, but this is taking quite some time. I'm hoping you like what you see/hear and consider me. I live in Singapore, but I am planning to move as soon as possible. I'm even willing to move there in the middle of my school year. For me, singing/songwriting and acting/performing comes before anything else as it is my passion and love. I'm hoping this application isn't too formal and fruity. Thank you for your time. Lina."

I'm embarrassed to read this today. No one would have cast a deluded daydreamer without references, experience, and certification, especially a foreigner without the right to work. I had so much drive, but I didn't yet understand the world well enough to see that my dreams faced impossible obstacles and were unattainable based on my path. I'd received good advice from my old friends, and I could give good advice to my sister, but I couldn't give good advice to myself.

I cleaned my room to make my mom happy, then I told my mom I wanted to drop out. I told her my time in school was wasted, while in my room I was writing five songs a day, recording my music, chunking away at Myspace, uploading videos to YouTube, and sending off demos to try to go somewhere. My mom said if there was an opportunity of a lifetime, then I could grab it, but until then I needed to continue school. Then she started bitching about *her* problems, telling me that it wasn't fair that I didn't consider her feelings, and saying if her yoga hernia got bigger or she got breast cancer she would blame my dad.

I kept reading about teen actors whose parents let them quit school to try acting. I wanted my dad to say, "I support you! Drop out of school to give your dreams a shot!" I knew if I got into some prestigious college my dad would be happy to pay for it, but not for *my life's passion and love—my acting career!* My Myspace page said:

> "I'm a singer, songwriter, actress, writer, artist and basically anything creative, and I'm trapped in Singapore. I can't wait to get out of here. I'm planning to move to Hollywood. I'm married to my work. My work is music, acting, writing, and performing. My dream is to be a successful singer and actress and to publish my books and turn them into movies. It's a long shot, I know, but I'm going to live my dreams or not live at all."

In reality, my "life's passion and love—my acting career" at the age of sixteen was only fourteen months old. When the principal asked me again and again what I wanted to be, in the meeting with my parents, I'd answered, "I want to be a tattoo artist" every single time; I never mentioned actress, singer, songwriter, or musician. I was fifteen when I first wrote the word "actress" to anyone and almost sixteen when I first wrote the word "songwriter," after writing "tattoo artist" dozens of times starting at fourteen. My "life's passion" for acting was another false memory.

I hatched a plan to get my dad to pay for me to live in Hollywood: I would apply to Musicians Institute there. An American online friend got in when he dropped out at fifteen, and then his life was awesome. He told me I didn't need a high school diploma to get in, and then I could get a GED, which is just like a high school diploma. So I decided to apply for their Independent Artist six-month part-time program. My dad wouldn't say no to me if it was a college! After I got accepted, I would drop out.

I told my dad it was a school I really liked, they arranged rooms for international students, they didn't require a high school diploma, and I would get a GED while I was in Hollywood. I begged my dad to let me drop out and take the course. I didn't care about the actual school; it was just my ticket to Hollywood, and then I'd be like, "Fuck you, Singapore!"

My dad checked out their website. He said their music school looked great and their four-year Bachelor of Music in Performance looked perfect for my talent and interests—after I finished high school. But he said the six-month part-time program was from their business school and made no sense when taking the damage to my high school diploma into account. I wanted to punch something.

Two of my grades improved, and the rest got worse. I failed the science test. It asked why the mouse population went down. My answer was that they used up their resources and the neighbor got a cat, and then I drew a cat on the exam paper.

My mom was acting like a teenager with mood swings. Everyone mistook us for sisters, no shit. My allowance was fifty dollars a week. She always forgot to give it to me, then insisted that she did. My mom was tight about money for me, even though she spent heaps of it on teeth whitening kits and $400 bras for herself.

My dad started dating as soon as the divorce was final. My mom didn't take it well. I suffered the worst of her complaining because I lived with her. I shared my misery with my sister:

"Whenever Dad is mentioned in this house, Mom always gets depressed or pissed, or I just walk into the living room and she's crying and she's like, 'I'm going to die alone!' I hate it!"

"*She* cheated on *him*, so I don't see what *she's* bitching about!"

"I know! I just don't get it."

"I'm still pissed that she decided to throw hissy fits about how she doesn't love him anymore during my study leave, so I seriously thought I was going to fail—and then *this!*"

"And whenever I tell her to stop bitching she's like, 'So now it's all my fault!' and I'm like, 'Well, yes, the divorce *is* your fault but, seriously, you were fucking depressed, so it's either divorce and you're depressed or it's marriage and you're depressed. Please, get over it, God fucking damn.'"

"At least Daddy's getting on with it."

"She is too, but she moans and bitches about it."

Before she started dating, my mom got breast implants. My dad was the first to notice. He was like, "Where did you get *those?*" At first she denied it, but then she admitted it. It shocked me that she hid her cosmetic surgery from me while I was living with her. Then she said farewell to cyber boy, after a year and a half of cyber love, and she started dating real physical men using a dating website.

I WAS GOING CRAZY! I decided I was *not* going to bother with my education. I wrote a letter to my dad pleading for him to let me move to Hollywood, as if relocation would solve all my problems:

"My entire life I have wanted to be a professional and successful singer/songwriter and actress, and although I was content with being stuck in Singapore, I can't take it anymore. If I drop out to pursue my career, you'll cut me off. Even if I finish high school, if I choose not to go to college you'll cut me off. If I'm forced to go through college, in the end you will still cut me off because I will always pursue acting and singing.

For every success story there are a thousand who don't make it, but I would rather put a bullet through my head than not do what I love. I need your support, financially and emotionally. Every time I mention my dreams, you put me down, and it hurts. I used to listen to you and hide who I really was. The more confident I got with myself, the further we grew apart.

I have to be in Hollywood. I'm missing opportunities all over the USA. I'm missing the casting call for the TV series called *Glee*. The lead actor dropped out of school in ninth grade, and never even sang until his agent told him to try it, and now he's on the number one show on television. I know it's a one-in-a-million chance I'll become successful, but I'd rather die trying than sit back and wait.

I care more about YouTube than school because I have the chance of being spotted. Acting and singing is my entire life and I will do whatever it takes to make it. Hollywood loves high school dropouts. Hollywood cares about talent and passion, and I have a deckload of both. I was born with genes that could make it to Hollywood. I just need to move and get an agent. I choose sitting at home and writing songs over socializing, so I've lost almost all my friends.

I can never concentrate in class because I'm worrying about my career and how I'm rotting away in Singapore. I'm begging you to let me move to Hollywood. I can get a GED in America, but first I need to get there and find lodgings and settle down. Every day I wake up with a sick feeling and just want to get out of here and start pursuing my career. I'm crying as I'm writing this. Please, consider helping me with my dreams.

Thanks, Lina."

This was magical thinking for a girl who failed her only audition for a speaking role (dubbing cartoons), never even tried auditioning for a speaking role in a school play, and spent her time alone in her bedroom. For a year I'd been expecting to leapfrog experienced American teenagers who spent their lives taking all the music, singing, and dancing lessons, and competitions, courses, workshops, auditions, performances, and certifications they could get, inside and outside of school, and networking, often building on the networks of their relatives in the industry. Even for *Glee* I would've needed credentials and experience, not to mention an American visa, to be considered for the show.

My dad replied while he was on a business trip, and we talked by email:

"Lina, I have always wanted to give you the best education because this will give you the best options, but if you believe I have overlooked your passion and dreams, please forgive me. To ensure you stay safe and have a happy outcome, please give me time to research places for you to go and how to go about getting there. Have you registered with agents or talent shows, like *Singapore Idol?* Agents and auditions will be good for experience, exposure, and your portfolio. Do you want to resume voice or instrument lessons or take acting lessons? Everything helps. I will support you."

"Thank you for your understanding. I'm taking up singing lessons again. That's the only thing I have planned right now. Anything happening about moving country? I'm kind of going crazy. Please let me know what the situation is regarding moving to Hollywood. I'm beginning to freak out. I'm really desperate to get out of here. Is there anything I can do to help?"

"You can help by putting a portfolio together. Your competition for auditions will have portfolios of roles they have done. Apply for every local role that comes up that you may be eligible for. I wrote to friends who live in Los Angeles to get information. I'm checking with a contact in the entertainment business on acting possibilities here. These would require auditions. To succeed in the world's most competitive industry in the most competitive country, you should be able to win nearly any audition in this less competitive country."

"I don't have a portfolio. I've looked around for casting calls and agents but can't find anything. There's nothing for me here. There are auditions every day in Hollywood. I can't stress how sick I feel every time I think about it. Maybe you and I could move to Hollywood together? I'm desperate. Acting and singing are my life and I feel like I'm beginning to die. I know I'm only sixteen, but Hollywood loves young talent and I really need to get out of here."

"It is fantastic that you have a dream, but buying a plane ticket should be more than trying your luck at some foreign auditions. You must offer more to agents than your competition.

Do you need to enroll in dancing and acting courses? You have had no dancing or acting lessons other than ballet when you were small and some belly dancing. I found some agents in Singapore. Once you put your portfolio together, you can audition for them. You can also go for auditions in lounges where they need singers who accompany themselves. Have you noticed these opportunities?"

No, because I couldn't understand that we couldn't just pack up and move to America because we weren't American, just as my mom never accepted that she couldn't stay in Europe as long as she wanted because we weren't European. I would keep on asking my dad for the impossible and be bitter when I didn't get it, just like my mom kept on asking him for the impossible and was bitter when she didn't get it. In Europe, she wanted to divorce him as her husband for not supporting *her* dreams. In Singapore, I wanted to divorce him as my dad for not supporting *my* dreams. I was becoming more like my mom than I cared to admit.

I was going insane wanting to move to Hollywood. I told my friends that I needed to get my head checked, but I didn't tell any adults. I started taking voice lessons again, and then I stopped again.

I was in such an apathetic state as the end of grade eleven approached that school didn't bother me. I thought school was such a waste of time that I spent six hours a day writing my novel as a way to escape it. I solemnly swore to my sister that if I failed to become a successful actress and singer-songwriter within ten years, I would kill myself.

I wanted agents and record companies and talent scouts! I wanted auditions every day! I secretly wrote to the producers of *Maximum Ride*:

"Hello there, I'm Lina. I heard about the auditions for *Maximum Ride*. I have to admit I wasn't entirely sure of what it was but as soon as I read the background information I couldn't stop my excitement. I went out and bought the book and I haven't been able to put it down. I'm a sixteen-year-old British-Filipino actress/singer-songwriter and it would be a dream come true to be in a film like this. I currently live in Singapore but I move all the time and I'm allowed to pack my bags as soon as anything calls, and I would never put off an opportunity like this. I would like to audition for the role of Max and I hope I'm what you're looking for."

I cringe when I read this as an adult. No one could have taken my application seriously.

EVERY AFTERNOON WHEN I CAME HOME from school, I sat down, stared at my computer, and started crying. Then I would get in bed and lie there feeling like utter crap, and my mom would never notice. She'd babble to herself until I got annoyed:

"Stop complaining!"

"Our life is in ruins!"

"Well, no shit, woman!"

"I have another date—bye!"

"... Bye."

And she'd run out the door. She was more like a friend with attention deficit problems than a mom. I could see the issues my dad had lived with. My sister and I discussed them:

"When we were kids," I said, "our mom was all nice and normal at home, but whenever people came over she seemed to be a completely different person, trying to impress them and acting like someone we didn't know. She *became that person!*"

"I remember clearly how rude Mommy was to Daddy before the divorce shit, and then when it happened, she became so nice to him it was sickening."

"I don't get her anymore. She's like this little kid with all her bitchy friends and they go out all the time and they dance like crazy, and then she freaks out and refuses to go clubbing anymore when she finds out people think she sleeps around. Fucking hell. And because we give each other the cold shoulder at home, she gets surprised when she finds out that something happened. She was surprised to find out that I restarted voice lessons and then stopped again. When we talk, it's her yakking and me going, 'Stop complaining!'"

"And then she gets depressed because nobody listens!"

"Of course nobody wants to listen to someone banter on like a Barbie that snorted Pixy Stix! She always talks about the different men she goes on dates with, complains how none of them are perfect, how some are nice but they're shit kissers! I'm like, 'What the fuck!' And she goes like, 'I want someone that's good at ... you know.' Laugh, cackle, stomp—foot hits table. Mom's going damn Benjamin Button, only it's her mind that's going backward."

I dreamed that I was yelling at my mom about being an idiot and a cocktease, and then I was adopted by Lynette from *Desperate Housewives*. I wrote a song about my mom called "Relationshit." I was beginning to form a relationship with my mom like I had with my dad: none, emancipated now from both parents.

I applied for the part-time program at Musicians Institute that my dad had rejected two months earlier. I didn't tell my dad, but my mom supported me because she was depending on me to get famous so she could leach off me for money. She actually said, "I hope you get rich and famous so you can buy me a mansion." She didn't mind that I would have to drop out of high school to attend that six-month program, and I didn't tell her that my dad had already refused it for that reason. My mom co-signed my application form as my parent and paid my application fee. If I was accepted and my dad refused to support me, then he would no longer be able to call himself my dad.

I felt exhausted. I felt like I had a gigantic rain cloud over my head. I felt like I was going to fail at life. I was still getting random mood swings, where one second I was happy and felt like I could conquer the world, and then absolutely nothing in particular happened and I switched, broke down, and cried. I couldn't talk it over with my mom because she was psycho, and I couldn't talk it over with my dad because he wouldn't listen. Plus, both were my parents, so they always treated my sister and me as children.

My dad reminded me about the Tisch Filmmakers' Program I'd applied to three months before. I told him I hadn't heard from them. He called them, and they told him I hadn't sent in my letters of reference and transcript and so they assumed I'd dropped out. Then Tisch emailed me to hurry up and complete my application, and my dad called me:

"Tisch told me they have reserved a place for you because they need more Singaporeans. Just send them any two letters of reference and any transcript, and you're in. Grades don't matter for Singaporeans. You only have one week!"

"I don't want to do that now."

"What? You're not interested in filmmaking now?"

"I don't feel like doing the program anymore."

"I don't get it. One day you want to do filmmaking, and the next day you don't!"

The Tisch Filmmakers' Program became a false memory. I remembered that I applied without knowing the cost and had a panic attack *when I discovered the cost* because I thought my dad would have control over me if he spent so much money, so I *withdrew* my application. In fact, the cost was on the brochure, I'd had the brochure for a week before I applied, and my dad never bought anything without knowing what it cost. My panic attack came *when I realized Tisch would assess my grades.* I would never have heard the end of it if I'd been rejected because my grades were low. My self-esteem would have been devastated. I never withdrew my application; I abandoned it and hoped my dad would forget about it. I remembered my dad *never supported filmmaking,* even though he was the only parent in Singapore who had agreed to sponsor his child to attend that course; all the participants came from overseas.

LIVING WITH MY MOM DROVE ME CRAZY. She always picked the chunks of chocolate out from the chocolate chip cookies. She bought muffins, ate the top, and left the shitty bit for me. I'd open the Ben & Jerry's tub and the ice cream would be torn apart by what looked like a pitchfork and all the pieces of chocolate fished out and eaten, leaving the normal ice cream for me. When I complained, she'd be like, "Stop talking to me like you're the boss of this house!"

Whenever I asked my mom for money, she'd freak out. But she was always bringing home new things for herself, like dresses, shoes, bags, and makeup, and getting her hair done. I couldn't stand it.

She talked about all the plastic surgery she wanted. I felt like saying, "You don't need it, you stupid poodle!" I swore if she got more cosmetic surgery I was going to walk out. She wanted to spend thousands of dollars modifying her body, but when I asked for money for my chicken rice, she was all, "We have food in the house!"

My mom was always on Skype sitting in her underwear, talking to different guys each time. They could see her underwear when she stood up, and I complained about it every time I walked by. She said they couldn't see her underwear, but she found any excuse to stand up and walk around.

She was so desperate, it was disgusting. She was so close to whoring herself out that I didn't want to imagine what she might be doing if I wasn't living there. I couldn't even think of her as a mother anymore, let alone a role model. Most single moms try to be independent, but every time I said, "You don't need a man to complete you. Try to be independent, for once," she'd be like, "No, I can't."

I finished grade eleven without English and French, with a C+ average, compared to C at my old school in a proper grade ten. I went over to my dad's place to cook dinner for his birthday, and we had a nice talk. He thought I'd matured because I no longer mentioned Hollywood and dropping out, but that was only because my application to Musicians Institute was still secret.

I went to see my dad again a week later. Now I told him I'd applied for the six-month Independent Artist program and been accepted, so I just needed $20,000 for tuition, $10,000 for transportation and accommodation, and permission to drop out. I promised to do my GED while I was in Hollywood.

My dad was shocked I had applied behind his back and was furious my mom had signed the application. He reminded me that he would support me through school and college, pay for courses along the way, and, after I graduated, help me launch my career or a business. He reminded me that he'd already told me that he would support me studying at Musicians Institute for a *four-year* Bachelor of Music in their music school. I went home and wrote a song about it, "Everything I Am Is Nothing That He Likes At All," blaming my dad for fucking up my life.

My dad met up with my mom for cappuccino. He told her that no other mother would assist her child to drop out. He told her I was too naïve to know what I was doing and too lazy to do the research to find out, and I just wanted to escape to a fantasy world.

My mom, running her fingers through her rebonded hair, told him I could drop out if it made me happy.

He accused her of sending my emotions on a rollercoaster ride and of taking my attention off my schoolwork by not thinking through the impossible consequences of her actions.

She accused him of always wanting to have things his way.

My dad accused her of destroying his relationship with me, even though it was I who was destroying whatever was left of my dad's relationship with my mom.

She still tried to convince him to let me drop out, so he got so fed up that he called her an idiot for the first and only time.

She stood up to leave, and he grabbed her wrist and ordered her to sit down until they agreed on what to do about me. People in the coffee shop stared at them. He refused to pay for Musicians Institute until I finished high school.

She gave in and agreed that I had to finish high school first. Then she asked him to reimburse the application fee.

My dad came over that evening and together they gave me their decision. As he was leaving, he asked for a hug like the one I'd given him on his birthday, but I was like, "Eew, no!"

I knew in my brain that my dad wasn't always bad, but something in my heart always broke down whenever he got involved in my life. When I watched family videos sometimes I got sad and thought, "Lina, he isn't all that bad!" And then he'd phone me up, and after we hung up I'd break down in tears. I hadn't said, "I love you" to my dad in years.

The Musicians Institute episode became a bitter false memory. I remembered I got *accepted* by a *music school* so I could escape to Hollywood, and I would have gone there to take that course, get my GED, and pursue my dreams—but it didn't happen *because my dad said no*, so I blamed him for not supporting my dreams. In reality, it had been impossible from the start. I would not have been *admitted* even though I'd been accepted: the application stated "international students are *not eligible for part-time programs*" and "admission is upon *submission of a high school diploma* or GED." And getting a GED in California was impossible because only residents can earn GEDs and only after they are eighteen. The course wasn't given by the music school but by the business school. My dad had chosen to argue that high school was more important than part-time courses, not that my mom and I didn't know what the hell we were doing.

I put a profile on Model Mayhem seeking modeling work. I soon realized it was for hookers, so I took it down. Modeling wasn't something I was passionate about. I preferred music, singing-songwriting, and acting.

A friend tipped me off about a casting call for extras in a Bollywood comedy movie being shot on a huge cruise ship from Singapore. Three of us auditioned and won non-speaking roles, not that we could speak Hindi. I made $1,400 in ten days, my first salaried job. My dad's girlfriend printed business cards with my photo to hand out on the ship to promote myself, but I didn't hand out any of them. The movie was a commercial flop. My dad bought the DVD so I could study my performance to improve my acting, but I told him he wasted his money because I didn't even want to watch it.

For my seventeenth birthday, my dad offered me a trip with my sister, his girlfriend, and him to Thailand or Indonesia for scuba diving, but I preferred to stay home, no family holidays. Then he offered me a trip to Universal Studios in Singapore, and I turned that down too. So for my seventeenth birthday he made a sixty-page hardcover book full of photos about my life. It was really nice.

As soon as I went back to school for grade twelve, I dumbed down my program again. I'd already dropped French and English. Now I dropped maths, science, and theater arts, replacing them with art design, business practice, and computer applications, which were vocational courses. My parents were like, "You wanted to drop out to become an actress, and now you drop theater arts!"

I didn't have any friends in grade twelve, so I hung around with my Mexican friend from my old school. We bonded over our mental issues. I earned spending money from YouTube for my songs, except for those with swear words, like "You Little Shit." When I wrote songs I scribbled down the lyrics and memorized the music. So much for being a songwriter. I never wrote the music down.

I didn't do homework because I thought classes didn't benefit me. When my mom complained she never saw me doing any homework, I lied that I did it at school during recess and lunchtime. I was actually writing my fantasy novel on the laptop computer my dad gave me for my homework.

Teenage Escape

My mom was practically a call girl in her numerous attempts to get a boyfriend. She started on Botox, but she called it "going for facials." She was on Skype whenever she was home, typing away and giggling.

She'd come into my room and be like, "Does this outfit look okay?"

"Yes, it looks fine."

Then she'd come back a few minutes later with another outfit. "Does it look good?"

"Yes. That's what you came in here for?"

"Why are you being so bitchy?"

My mom often asked my sister and me for relationship advice, but she never followed it. She couldn't keep friends because she was so busy wallowing in self-pity to stay the center of attention. She whined to me about her problems constantly because she needed someone to whine to. Her behavior was pathetic. She tried so hard to be the victim, all the time. I wished I could smack some serious sense into her head. I was constantly telling her to get a shrink, a female shrink.

I was watching a TV show called 90210 where this girl said, "The person I admire most is my mother," and she talked about how when her parents divorced her mother remained composed and strong. I was like, "If only it was the same for me!"

My grade average improved to where it was before my breakdown, three years ago, but that was because I'd replaced five hard courses with easy ones; the grades in my other courses stayed the same.

My sister was doing well at LaSalle, taking animation art. She had my dad's apartment mostly to herself because he was away so much on business trips. She encouraged me to join her at LaSalle to study acting, film, art, or music, and suggested we ask my dad for an apartment for the two of us. But I wasn't interested. I wanted to move to Hollywood or London.

All grade twelve students had to see the school academic advisor about their college choices so she could help us with our preparation. I told her the only school I would consider was Musicians Institute in Hollywood. She suggested Berklee College of Music in Boston or a conservatory. I said I was not going to go to a conservatory to become a musician because it would probably be really hard, and I hated having to learn stuff about classical artists and fusion music and shit. I didn't even read music properly anymore.

She told me that if she were my mom, there is no way she would pay $30,000 per year, plus accommodation, for Musicians Institute because its credits weren't transferable if I failed to complete all four years. She said I had potential for business and suggested I get a business degree while pursuing my musical interests. I told her there was no way I was going to college, and I would consider getting a job in Singapore while I tried to break into the music industry. Our one-hour career coaching session was over in twenty minutes.

The music teacher at my new school offered to mentor me and to nominate me for admission to the Royal Conservatoire in The Hague, where he did his PhD. He suggested I take a degree there in pop music and jazz, with a vocal option. The courses were in English, the location was fantastic as a lot of performers, artists, and producers went there, and I would have time to work as well as study. If I said that I was interested in applying he would contact the head of admissions to arrange a meeting for us in February. He advised me to restart my voice lessons to prepare for an audition.

My dad got so excited when I told him. He said an education in Europe surrounded by musicians from around the world would be much more fun than high school. He offered to send me to Holland with my mentor for the meeting and audition. But I told my dad I wanted to take a gap year because I needed some time away from the whole education system, during which time I'd work on making myself known. If nothing kicked off during my gap year, then the Conservatoire looked good.

I emailed the Conservatoire to ask if I could drop by during the Christmas holidays, in two weeks. They said the school was always open, so I asked my dad to book my trip. He lectured me on meeting the right people with the right introductions at the right time, which was in February with my mentor, not just dropping by during the Christmas holidays when no one was there. But I wanted a Christmas vacation, not to meet people.

My dad and my music teacher were dumbfounded I let a once-in-a-lifetime opportunity to be mentored to become a professional musician, and to live in my beloved Europe for four years, pass me by. But I would not have survived being surrounded by people who were as talented as I was and who probably studied a lot harder.

I went over to my dad's place for Christmas. My sister and I cooked a turkey dinner. My mom and my dad's girlfriend came over, and we ate together. The food was good, but the corn turned green because we boiled it with the beans. My mom acted like she owned my dad's kitchen, and she made faces at my sister when she asked my mom not to pick the sausages out of the stuffing. Then we took taxis to my mom's place, where the piano was, to play piano-violin duets.

My mom was acting bipolar. Sometimes she would scream like a banshee and the neighbors would open their doors and stare at her. Sometimes she would speak to the air around her and I would think she was talking to me, but she did it so often that I realized she was talking to herself.

She kept bitching that she didn't have a family anymore, but whose fault was that? She absolutely needed a man in her life or she felt unfulfilled and vulnerable. Her self-pity made my sister and me angry because it was her lying and cyber sexing that brought about the divorce in the first place. She told me she wasn't even trying to find a decent guy anymore, so she went out and she had "flings," even with men she knew were married.

I wrote a song about my mom called "Stop Whining, Bitch" and uploaded it to YouTube. My sister was happy she didn't have to live with my mom. I was happy I didn't have to live with my dad.

In addition to my regular gynecologist, I began seeing an endocrinologist to try to find out why I never had periods. A test was done in a hospital, using insulin, and was so dangerous a parent had to be there. All my results were normal, except that my thyroid level had dipped slightly to just below normal, I had low bone density, and I had low Vitamin D, which is rare when you live under tropical sunlight. I started taking levothyroxine, calcium, and vitamin D, in addition to the hormones I took every six months to induce a period. The endocrinologist wondered if my odd hormone problems and my psychological problems might be related, because both started at the same time.

I got depressed again. I just wanted to curl up into a ball and dream. My makeup, hair, clothes, homework, YouTube, and artwork were pissing me off. I had a thousand subscribers on YouTube, but most of the comments I got were about my tongue piercing and hair dye, not about my songs.

I emailed a list of six colleges in Britain to my dad and told him that I wanted to move there a year before I applied. I said I wanted to settle in Britain, learn to be independent, learn the value of money, see more of what real life is like, get a part-time job, gain working experience, send out demo CDs, get an agent, and do acting, music, and writing. He replied that the first college on my list was excellent but the rest weren't accredited. He encouraged me to apply to the excellent one and get a deferral; it was the same college from which he and all his siblings had graduated. He reminded me that he would also support music degrees at the Conservatoire and Musicians Institute.

Two months of thyroid therapy changed nothing. I still coasted at school. I would tell my mom I was sick when I was fine but just didn't feel like going to school. My dad and his girlfriend found me more auditions for singing and acting. I wasn't interested.

When my dad came over to help me with my computer, he asked me why none of my documents and bookmarks were about college; they were all about clothes, hair dye, record labels, and social networking. I said that was because I was interested in applying to the excellent British college. I didn't tell him that was because my Mexican friend was planning to apply there with me.

My dad was happy with my choice and asked me if, after I graduated from high school, which was when his and my mom's leases expired, I would like to move in with him and my sister so he could better support me with college logistics. If yes, they would get a larger place for me. I agreed to move. My mom was happy because she'd have privacy for dating. My sister was even happier.

Without telling my parents, I applied to the excellent British college with my Mexican friend. My program choices were Bachelor of Arts and Bachelor of Fine Arts in Performance. In our applications we declined campus housing because we wanted to get an apartment together. I saved my application in my computer as *ApplicationKissass.doc*.

I emailed my dad and asked for all my school reports and extracurricular certificates. I didn't tell him why I needed them, and he didn't ask. He scanned everything and sent it to me. Then I went to the academic advisor to ask her to send my official transcript to the college. She told me I had to write the SAT before I applied, because my diploma would be neither British nor International Baccalaureate. She checked the SAT website and found I had *one hour* to register for the next test! We did it together, she paid with her credit card, and I told her I'd pay her back. I wrote the SAT secretly three weeks later and paid her back from my allowance.

I graduated from high school in a program with no English, maths, science, or language. My one-year average was B+, but my four-year average was C+. My graduation ceremony was held in the gymnasium, with no formals, dinner, or dance. Compare that to the Shangri-La Ballroom, where my sister and old friends graduated with their International Baccalaureates. My parents and my dad's girlfriend took my sister and me to Hard Rock Cafe to celebrate.

I received my SAT results: the fifty-seventh percentile.

My SAT became another false memory. I remembered I kept the SAT a secret because *my dad would tell me to study for it*, even though it was secret because my college application was secret. I remembered that *my dad opened the envelope* and he was first to see my results, even though I was living with my mom when the results arrived, I didn't tell him I'd written the SAT until four months later when I was living with him and asked to go to New York, and then I sent him the results by email. I remembered *my score was good*, even though it was below the cutoff for the British and other first-tier colleges and was poor for anyone bright; people above the ninety-eighth percentile for intelligence generally score above the ninetieth to ninety-fifth percentile on college admission tests, so my fifty-seventh percentile score had only proved how little I learned in school.

Because my dad didn't know I'd already applied to the British college, he was still doing everything he could to help me get accepted when I finally did apply. He had the idea to ask my endocrinologist to write a letter of support for my college applications. So the doctor's office printed a letter on their official stationery, and it said:

> "Lina was experiencing lethargy and apathy toward her schoolwork, and her grades faltered. Tests of pituitary function revealed secondary hypothyroidism. The effect would be lethargy, poor motivation, and possibly memory, mood, and personality changes. It may be prudent to consider that her preceding years of poor performance may be attributable, at least in part, to her medical condition. Within the short time after her consumption of levothyroxine there has been a noticeable change in her energy and drive."

The doctor's letter became another false memory. My dad didn't tell me *he wrote the letter* and the endocrinologist hardly changed it! It fooled me as my dad intended it to fool colleges: I thought my grades went up *after I took levothyroxine*, even though I had all my medical and school reports. If I'd read them, I would have realized my grades went up *two terms before* I took levothyroxine; they went up after I dropped maths, science, and theater arts. All three thyroid tests while my grades were at their lowest had shown no hypothyroidism. My dad had tried to give me practical support for college admission, and emotional support by helping me believe my future looked brighter than my past. But because I never used the letter, its only result was to make me *blame my dad for maltreatment* for not having my thyroid treated earlier.

The British college rejected my secret application because I lacked English. I could repair this in a few months by writing the English AP exam, but my Mexican friend was rejected because she failed to graduate from high school, and resolving her problem would take her at least a year of studying in a community college.

My Mexican friend then worked as a waitress, took a make-up year at a community college, worked again, and then earned a four-year degree in creative and professional writing. It took her five years plus a gap year to earn a BA degree, *six* years that would have taken her just *three* if she'd graduated with her International Baccalaureate. Her anti-depressant, anxiety, and concentration medication—her "happy pills"—controlled her moods but couldn't make her smarter.

Because both her parents expected her to go to college, and she was making the effort, they could see that she needed help to control her moods so she could focus. She got psychiatric help and medication. But not me. I was smart enough to do the International Baccalaureate, as everyone told me until I got fed up and sick of hearing it, but I didn't get help to control my moods because everyone thought I just wasn't trying and no one could see what was wrong.

At eighteen I moved in with my dad and my sister, who had moved to a bigger place for me. I brought our dog and piano. My mom moved to a smaller place that she bought with her divorce money. Everyone was hoping that my sister would lift my attitude and help bring me closer to our dad, but instead I dragged her attitude down and pulled her away from him.

At first it was small things, like he stopped kissing her on the top of her head because I hated being kissed there, and he was trying to treat us equally. I became unable to touch and to be touched by anyone after I became a teenager, even by my dad, so gradually everything got colder between my sister and my dad too. It was heartbreaking for them, but I'd always been a relationship destroyer. It wasn't just that I couldn't keep friends; there was something about my behavior that always polarized everyone around me and made it difficult for them to remain friends with one another.

My dad told me to relax for a month before working on my college applications. He would keep giving me an allowance as long as I was a student or a deferred student for a degree from an accredited college in Singapore, or abroad if it had campus housing. My sister had been accepted by four universities in Britain, and she had then deferred her admission. If I needed make-up courses or tutoring to get me accepted, he'd support that too. He suggested I get a general degree because I'd be a good lawyer. The principal at my old school had said I'd make a good psychologist.

My dad wanted us to have a profession on top of being artists and musicians, what he called "Art Plus." He didn't want my sister and me to become JAFAs, as my sister mocked them: Just Another Fucking Artist, earning low wages one drawing at a time, money by addition not multiplication. He said that pairing two competencies would give us more options, income, and security than "Art Only." What would happen after a hand injury? Or if we got tired of drawing all day? He suggested art plus advertising, or music plus psychology, like what he did with his engineering plus business degrees.

My dad's "Art Plus" became another false memory. I remembered he would *never allow us to become artists or musicians*, even though he'd offered to sponsor me at Musicians Institute in Los Angeles and the Conservatoire in The Hague to become a musician, he'd offered to sponsor my sister at the School of Visual Arts in New York to become a graphic artist, he'd sponsored her studying in Britain for the degree in fine arts that she had chosen herself, and after she dropped out he'd sponsored her studying at LaSalle as an animation artist, where she graduated.

My dad was often on business trips or on holidays with his girlfriend, and my sister was working hard at school, so I usually had the house to myself during the day. I lived in my bedroom, trying to become famous by composing, recording, and uploading songs to YouTube. That is, when I wasn't cooking and leaving the dishes in the sink, working out in the condo gym, or talking online to my American friend, who had graduated from my old school and repatriated. She'd started studying graphic arts at the School of Visual Arts, taking the program my dad had recommended for my sister but she had rejected because she refused to write the SAT.

TWO MONTHS WENT BY, and then my dad started nagging me about college research. To get him off my back, I told him I'd already applied to the British college three months ago but I had been rejected for lack of English. He asked me if I wanted to reapply there. I told him I didn't want to discuss college anywhere. He said I had to get moving, and he sent me the spreadsheet of the best universities in the world he made for my sister, with filters, rankings, and website links. I didn't bother to look at it.

"Keep calm and discretely throw shit at walls," I wrote in my journal. "When people walk slowly surround you, be swift and fart." Such was the state of my mental health while all my old friends were off to college, except for my Mexican waitress friend.

My dad asked the academic advisor at my high school for suggestions. She suggested I do one year at a community college to pull up my average and make up for my lack of English, and then I should transfer to a four-year college in the second year. When my dad told me this, I emailed her directly:

"Hi, I've been looking into the 'Video and Film' course at the School of Visual Arts in New York City and I emailed them about the English 12 issue. I've forwarded all the emails so you could see what they said. I've been advised to send my transcripts in as soon as possible so the application process can start. Thanks for the help."

I didn't tell my dad what I was doing, so he took me for a tour of the community college that the academic advisor had recommended. He reminded me that I hadn't had a single year with four good terms since grade eight, despite seven tutors, two schools, and four course simplifications from academic to vocational. He promised that if I could complete one year of good grades at that community college, he would support my transfer to any college, anywhere, in my second year.

The next day I revealed my latest scheme in a food court with my sister:

"I've decided to take film studies at the School of Visual Arts in New York City. I've already written the SAT."

My dad looked up from his chicken chop. "And what are your second and third options?"

"I don't need *options*. This is the only thing I want to do."

"If you don't have options, then you are not serious about your education and career. I'm still waiting to see your college research. What are you going to do with film studies?"

"Screenwriting, acting, directing. My American friend is studying graphic arts there, and she loves it. She said the dormitory would be too noisy for recording my YouTube videos, so we plan to get an apartment together. She's already out looking."

"Then you aren't going for a degree; you are going for an apartment with your friend while recording YouTube videos. I'm not going to allow that, and I doubt her parents would allow it either. For $300,000 you have to be *passionate* about film studies. If you only want to take film studies under certain *conditions*—like an living in an apartment in Manhattan with your friend—then you have no passion for it. You didn't have enough interest in film studies last year to attend the Tisch Filmmakers' Program; you dropped it. Then you dropped theater arts. You have shown more passion for art and music by taking it every year. Before living on the other side of the planet, you have to know how to study independently. You could show your passion and maturity by doing your first year at the community college we went to, or at LaSalle with your sister, if you insist on film studies."

My sister shouted, "Lina doesn't want to go to LaSalle!"

My dad kept his focus on me. "After the first year, if you still want to go to New York, I'll be retired and could come with you to help you get set up. I couldn't help your sister because I was working when she started college—and look what happened to her."

"I don't want you to come with me! *Eew!* Mom told me she approves! You have to support me!"

"Then let Mommy support you, and I'll repay her after you graduate. Career discussions should be between two parents and one child, at home, not between two siblings and one parent in a food court. This is not the place. We never talked with your sister about her plans when you were sitting there."

My sister and I started blaming my dad for everything. We spent an hour beating it into his head that he was a stupid, arrogant prick. He stayed calm and businesslike, but we were both in tears at the end of the discussion.

As we walked home, I shouted, "You never care about me! You are comparing who I am now to who I was when I was crazy! Every time I considered suicide it was because of you! I was slitting my wrists in the bathroom because of you!"

"Are you asking me to send a girl who was slitting her wrists to New York City, alone?"

He was concerned about my health and safety, because I sure wasn't, but that triggered an emotional breakdown and I collapsed on the sidewalk, gasping for breath. My dad tried to help me stand up, but I shoved him away and shouted, "Don't *touch* me!" He looked crushed.

As soon as we got home, I went out to walk the dog so I wouldn't have to face my dad. While I walked over the overpass I contemplated how easy it would be to throw myself off to be run over by the oncoming traffic. I regretted moving in with him and my sister, because of him. My sister regretted it too: during the two years she and my dad lived together, they got along fine without me. Three months after I moved in with them, my sister hated the atmosphere and the relationships between everyone.

While I was out, my dad lectured my sister on how she might have thought she was helping, but she'd only made things worse by being uncompromising, not helping to look for solutions. She got so pissed at him because she had only been standing up for me against my dad, which is exactly what I asked her to do.

When I came back I wrote him an email:

"Program costs are US$50,000 per year, plus accommodation. My SAT scores are Reading: 470 (40%), Math: 500 (46%), Writing: 600 (82%). Sharing an apartment would be cheaper, and I promise I could take care of myself. My American friend's parents are also worried but they plan to move her out of the dorms. I'd do recording in my free time, so dorms are a bad idea because noise ruins recordings. I've already filled out the online application. I'm just waiting to hit the send button, which I won't do until you say I can."

When my dad read the email, he walked into my room and said my SAT should be good enough to get into college. He was trying to sound optimistic, but I put him in his goddamn place.

I looked him dead in the eyes and said, *"I know!"*

This became a false memory. I could not have known. My

British college application had been rejected because I hadn't met the English requirement, and their website said my SAT score was below the level submitted by successful applicants.

My dad emailed me the next day. When he emailed instead of talking, it meant he was really serious:

"Lina, I'm sorry the college discussion has upset you, but I worry about your future. I'm disappointed by some of the comments you and your sister made, but let's move on. These are the steps to moving forward with your education:

1. Research careers and their education possibilities.

2. List three or more schools and their programs.

3. Agree on some programs with Mommy and me.

4. Apply to those programs.

5. Get accepted into at least one.

6. Execute the respective plan.

The purpose of higher education is to get you the knowledge and certification you need for a career so you can be independent after you graduate.

I would support you at a Singapore college while living at home. I would support you at a British college which has a good proportion of international students and knows how to take care of them. I would support you in other countries at residential universities when I'm sure you are mature enough to cope with the stress of the academics, living in a dormitory, cooperating with your parents remotely, and managing money.

You could show me you are ready for other countries by doing a successful first year here at a local college or by working and bringing home a good reference.

Love, Daddy."

My dad would not follow my plan, but he expected me to follow *his* plan. I forwarded his email to my sister, who replied:

"I fucking hate our dad. There's no forgiving him now. He's completely ignoring the points we made. I'm going to divorce him as a parent once I'm on my own. I used to be angry at Mommy for divorcing him, but now I can see that she was justified. His wives are trophies, and we're investments. As kids he didn't love us, his priority was raising us. Mommy is the one who loves us. She's unstable, but she'd die for us. For Daddy it's all dollars and cents.

He's telling you film studies has no future so you should do art, when he was telling me art had no future unless I planned to go into advertising. It's your life, and it's your choice. When I told him to support you, he got offended that we don't consider our moving to this big apartment to accommodate you as supporting you. That's not supporting you; that's called doing what you have to do to avoid the authorities coming down on your ass for neglecting your children. He tries to put a bullshit veil over our eyes but I'm not buying it. After a year and a half I'll be out and he can go fuck that stick up his ass all he wants. Daddy keeps going on that you haven't done any research into college options—no research my ass, you've been devoting your time to college research for weeks!

He doesn't apologize, or doesn't mean it when he does, and then acts like any act of repentance should be enough to get him off the hook. Asshole. I hate him. The minute I can support myself, I'm on my own. I'm just wondering how he plans on enjoying life when his only concern is hoarding millions. If he doesn't pass it on to us, then he can scatter his own damn ashes."

Telling lies was one of the ways I nudged my dad away from my mom and my sister without even trying, because my dad usually saw through the lies they believed. They believed my lie about having done weeks of college research, when the only research I did was for hair dye: I ordered so much I only had four dollars left. In just two years, their failure to see through my lies, and my dad's failure to follow my plans, had aligned my sister's thinking with mine: bitter and ruthless.

I wrote my dad an essay addressing every one of his concerns *except* for me getting an apartment with my American friend, because that was my goal in New York City, just as getting an apartment with my Mexican friend had been my goal in Britain. I'd give studying a try if my dad sent me there, but it was the apartment I was after. My mom and sister didn't see that either, and they backed my plan.

My dad said there was no way two eighteen-year-old girls were ready to live on their own in Manhattan, non-negotiable. He tried to find other solutions for film studies. He emailed SVA and learned that *half* of their graduates didn't do their first year there but were transferees, just like what my academic advisor had recommended for me. He called the program coordinator at LaSalle, who suggested I study at nearby LaSalle or Chapman for the first year to show my passion and prove I could study, then transfer to SVA, also like what the academic advisor had recommended. I refused.

I didn't want to study; I didn't know *how* to study; I couldn't function in a classroom environment. I just wanted to leave home, leave Singapore, whatever the cost. My dad brought up my former choice, the British college, and so I revealed my secret application and rejection and told him that was why I had written the SAT. I said I didn't want to write the English AP and reapply because my friend wasn't going to go there anymore. He brought up Musicians Institute, but I wasn't interested, and I admitted I'd been lying when I applied there because it was only for the location in Hollywood, not the program. I didn't want to go there anymore.

My mom met up with my dad in Starbucks to try to help me with my plan:

"You will lose Lina for good if you don't send her to New York City."

"Lina won't be safe outside a dorm, but she won't drop her condition of sharing a private apartment with her American friend. That means she is going there for the apartment and she might not even study, just make YouTube videos."

"If you don't send her to New York, Lina will hate you forever."

Both my parents were right. It was the last time they ever met privately.

My sister was totally with me: it was film studies in New York with my American friend, or nothing. I got nothing. We wanted my dad to die. I called the house Auschwitz, my dad Hitler, and my sister Switzerland. I never mentioned acting or film studies again.

I understand in my brain that my dad loved me so much that he prioritized my safety over my affection—my mom, the opposite—but I couldn't feel his love in my heart because he didn't love me the way I wanted to be loved. The result of his love was that our relationship was destroyed, my education was terminated, and the only non-loser was, and remains, my mom.

My American friend graduated four years later. Then— despite her $300,000 degree—it took her two years to get a job, as a kindergarten art teacher in Hong Kong. The only winner from her expensive education was the School of Visual Arts.

My dad and his girlfriend kept pushing me to consider other options. They offered me a career coach and, to shut them up, I accepted. I took the *Myers-Briggs Type Indicator* and *Strong Interest Inventory Profile* tests for the coaching center and waited for the first coaching session, where the results would be given to me.

Meanwhile my dad told me I should stop sitting in the house and go out and work. He told me what his father told him when he finished high school: I could go to college and live for free, or go to work and pay rent. I kept making YouTube videos, so my dad stopped paying my gap year allowance. He said he would continue to pay for my room, board, and medical expenses until I got a job.

Despite the tension in the air, my dad, my sister, and his girlfriend tried to make Christmas happy, with decorations and lights, and gifts piled under the tree. While they decorated, I stayed in my room making YouTube videos. On Christmas Eve I marched out of my bedroom past the three of them and said, "It's not very Christmassy around here," as I walked out of the door. They wanted to enjoy what would be our last Christmas together, so I wanted to spoil it.

I was no longer interested in being a professional singer, so I got a second tongue piercing. It caused a keloid and had to be removed. I started an apprenticeship at a piercing salon, making $1,200 a month, half of what my Mexican friend was earning at Kenny Rogers Roasters chicken restaurant. As soon as I started working, my dad started charging me $700 a month for room and board. It was a quarter of my actual cost, he said. He kept paying my medical expenses, but he warned my sister and me that if we got pierced or tattooed we would have to pay for our medical expenses ourselves, because if we didn't care for our bodies—like by sticking needles into them—then why should he care for them?

My dad still didn't give up on me going to college. He asked me to register for the English "Advanced Placement" (AP) exam to make up for my lack of English 12 and open more college options worldwide. I agreed to take it just to get him off my back, and he bought me a massive study guide.

My dad's girlfriend became his fiancée and moved in with us. They invited me to their June wedding in Britain (my sister would be away with her boyfriend) and to drive me around to studios and colleges there. I accepted.

A couple of weeks after my dad booked our flights, I dyed my hair green and got piercings around my face, along my arms, and down my back—mostly dermal piercings. My dad asked me to look natural for their wedding and said it would also make a better impression on studios. I agreed to dye my hair brown but not to remove my piercings. Even my mom asked me to remove some of them. I told them my piercings were part of me and I couldn't live without them. My dad canceled my flights. He was like, "First be successful, then get pierced."

Because of my multiple piercings, my dad told me to pay for my own medical expenses and to budget about $250 a month for them, including vision and dental but mostly for my specialist care. Yet my dad never stopped paying for my sister's and my medical expenses while we lived at home. It was a bluff, to try to give us reasons not to get pierced and tattooed before we were successful in our careers. He was trying and failing to change behavior he thought was self-destructive.

I wrote the English AP exam without opening the study guide, and I scored four out of five. My dad urged me to reapply to the British college, but I hated high school and never wanted to do anything like it ever again. I thought education was a waste of time and effort, and that it caused huge drama at home. So I stuck with the decision I'd made at fourteen: no college. I knew my dad wanted me to go to college more than anything else in the world, but he went about it the wrong way. I didn't confront him, I just told him my decision and then ignored him. I never went to see my career coach so I didn't find out the results of my psychological tests for many years.

My body rejected my dermal piercings, leaving me with a dozen scars that I would later mask with tattoos. I got my first tattoo where my dad and his girlfriend wouldn't see it: the words "Jagged Little Pill" written under my bra line, the name of the angsty Alanis Morissette album that I loved. I began gauging my earlobe piercings with black grommets, stretching them open.

Sometimes my dad and I would get along for a while, but we eventually clashed because of his unwanted parenting. My mom kept telling me to use him for his money by listening to him and going to college to have a good life, as my sister was doing. But I didn't want to use his money because I couldn't get along with him.

My dad and his wife flew back from their wedding, jet lagged and exhausted. The next day, on Facebook, I cursed them with a death wish:

"Some people are fucking inconsiderate. The people I'm currently living with returned from overseas. I let them sleep yesterday morning. This morning I woke up at 6 a.m. and warmed up my voice because it fucking sucks in the morning, and then one of the said people chooses to go back to sleep because of her fucking jet lag. Fine. Fuck you. Then

I waited two hours. Still not up? Deal with it. So I started recording at 8 a.m. The other one barges into my room and starts complaining. Excuse me? I'm the one that works ten fucking hours a day. You have all day to sleep. I'm trying to be productive here. I'm trying to finish my fucking albums so that I can move away from you assholes and pursue my career. I didn't record last night because you wanted to sleep, so I woke up early, and now I can't even record in the fucking morning? And now you complain that I'm being inconsiderate? Fuck you! Sincerely, always hoping you'll get hit by a bus, Lina."

My mom immediately "liked" it!

My thyroid pills ran out three months after my dad told me he would stop paying for my medical expenses. I went to the endocrinologist's clinic to buy more pills, and I was crying on the bus. I was trying not to burst into tears when I told the receptionist that I needed a medication refill. She brought me the pills:

"Here's three months of levothyroxine."

"Could I just buy one month?"

"Sorry?"

"I can't afford three months."

"Three months is thirty dollars."

I was stunned, then furious! Instead of realizing I hadn't been paying attention when my dad said $250 a month was for my *total* medical costs, and instead of asking him for a list of my expenses, my brain produced another false memory: because he wanted to control me, my dad was *maliciously fearmongering* me into believing I couldn't support myself by telling me *my pills cost hundreds of dollars a month.*

But fearmongering means manipulating a person though

deception to fear something when fear is not reasonable or necessary, while it was both reasonable *and* necessary that my disordered mind become concerned about being able to afford to maintain my disordered body. My dad had been honest and correct to be concerned that my health would suffer for lack of money. This paranoid false memory stayed with me even after my dad gave me my medical files when I moved out, because I didn't read them.

I met my first boyfriend, a friend of a friend of a friend, while we were clubbing. On the night we met, we snapped elastic bands at each other, getting welts everywhere. One of my cuts went deep, and it felt amazing. He stroked it and I closed my eyes.

The next day he came into the salon where I worked, and I pierced his ears and eyebrow. He told me he would come back and visit me. He flew home to America a couple of days later, and we fell in love by talking online. My first boyfriend would become my first ex.

My first ex spent his childhood feeling suicidal. Ever since he was twelve, he wanted to escape. He'd had a tough childhood, a rough past, and bad friends, and he wanted to start his life over. He was insecure and had no friends until he started making friends online, through World of Warcraft. He used to be a bodybuilder, then he met this girl and fell in love. She fucked his best friend, so he got depressed and crashed his car. He was still working off the debts for the crash, so he couldn't afford his gym membership and steroids. His parents were paying for him to go to a two-year vocational program. Then he planned on emigrating.

So we made a plan: I would go to Britain and start a band, and he would follow me and be my bass guitarist.

My dad continued nagging me about going to college. My first ex told me to stop bullshitting and tell my dad the truth. So I told my dad I would be moving to London in two months to pursue my singer-songwriter dreams while apprenticing as a tattoo artist, without mentioning I now had a boyfriend. My dad took it well, and I was so happy. He said if I ever changed my mind and wanted an education, he would provide it.

Adult Turmoil

I BOUGHT A ONE-WAY TICKET TO LONDON on my nineteenth birthday. Independence, fame, and fortune beckoned.

A week later, when I told him I was leaving, my dad spent a thousand dollars in *one day* at my endocrinologist, gynecologist, ophthalmologist, and dentist. He handed me my medical binder and said it was a good thing I was moving to Britain, because there my medical care would be free.

Three weeks later, while I was still living with my dad, I published my farewell on the internet:

"I'll be moving to London. London is big on music and that kind of stuff. I consider my songwriting and my music being like poo: you just have to let it come out naturally. There are dry spells when you are constipated, but you wait and relax, and it flows out naturally; that's why all my music sounds like shit. I have the right attitude for making it a business. I haven't met anyone else like me.

I'm a gypsy. I don't have a home. After I graduated high school, I started working to save up so I could pursue my dreams, because my family doesn't support me. I made enough, and I'm moving to London. I'm an artistic being; anything creative, nothing academic. I play violin, piano, guitar, bass, and pretty much any other instrument you can shove into my hands. I'm an artist, mostly digital. I write songs. I act, direct, film, and edit. I've written three books. My plans are to become a singer-songwriter, publish my novels, and turn them into movies. Tattooing is something that I've always wanted to learn and do, but it's not the big picture for me. I'll do tattooing while I pursue my music, singing, and acting.

When my parents separated, I wasn't upset. Even as a kid I knew my parents weren't meant to be together, and though it was a surprise when my dad broke the news, I was happy. It meant I didn't have to live with him anymore—two strong-minded people in the same house. Everything I love, he hates. My father is all about education, which I am not. I dreamed of dropping out because I felt my life was passing before my eyes and I was stuck in a cage. I got kicked out of a private school because of my attitude. There were other terrible students there but none of them had parents that ruined their lives. I moved in with my mom and went to a school that was more chill.

My dad didn't just not support my dreams, *he held me down and stopped me* from pursuing them, so all he ever gave me was anger and hatred toward him. I wanted to study film, but he said no. I refused to take anything else, so he cut me off. When I got a job he started charging rent, so it was taking me longer to save up to move overseas. My father tried to make me drop to my knees, crawl back to him, and follow his rules. He thought I would continue living with him for eternity but it backfired. If I followed his rules he'd love me, but I don't because his rules stop me from being who I am.

When I was depressed and suicidal, all he cared about was that my grades were dropping. I seriously considered murdering him multiple times over the years. *I was seriously planning on killing him.* I thought about poison, stabbing, gas, arson. My dad is a *racist, sexist, homophobic, closed-minded bigot*. When I move, he's not going to be a part of my life anymore. As much as I'd like to have a relationship with my father, I can't, because *he's not good for my mental health*."

I understand now that I had it backward: *my mental health was not good for relationships, especially with my caregivers.*

My first ex came to Singapore and I threw my London plan out the window. Instead of me moving to Britain to focus on singing-songwriting and starting a band, and him joining me a year later when he finished school, I would move to America to live with him as a tattoo artist while his parents supported him, and then we would move to London after he finished school. So I got a one-year visa and changed my ticket from Britain to America.

That's when I realized I would never be famous.

With this plan I would be happy for a while, but not as happy as I would have been if I'd been famous. In exchange for what would become two years with my abusive first ex, I gave up my fame-and-fortune singer-songwriter-musician-actress dreams to be an apprentice tattoo artist.

I moved out of my dad's apartment while my dad was at work. I left an envelope with $1,000 inside and a note: "I've moved out. I was going to move out at the end of the month but it made more sense to do it on my day off today. This should cover my rent for the last few weeks. Lina."

With that, I abandoned my dog and my dad. I knew my dad wasn't all that bad, but I broke down in tears after every time we talked so I walked out without even saying goodbye to him.

For more than a decade I remembered the events leading

up to our estrangement differently. I remembered that my dad *manipulated me* into moving into an apartment with him and my sister by promising to send me to college. But there had been discussion and support from everyone in the family. I chose to move after discussing his offer with my mom, who preferred to have her privacy for dating, and with my sister, who wanted me to live with her, and it was generous for my dad to arrange it. I remembered my dad did everything he could to *stop me from pursuing my dreams*, even though the only thing he refused to discuss was an apartment in New York City. But I refused to go to college unless I could live with my friend, and I turned down every suggestion he made for my first year, including going to LaSalle with my sister. He'd promised to send me to college, but not to *any* college *anywhere* in the *first year*. If I'd said I wanted to study filmmaking with enough passion to live in the dorm, he would have sent me. I remembered my dad did everything he could to *prevent me from leaving home*, even though he was the one who told me to get a job and pay rent if I wasn't going to college, which was the opposite of what you would say to a child who you wanted to stay home.

I was in transit at my mom's for a few weeks. We laughed to hear from my sister that it cost my dad hundreds of dollars to repair the gouges I made in the parquet floor in my bedroom by dragging my furniture. My mom wouldn't have laughed if it was *her* floor, but she couldn't abuse my dad anymore so she did it vicariously.

Of the five goals I'd written down at thirteen—to stay in the same school, earn an International Baccalaureate, scuba dive in the Great Barrier Reef, go to college, and move out—the only childhood goal I ever achieved was to move out.

I flew to America, moved into my first ex's parents' house with him, and found work as a tattoo apprentice. It was nothing like *Miami Ink*: I got hired without experience because they needed artists in the seats so that anyone who walked in could be inked before they had second thoughts. They told me I could make $4,000 to $8,000 a month, but I was paid by the hour and mostly waited for customers—one or two a day—and spent my time on the internet. Then, whenever I was given a customer, I would have a panic attack: I would walk into the bathroom, have my meltdown, gather my wits, and then walk out and pretend to be okay.

A month after I moved in, my first ex's public Facebook profile said:

"I'm in an open relationship. I'm a total loser. I've loved being taken in the butt from an early age. The first time was while I was climbing up a rope in gym class and the coach was helping me and slid three of his fingers into my tight rectum. I loved it!"

That screamed trouble. But I made myself at home even though my visa was non-renewable, and I bought a puppy. For a few months my $200 YouTube checks continued to arrive in my dad's mailbox, and he deposited each one into my bank account. I never thanked him. At Christmas he put a gift into my bank account. I never thanked him.

I began suffering from dyspareunia, painful sex. Penetration was excruciating. Even touching my vulva was painful. My first ex wanted sex every day, so he took me to a family doctor. I told her I'd never had a natural period and I couldn't afford any tests or specialists. She prescribed birth control pills. Sex still hurt but it wasn't excruciating.

I wrote a special song to my dad, recorded it, and uploaded it to YouTube:

"Your bullshit makes me laugh
More than it pisses me off, which pisses you off
Try if you will, try if you can
Try again, block me, then give me your hand
Use all your might, use all your strength
But I am stronger, you know, in the end I get it, I get you
You cannot stand that you cannot control me, boohoo
I see it in your eyes
Every time that you look at me, I know you despise
everything, every inch
Every piercing and bar through my skin
You hate my hair, you hate my style but I don't give a shit
and I just smile
And I can tell that it drives you crazy
That it doesn't phase me [sic] when you're a prick
Well, I should tell you that it's not surprising
'Cause you've always been nothing but a dick
And I can tell that it drives you apeshit
That I'm independent
And now I'm gone
Well, I should tell you that this is my life and I am all mine
and
This is so long."

My mom "liked" it immediately.

A few months later, my first ex quit school and his parents stopped supporting him. He got a job as a casino bouncer and we moved into an apartment. Now that he had his own money, he resumed taking steroids. I did his injections.

Back in Singapore my sister became happier living with my dad and his wife after I moved out. My mom was getting crazier, stocking up on canned food for the apocalypse—as if that would help at the end of the world. She found a boyfriend who could put up with her. They got engaged on an auspicious date she picked according to *feng shui*.

My sister graduated from LaSalle with a bachelor's degree in animation art and was class valedictorian. She received what she thought were three job offers. My dad said they weren't offers but letters of interest, so she should follow them up but keep looking. She told me that the way he spoke made her feel like she was never going to go anywhere in life. He was trying to be realistic because we weren't and my mom never was, but the way he tried to be helpful always made us feel like he was putting us down. None of those "offers" came true, but his lack of empathetic coaching didn't make my sister feel any better.

My sister couldn't find work as an artist after she graduated, so LaSalle hired her as a temporary teaching assistant. A year later she got her dream job: an artist for a computer game software company in Singapore. She worked there for three years, then she quit to freelance online. After several frustrating years of competition for commissions from artists living in low-wage countries, she found work as an artist for a computer game software company in Europe, and moved there.

My Art Plus—art plus skinprinting—has served me better than Art Only has served my sister. Most of my income comes not from the Art but from the Plus, paid by the hour, and I'll never have to worry about foreign competition from over the internet.

Under my visa I couldn't be employed by one company for longer than six months. I liked where I was working and I didn't want to marry for a visa, so I tried to switch to a "de facto" visa. It was denied, so I found work in a different tattoo parlor, owned by an outlaw biker gang. It was busted by the police a few months later, so then I found work in my third tattoo parlor.

Because of the birth control pills, my B-cups quadrupled in size to C, D, E, F, G, H, and, finally, I-cups, hanging like useless sacks with gigantic areolas. They looked hideous and gave me backaches. My bras cut into my shoulders. I was too proud to ask my parents for money for the specialist care my high-maintenance body required, so I stopped taking the birth control pills and suffered through excruciating sex again. My formerly perfect breasts would pay a high price for my pride on the operating table six years later.

The only way I could stay in America for more than a year was to marry a citizen. I wasn't dumb enough to hitch myself to a guy I didn't love at all, but I married for a visa, like my mom. I was twenty when we announced our engagement. My mom was happy for me, my sister hoped for the best, and my dad knew nothing about it.

My sister, my mom, her boyfriend, and my first ex's sister and his parents came to our wedding. Before my mom and sister arrived, I cleaned the apartment and bought a giant TV because my mom likes watching TV. My mom complained our apartment was dirty, and she and my sister started vacuuming. She complained my TV was too big, and when she saw my boobs, she complained they were too saggy. She never stopped damaging my self-esteem.

While my sister was there I tattooed her with a colorful tryker from her Ryzom game that covered her left thigh. Six months later, when my dad took my sister on a scuba diving holiday in Borneo, he became quiet when he saw her first tattoo. He didn't say anything about it.

I got married just before my visa expired, and I replaced it with a spousal visa. My dad had often counseled my sister and me never to become dependent on a man, but I didn't think of myself as dependent.

When my Mexican friend told me about how much she loved being independent at college in America, I replied, "*I'm* independent! *You're* dependent on your parents for college." A perfect retort from her would have been, "No, *I'm* independent. *You're* dependent on a man for your residence. But I'll always have my parents."

After she graduated, my Mexican friend was able to work in America, thanks to her degree and years of residence, and she immigrated there on her own, single. *That's* independence.

I was so confident about my future that I adopted a second dog. But my visa depended on keeping my first ex happy—and he knew it. He would rape me whenever I refused sex, and he didn't listen when I told him to stop. He physically, sexually, and psychologically abused me. I became so paranoid about being touched by men that if someone so much as brushed my arm on a bus, I would have a panic attack. I thought I was going crazy, and I started thinking about suicide for the first time since high school.

MY MOM MARRIED HER BOYFRIEND a few months later, and I flew to Singapore for their wedding. Even though she always complained that we didn't want to go to church, and she ruined our *Phantom of the Opera* experience over church, she remarried in a *Buddhist* ceremony. My sister and I met our new stepsister at the reception. She told us that her mom said that our mom "managed to raise two juvenile delinquents." I thought that was hilarious, but my sister was pissed because she didn't think her image was as bad as mine.

At twenty-one my emotions were still beyond my control. My stepsister gave me a mental breakdown—by giving me a pillow. There was a little rainbow pillow that I liked in a shop, so my sister and stepsister went in to buy it for me. They came out with two pillows because my stepsister wanted to give me a gift too. I had a meltdown in front of my little stepsister over a purple lollipop pillow just because I hadn't asked her for it. I felt like an absolute ass.

I couldn't keep my first ex happy every day, so he retaliated on Facebook:

"Looking for willing participants for threesome with self and wife. Apply below with photo resume and video of your maneuvers. Preferably hot and dripping Latino males."

I tried to make it look like a joke by uploading a video of myself bouncing my bulbous boobs. But three weeks later, just before our first anniversary, I discovered his affair. I retaliated on Facebook:

"He cheated on me with a home-wrecking whore. She knew he was married when she took him home. Of course, he did too. London could be short term or long term. I have no home. I'm a nomad. I go where the wind takes me."

In minutes, my mom "liked" my posting! What was that supposed to mean? My spousal visa was canceled so I had one month to leave the country. I had to move to Britain because my Singapore residency had lapsed.

On my way to London I stopped over in Singapore to see my mom and tattoo my sister again. While I was there I inked the outline of a cartoon, "Pain," across my sister's breast and shoulder. It would take twenty hours and cost her $1,500 when it was completed and colored.

I stayed for a few weeks with my aunt and then with my cousin, a student who was going away and allowed me to use her London apartment for a month. I emailed an acting agency, met the agent the next day, and signed on. I got an audition, memorized my single line, and passed.

When I told my aunt, she started freaking out. "This is amazing! We have to celebrate!" She spoke to me like I was a schoolgirl—and I loved it, even though I used to hate it when my parents talked to me that way. I felt emotional support for the first time in my life, and I cried. I'd never felt emotional support from my family because every compliment had been followed by a "but," as in, "Great performance, but you have no lines." I felt like I was never good enough for my family, but I was good enough for my aunt.

Now I realize my family had given me emotional support by watching and recording every high school performance and always taking me out to dinner to celebrate, and they didn't mind *until I started demanding to live in Hollywood* that I never auditioned for speaking roles. Then they nagged me to audition for speaking roles, but then I didn't see that as support for my dreams. I had always been good enough for my family, but never good enough for Hollywood.

When I tried to register for the National Health Service, I realized I needed some documents I'd abandoned. I asked my cousin to email my dad for them so I wouldn't have to ask him directly, but my dad emailed back to me:

"Dear Lina, I heard you are in London and need documents to assist you in getting settled as a citizen. Please confirm what you need with me directly. I offer assistance to advance your situation, including financial support if required to get settled and find employment or support to return to school in support of a career, including accommodation. I love you unconditionally, I miss you, and am prepared to move on and start over with our relationship if you are. Love, Daddy."

I wasn't ready to have my dad back in my life, but I needed the documents urgently so I replied:

"Hello, I require all my original documents, like my birth certificate, citizenship certificate, and all others. I do not need money but thank you for the offer. I can wire you the payment for postage. Thanks, Lina."

My dad sent me the documents.

When my cousin returned, she was furious: "You treated my place like shit! You stuffed dirty pans in my oven. You spilled nail polish remover on my table. What kind of idiot uses nail polish remover on a wooden table? It stripped the paint! You didn't fix it and were hoping I wouldn't notice. You've got no respect for people's property! All the YouTube followers in the world won't change the fact that you are lazy, self-absorbed, and cheap. You aren't looking to find a job. You prefer to live off your YouTube account and sporadic one-day acting jobs as an extra. You sit at home all day doing makeup, taking photos of yourself, and writing songs. Get out!"

My dad and his wife could have said exactly the same thing while I was living with them; I hadn't matured in two years of working and living with my ex. I moved back to my aunt's place until I found work in a tattoo parlor, where I worked for ten hours a day to support myself.

I had my dogs shipped over from America, and I found a boyfriend. He worked from home, so I used him as my dog sitter in return for free rent. I liked him only when he was high on cocaine, and for a month I was on cocaine with him. Sex with him was better than with my first ex because his dick was small, but he gave me chlamydia. After three months I threw him out, and then I spent six months pining for him. I call him my second ex.

BACK IN SINGAPORE, MY SISTER went to our dad's place to play the piano. She knocked on his door with bright pink hair, a septum ring, and the "Pain" breast-and-shoulder tattoo I'd just done for her. He was stunned by her appearance. It was the only time she ever saw my dad struggle to speak.

"You look awful. We don't want to see tattoos here. Please cover them."

My sister flipped out. "If that's the way *you* feel, then I'd better leave!"

"If that's the way *you* feel, then I guess you'd better leave," he replied.

"Mommy has no problem with the way I look! It's only you!"

"That's because I was the one who did everything I could to help you reach your potential. If you want to handicap yourself by looking like a cool loser—*permanently*—you have that right. You are welcome here, but your vice is not welcome. Please keep it to yourself. I'll lend you a T-shirt."

"I'm never coming here again! Sell the goddamn piano!"

My sister stormed out. Then *he* flipped, and he bolted the door behind her.

The next day he called and apologized and emailed her:

"My love for you and Lina is unconditional. Nothing changed last night even though our emotions ran high. But I detest tattoos outside the circus and look down on people who are so short term in their thinking and so narcissistic, misanthropic, and stupid as to get them. Until last night I ignored the mutilation that has been spreading on your skin like cancer. I care, and a caring person gives honest feedback. I don't want to see you reduce your chances for long-term happiness by participating in a fad. If you drink or smoke, you can stop; if you tattoo, you can't. Have you seen old people with old tattoos? They look awful. Suppose your professor had pink hair, fishing lures in his ears, nose, mouth, and lips, and graffiti on his arms and legs under a tank top and shorts. If he applied for a job as an artist, could he get it? Sure—he can draw. If he applied for his professor job, with four times the salary, would he get it? No way! After you become successful you can look as you like, but you are not yet successful and your appearance is handicapping you professionally and socially. Please visit us, but respect us. Love, Daddy"

My sister posted her reply to him on Facebook: "Fuck you."

She estranged herself from him and is still estranged. Our tattoos were symbols of our rejection of the values he tried to pass down to us. Our alignment against him was complete.

It was a long time coming. We were surprised he managed to hide his disappointment as long as he did, while we became tattooed, pierced, black-wearing, spike-sporting, dyed-hair artists he wouldn't want to be seen with, and not the debonair professionals he'd given us the opportunity to become. To realize what his dream children had become was more than our dad's heart could bear.

I uploaded this condescending tribute to my website:

"My dad is a shit human being; a racist, sexist, bigot. If you did something or were something that he didn't want you to be, he would try to stop you from doing it or being it. There was a lot of manipulating, power-hungry bullshit. He ruined my school experience because I didn't try very hard, and he was so obsessed with grades that he would call my teachers every day to ask how I was doing in class. So my shitty grades got noticed. I got kicked out of that school that my father was so proud of me being in, because everybody noticed me so much. That is his fucking fault.

I stopped talking to him when I left Singapore, but then I needed him to send me some documents. He held them hostage because it was his last power over me. I was surprised he gave them up with no ransom or negotiation. He was all, "I love you no matter what. I want to try again if you're up for it." I was thinking maybe he'd grown up and learned to accept me for who I am, and we could get along. Then he and my sister fell out.

She got good grades, never partied in school, and she listened. She'd been the golden child. Now she's like, "I'm working, I'm independent, and I'm going to do what I've always wanted to do," like getting a bunch of tattoos and dyeing her hair bright pink. She went to hang out with our dad and his wife. She took one step in the door, and he looked like a volcano about to explode. He never yelled at her. He only talked. It's terrifying. He told her she looked disgraceful, and she should cover up in public. She said no, so he told her to get out, and she did.

People are governed by their fears, whether they know it or not. The reason I am so free is that I know what my fears are, so they don't rule my actions. I'm aware of who I am and what's going on inside me. My dad ended up afraid and controlling because something happened in his past that left him so broken he became unable to bear the thought of betrayal. He doesn't know this himself. My dad is governed by his fears, and I am not. I'm stronger than he is. I'm the bigger person because I can be. I'm not letting my past destroy me like he let his destroy him.

If people are fucking up your life, get rid of them—friends, teachers, or family—because that's what's best for you; blood and DNA mean nothing. Do what you need to do to keep your mental health intact. My dad made me want to kill myself and want to kill him, and many times I plotted his murder. I cut my dad out of my life for my mental health."

My screed was read thousands of times. Because of the websites I followed, I'd written, "something happened ... that left him broken and governed by his fears," and he "let his past destroy him" but "doesn't know this himself"—a contradiction because you can't let something happen that you don't know about. The websites I followed viewed psychological problems through the lens of childhood trauma caused by dysfunctional families. I couldn't accept that my dad and his siblings and parents all showed their love for each other throughout their lives, and none ever mentioned anything like family dysfunction, abuse, or trauma. If these had occurred, some of the six would have remembered it, which none of them did, and not only my dad would have been "broken" or "destroyed," which none of them were. I'd labeled him a "racist bigot," even though he lived and worked all over the world, his wives were Caucasian, Filipina, and Chinese, and my sister and I are *mestisas*. In fact, my dad's "controlling" behavior was like that of the parents of my overachieving friends, but I couldn't have overachieved no matter what he did. It would take professional therapy to change my mind about myself, about him, and about self-help websites.

Six months after my abusive broadcast, I sent my dad a "happy birthday" email! I found a copy in my archives. I forgot that I did it and don't remember why I did it, so I may have been on a manic high, perhaps on cocaine. My dad replied, but I never emailed him again.

I finished my novel, now as long as *Lord of the Rings*, then asked my followers to donate $5,000 on GoFundMe to pay for an editor. I raised $1,200, mostly from my mom, and self-published my book on Amazon seven years later. It sells several copies a year.

I PUT A BAND TOGETHER. When I was a teenager I'd dreamed of having a band with best friends and touring the world, but when I actually *had* a band, at twenty-two, it made me want to kill myself. My mental health couldn't handle it. I thought twenty-two was when I discovered I hated working with people and I was terrible at it, but at thirteen I'd quit ensembles, choirs, and orchestras because I couldn't deal with being in groups. The *Strong Interest Inventory Profile* test I took when I was eighteen had reported: "You are likely to prefer working alone as an independent contributor," but I didn't see it until I received my archives. I learned the hard way that working in teams of people, let alone *directing* teams of people, which is where the big money is, isn't for me.

I shut my band down and cut all the musicians out of my life, except for one with a full body tattoo, with whom I fell in love. He became my third ex. Sex with him hurt, so I resumed taking birth control pills. They weren't enough for the pain, so I researched dyspareunia on my own and started taking three birth control pills a day. Sex became less painful.

I went to see a doctor at twenty-three. She had my hormones tested for the first time since I left home. My thyroid level was normal, but my baseline estrogen was too low, so she stopped my levothyroxine and birth control pills and put me on estrogen-progesterone. I was angry to think that years of sexual trauma from dyspareunia and the ballooning of my breasts could have been prevented if I'd been correctly medicated, and I accused my dad of years of neglect of my medical care.

This was another massive false memory. I remembered my hormone tests *starting at sixteen*, when they had started at fourteen; and at fourteen, fifteen, and sixteen, they had all been normal. I'd even had a chromosome test to see if I might be a pseudo-hermaphrodite! My thyroid level had been slightly too low at seventeen, so I was put on the lowest dose of levothyroxine. By the time I left home, my thyroid had been tested ten times. I remembered my lack of estrogen was diagnosed *only because I demanded to be tested*, when my estrogen levels had been tested five times starting at fourteen and were still normal when I left home; I lack only the cycle where baseline levels increase to create periods. That's why I hadn't been prescribed estrogen: it would have been an overdose, which is what I got in America from birth control pills. The reason I hadn't been correctly treated *wasn't neglect by others* but *neglect by myself,* because I abandoned my specialist care. My dad gave me my medical binder when I left home, including my hormone tests, but I threw it out because it was so heavy.

My mental health couldn't handle my third ex. I changed my behavior and clothing to try to be good enough for him. I became jealous when he developed friendships because I'm jealous of those who have friends. Like my second ex, my third ex triggered my mood swings. I suffered separation anxiety when he was away and I threw tantrums whenever he was unresponsive. This pushed him away, which triggered my fear of abandonment, which pushed him further away. I got jealous and thought, "Am I not good enough?" One night he took a woman on a date, and I cried the moment he left. I woke up in the middle of the night to the sounds of them having sex in the next room, so I cut my third ex out of my life.

I blamed my failed relationships on my parents: they didn't have a healthy relationship, so I had no idea what a healthy relationship looked like and I craved people who were horrible for me, people who had been abused by their family, friends, or teachers. I saw all love as psychological abuse, and I thought all three exes psychologically abused me by guilting me into thinking I needed them, and that I psychologically abused them because I wanted to nurture them to reach their potential. Later, during my therapy, I learned that much of what I'd perceived as abuse would not be perceived as abuse by someone in good mental health. I'd been oversensitive to abuse and trauma because of my psychological state.

Relationships hurt, romance hurt, sex hurt. I became celibate. In the past I'd labeled myself bisexual, pansexual, non-binary, and queer, but never gay or straight; now I labeled myself asexual. I controlled my mood swings by making myself emotionally unavailable, but at random times I'd get an overwhelming emotion, like from music, and then I'd break down and cry.

I hated being controlled by a boss, so at twenty-four I quit the tattoo parlor and became self-employed, working at home. My stress reduced, but my emotions were still uncontrollable. I had a meltdown in the gym because my favorite machine was removed; I went to the bathroom, hyperventilated, bawled for ten minutes, and quit my gym membership. I wanted to live alone, but I needed roommates to share the rent.

I had breast reduction surgery, paid for by the British government, to repair the damage I did when I went to America and abandoned my specialist health care instead of moving to Britain, where my health care would have been free. The operation left anchor-shaped scars on my breasts, but my backaches stopped and my appearance and self-esteem improved.

At twenty-five I thought I had figured out who I had been, who I was, and who I would always be: I would lead a simple life as a tattoo artist in a shared rented room with two dogs.

To keep my emotions under control, I estranged everyone who ever made me feel like shit: teachers, bosses, friends, roommates, ex-lovers, everyone in two tattoo parlors, everyone in my band, and, above all, my dad. My estrangements gave me time to grow, learn, heal, and understand myself. The British government would not leave me destitute when I retired.

I thought I had it made.

Recovery Journey

AT TWENTY-SIX I MET ANOTHER ASEXUAL: a social worker a few years older than me. They were my roommate, but they became much more than that. Slowly I began to trust them, and they, me. After all, asexuals rarely have affairs. To them, helping others was more important than making money, which is why they were as short of money as I was. It was in their bones to help others, and, gradually, they began to inspire me to change. They encouraged me to love others more than myself, especially themselves and my family, and to stop playing the victim and blaming others. I'm only attracted to people who inspire me, and *they* inspired me. They became my partner, who touched my heart but never my body.

My partner and I shared our stories of abuse. I told them everyone in my life was abusive—friends, family, lovers—until I met that partner. I abused everyone and everyone abused me. I told them I did horrible things to my friends. I regretted it, sought forgiveness and was granted it long ago, but I was worried they might still be damaged by the abuse I inflicted on them when we were children because I still felt damaged by the abuse my family did to me. I'd apologized to my friends before, but my partner said to apologize again, as an adult.

I contacted those I'd bullied, and I asked again for their forgiveness. None felt damaged; none remembered me as bad. All remembered me as a better person than I remembered myself. I realized I had abused no one, not seriously, and my bullying had affected *me* far more than it affected my victims. I cried because I hadn't forgiven myself. Since my friends hadn't been damaged by my abuse, I began to wonder if I had been damaged by the abuse I believed my family had done to me. My partner said that if I thought everybody abused me, that might mean that nobody abused me.

I realized I identified more with internet strangers than with physical people. YouTube made me feel happy and loved, even though I was alone and nobody cared. Now that I had my partner, I didn't need external validation through "likes" and clicks. I began to see YouTube as a human zoo and myself as an exhibit. I began to feel disgusted by the comments written by some of my visitors.

My first turning point was cleaning up YouTube. I pulled down every YouTube video that wasn't music or lifestyle (hair, makeup, tattoos, clothing, and cooking), and I stopped living my life in public. Encouraging voyeurism into my personal life had led me to exaggerate my problems instead of solving them. Now that I didn't need empty affirmation, my 150 videos about my personal life weren't worth the $50 a month they earned. I was still making $600 from my 170 lifestyle videos and $150 from my 450 music videos.

My partner encouraged me to remove the tattoos that reminded me of past traumas, so I removed some black ink ones and blacked out some others. Removing color tattoos hurts like a bitch, costs twenty times more than inking them, and leaves scars that turn a tattooist into an apostate.

My second turning point was getting a shrink. For half my life I'd been trying to self-diagnose on self-help websites. Social workers are not psychologists, but my partner told me to put my amateur diagnoses away, get professionally diagnosed by a psychiatrist with twelve years of training, and then, if she recommended it, get as many psychotherapy sessions as the British government would pay for.

So I did. I began psychotherapy—"talk therapy"—with medication for anxiety, like my Mexican friend had done a dozen years before. The more I explained my life to my shrink and to my partner, the more they spotted inconsistencies and asked questions about my past that I couldn't answer. Nor could my mom and sister answer, but I knew my dad could answer because he kept everything.

My shrink and my partner encouraged me to email him and ask him questions as though I'd nothing to lose. They were like, "Fuck pride, ask him! Fathers can say they're childless, but nobody can say they're fatherless. Estrange him again if he gives you any shit."

My third turning point was asking my dad some questions by email. He not only sent me the answers, he sent me all my backup files: a hundred thousand documents and photographs and millions of words of messages that my computer had saved. My digital archives included history that I'd forgotten about or I never knew, my medical and school records, almost everything that had been written by me or about me before I left home. It was amazing to see all these at twenty-eight, and it took me a year to read them all. And he sent me a draft of his memoir.

I replied with, "Thank you," but I wasn't yet ready to ask him for reconciliation, nor could I be sure that my dad would be open for reconciliation after the way I treated him. I was not in control.

Because I trusted my partner, I trusted my psychiatrist. I began my first appointment by telling her I was a fucked-up kid who did many fucked-up things. I admitted I was ashamed of being so terrible, and I thought I had mental disorders for many reasons; yet at the same time, I loved who I was so I wasn't ashamed of myself, and I wouldn't change anything. I got emotional, and I cried.

In the first few sessions, I outlined my life story while she took notes. In later sessions I explained my phobias and problems, which she grouped in themes. She cautioned me that making a meaningful psychiatric diagnosis is far more challenging than making other medical diagnoses. For most psychiatric problems there is no blood test or a brain scan, so psychiatrists have to match a patient's patterns of thoughts, behaviors, and emotions to documented patterns. That's why it was mainly me talking and her asking questions. She didn't want to come up with a diagnosis until she had heard everything I had to say.

I told my shrink it was easy for me to talk to her because not only do I love to talk about myself, I talk *to* myself if no one's around to listen. I'm always talking to someone, even if they aren't there. I once ripped my knee wide open because I was so deep into conversation with myself that I didn't see the giant rock in my way.

She said it's very common for intelligent people to get so focused on a problem that the world seems to disappear, like the absent-minded professor in storybooks, and she looked forward to listening to intelligent me talking about my absent-minded self.

I told my shrink about how my mental health plummets whenever anyone tells me what to do, and I lose control over my emotions. I can't stand it when people expect something from me, so I never tell people what I plan to do because they'll be watching me—then, if I fail to do it, they'll hold it against me. And I can't commit to long-term goals like college because, thanks to my mood swings, I'm constantly changing my goals so I know I will never achieve them. I thought this might be caused by spending my whole childhood being told what to do.

She said that all children spend their childhood being told what to do. My shrink asked if my sister experienced a fear of commitment. I said no. So, she said, my fear of commitment must have an internal explanation.

I told my shrink I had a fear of being abandoned, even though I loved to be alone. This made me abandon my friends before they could abandon me, and that is why I had no friends left. I manipulated my friends into turning against their other friends so they wouldn't turn against me. In middle school, when my friends came over to my house, they would follow my sister around, increasing my fear of abandonment. I needed to have other people with me when I encountered strangers, or I became a wallflower. That's probably why I refused to make any college plan that didn't include living with a friend in an apartment. I went clubbing in high school because everyone else was doing it, even though I hated being around people. But being with people who were acting like best friends while they were drunk, but not caring about me while they were sober, was too much for me to handle.

My shrink commented that there were a few disorders that show this symptom, which is called *autophobia*, fear of being alone, and we would look for them.

I told my shrink I thought I had social phobia because I become unstable when I'm with people—despite my autophobia! I quit every group activity I ever started, even my own band, and I need to spend most of my time alone. I have a hard time handling social situations. If a conversation is not about me or my limited interests, I wait for the other person to shut up so I can go back to talking about myself. I had problems at every job because of how I behaved toward others. I'm unempathetic, blunt, and rude.

My shrink asked if I'd taken the *Myers-Briggs Type Indicator* personality test. I said I had, at nineteen and twenty-one, but I only knew my personality type at twenty-one, INFJ, because I'd quit career coaching. I took the test again and I was type INTJ, with a ninety percent score on introversion. She said social anxiety is characteristic of extreme introversion, and it isn't necessarily a disorder. She asked if my sister experienced social anxiety. I said yes, but not as much as me, and my dad too. None of us are party people, except for my mom.

Then I found my coaching test reports in the files my dad sent me: I had been type ISTP at nineteen. So for nine years the only stable dimension of my personality type was the letter "I" at the front: *introversion*.

My dad, in his memoir, said he was type INTJ, the same as me, also with a ninety percent score on introversion, and his IQ was the same as my sister's and mine. As an introvert, careers like actor, filmmaker, director, and bandleader hadn't suited me any more than they would have suited him. It makes me laugh to imagine him in those careers, so maybe it made him concerned for my future when I'd aspired to them. I'd been so right when I thought we were the same.

I told my shrink my whole family hurt my feelings and made me angry and depressed, and my parents psychologically abused me by forcing me to be someone else. I was grateful for my schools and lessons, but I felt that my parents gave them to me in the wrong way. I said I spent my childhood devoid of true love and support because I was never good enough for them.

My parents convinced me I needed education to be able to afford the things I wanted, and they forced me to go to school, do my homework, and practice my instruments—and that abuse gave me childhood trauma.

I told her my mom taught my sister and me that we had to be thin to be attractive; her abuse gave us childhood trauma that made us hate our bodies. And when my mom became unfaithful because of her problems, she blamed her behavior on mine. My parents' marriage went through unbelievable stress because of my sister's and my melodrama, but she went too far in blaming her behavior on mine, and she ruined my self-esteem. Tattoos make me feel less vulnerable, and the more tattoos I have, the less insecure I feel.

I told her that my dad expected too much from me, and his abuse permanently damaged me so I couldn't function in school or even look at a school. I thought my nightmares and fear of violence were because I'd been under psychological attack by my dad, who made me think I had to defend myself and decide whether to fight or flee. He psychologically abused my family by fearmongering us into thinking we needed him so we would follow his plan. He dreamed of returning home to Britain, retired and wealthy, to his house, stable, and acreage with his erudite and cosmopolitan family, and everything went according to his plan until his children started having problems, his wife became unfaithful, and the family fell apart. He loved to give us presents but would manipulate us into feeling guilty if we didn't use them. This psychological abuse gave me more childhood trauma, so now I have a mental breakdown when I receive a gift I didn't ask for because I believe the gift giver will never forgive me if I don't take it and use it.

My shrink commented there might be a link between my

feelings of being traumatized by parental abuse and my teenage academic failure, but she suggested I might have the cause and the effect backward and therefore be too hard on my parents, especially my dad. She said that my dad's constant pressure to go to school, do homework, and practice music sounded like normal parenting by affluent parents, especially since he treated my sister and me the same way, and she had always performed well at school.

But what if I had a mental disorder that prevented me from performing in a classroom even though I was smart? Then, because I couldn't perform like normal kids, normal caregiving felt like abuse, and I felt traumatized. She said abuse is an *action*, like a punch, while trauma is the resulting *injury*, like a bruise, so abuse can lead to trauma, but not everyone who has been abused becomes traumatized, and, more importantly for me, not everyone who has been traumatized has been abused. She also said that overwhelming experiences can cause childhood trauma, but trauma can occur without abuse when parents do not meet their child's emotional needs—*even when they don't understand what those needs are.* Perhaps my parents hadn't met my emotional needs because my needs were abnormal, and so no one knew what they were. In that case I might want to think of myself as having been *traumatized by my feelings* but not having been abused by my family.

I told my shrink my grandfather sexually abused me. She was startled, and she asked me how it happened. I said I didn't know, but I'd been reading about people who suffered from mental health issues like anxiety, low self-esteem, dissociation, and visions, and who healed themselves by confronting their childhood sexual abusers even though they couldn't remember any details because they were too young and there was no evidence because it was so long ago. Like them, I had these kinds of mental health issues I couldn't explain. So, like them, I concluded that I had been sexually abused before I could have remembered it. That meant no older than five years old, and that meant it had to have been in Tokyo. The only people who could have molested me there were my parents, the maid, my grandmothers, and a grandfather; so it must have been that grandfather, who was seventy-five at the time. I said I'd read that I have no memory of child sexual abuse not only because I was so young but because my brain removed the traumatic memories to protect me from them. But my body remembered what happened and gave me signs called "body memories." For example, when my flight stopped in Tokyo I felt sick, and whenever I looked at pictures of Japan I felt sick. My aunt was shocked that I could think that her father, who babysat nine grandchildren, could be a pedophile. But my body knew.

My shrink explained that mysterious psychic distress does not always mean sexual abuse occurred, and her patients with sexual trauma from childhood are so *acutely* aware of the details of their abuse that they wish they could forget them. Trauma results in memories that flood back with the same horror as when the events occurred, so psychiatrists never use confrontation to help patients who remember trauma. Some blocking out of memories can occur, but no details plus no evidence almost always means no trauma, which means no abuse.

My shrink despises authors who explain away mysterious psychic distress with faith-based solutions that have been rejected by modern psychiatry, like "recovered memories" and "body memories." She asked me if I'd read *The Courage to Heal*, which says, "If you think you were abused and your life shows the symptoms, then you were abused."

I said that I don't read books, but many self-help websites quote that book.

"It's dangerous, destructive, bestselling, discredited rubbish," she said, "that was written by a creative writing instructor." She said my conjecture was undoubtedly a false memory, a thought you get from therapy or hypnosis or a website and come to believe happened to you, and I shouldn't be casual about accusing someone of a crime for which the punishment is fourteen years in prison. She said we would need to find a more plausible explanation for my anxiety, dissociation, low self-esteem, and visions.

I TOLD MY SHRINK I THOUGHT I HAD ASPERGER'S Syndrome because I am intelligent and articulate, but I am also socially awkward, narrow-minded, and hyper-focused. I identified with the "Aspie" label.

My shrink said the term Asperger's Syndrome was used to describe a childhood developmental disorder where those with normal intelligence had repetitive behaviors and impaired social interaction, but in 2013 that diagnosis was discontinued. People who would have been diagnosed with Asperger's are now diagnosed with "autism spectrum disorder without language or intellectual impairment."

She took out an old psychiatric manual, and we went through the *former* criteria for Asperger's Syndrome:

"1: Impairment in social interaction. At least two of:
    (a) Marked impairment in multiple nonverbal
    behaviors such as eye contact, facial expression, and
    body postures.
    (b) Failure to develop appropriate peer relationships.

(c) Lack of seeking to share enjoyment, interests, or achievements with others.

(d) Lack of social or emotional reciprocity."

No to (a). A qualified no to (b): I *developed* friendships but I abandoned them. No to (c). Yes to (d): my friendships are always all about me. With a score of one out of four, no to this criterion.

"2: Restricted, repetitive, stereotyped behaviors. At least one of:

(a) Preoccupation with a stereotyped pattern of interest that is abnormal in intensity.

(b) Inflexible adherence to pointless routines or rituals.

(c) Stereotyped and repetitive motor mannerisms, like hand flapping or body twisting.

(d) Persistent preoccupation with parts of objects."

No to all areas and no to this criterion.

"3: The disturbance causes significant impairment in social, occupational, or other important areas of functioning."

Yes to this criterion.

"4: No significant delay in cognitive and language development."

Yes to this criterion; my development was *not* delayed.

I met only two of the four criteria, so my shrink concluded that I would not formerly have been diagnosed with Asperger's Syndrome.

Then she took out a new psychiatric manual and we went through the criteria for autism spectrum disorder:

"1: Persistent deficits in social communication and interaction across all three areas:
(a) Social-emotional reciprocity; for example, failure to initiate or respond to social interactions and reduced sharing of interests and emotions.
(b) Nonverbal communicative behaviors used for social interaction; for example, abnormalities in eye contact and body language, lack of facial expressions.
(c) Developing, maintaining, and understanding relationships; for example, difficulties adjusting behavior to suit social contexts and difficulties in making friends."

No to (a) and (b) and Yes to (c), and therefore no to this criterion.

"2: Restricted, repetitive patterns of behavior, interests, or activities in at least two areas:
(a) Stereotyped or repetitive movements, use of objects, or speech; for example, lining up toys, flipping objects.
(b) Insistence on inflexible routines or rituals; for example, distress at small changes, the need to eat the same food every day.
(c) Restricted, fixated interests abnormal in intensity.
(d) Hyper- or hypo-reactivity to sensory input, such as indifference to pain, excessive touching and staring."

No to all these areas and no to this criterion.

"3: Symptoms must be present in early childhood."

Yes to this criterion.

"4: Symptoms cause significant impairment in social, occupational, or other important areas of functioning."

Yes to this criterion.

"5: These disturbances are not due to intellectual disability or developmental delay."

Yes to this criterion.

My shrink concluded I wasn't autistic, both because I didn't meet all five criteria and because autism wouldn't have caused me to crash suddenly at fourteen after doing well in every term in every previous year.

I TOLD MY SHRINK I THOUGHT I HAD BORDERLINE personality disorder. I said I had no control over my emotions, mood swings, and self-destructive thoughts, and I still cry almost daily. When I'm on a manic high, I feel on top of the world, but when I'm on a low, depression kicks in. At first I thought I had bipolar disorder, but bipolar's highs and lows come and go slowly for no reason. But mine have triggers.

My shrink read me a description of borderline personality disorder:

"A pervasive pattern of instability of relationships, self-image, emotions, and moods, and marked impulsivity, beginning by early adulthood, distinguished by self-destructiveness, angry disruptions in relationships, and chronic feelings of emptiness and loneliness. Paranoid ideas or illusions may be present. Chronic instability in early adulthood, with episodes of lack of control over emotions and impulses. Manipulative behavior directed toward gaining the concern of caregivers. Impairment gradually wanes with age. Some attain greater stability in relationships and vocational functioning during their thirties and forties, but the tendency toward intense emotions, impulsivity, and intensity in relationships is usually lifelong. The disorder is five times more common among first degree relatives than in the general population and is diagnosed about 75% in females."

I recognized myself—that's someone I know—me! We then worked through the criteria to make a diagnosis. A score of five out of nine would be enough for a diagnosis.

"1: Unstable and intense relationships alternating between idealization and devaluation. They may idealize others at the first meeting, demand time together, and share intimate details. Then they may switch to devaluing them, feeling that the other person doesn't care enough or isn't there enough. They may empathize with and nurture others only with the expectation of reciprocity. Dramatic shifts in their view of others often reflect disillusionment with a caregiver or lover whose nurturing qualities had been idealized or whose abandonment is expected."

Yes to this criterion.

"2: During periods of extreme stress, paranoid illusions may occur. Some develop psychotic-like symptoms (e.g., image distortions, ideas of reference, sensations that seem real, and hallucinations) during times of stress. Hallucinations occur and are vivid, like normal perceptions, and are not under voluntary control. Auditory hallucinations are usually heard as voices."

Yes, in adolescence.

"3: Dramatic shifts in self-image, characterized by shifting goals, values, and vocational aspirations. There may be sudden changes in plans about career, values, and types of friends.

They may suddenly change from the role of a needy supplicant to that of a righteous avenger of past mistreatment. They usually have a self-image that is based on being bad or evil. They may show worse performance in unstructured work or school situations."

Yes to this criterion.

"4: They display self-damaging impulsiveness, including eating disorders and substance abuse. They may have a pattern of undermining themselves at the moment a goal is about to be realized; e.g., dropping out just before graduation or destroying a relationship just when it is clear that it could last. Job losses, interrupted education, and separation or divorce are common."

Yes, especially in adolescence.

"5: Recurrent suicidal behavior or threats, or self-mutilating behavior such as cutting and burning. Episodes are usually precipitated by threats of separation or rejection, or by expectations of increased responsibility. Self-mutilation is regarded as a symptom of borderline personality disorder; however, most of those who self-mutilate also meet criteria for other diagnoses."

Yes, in adolescence.

"6: They may display mood swings due to intense unhappiness, irritability, or anxiety lasting a few hours or days. The basic miserable or dissatisfied mood is often disrupted by periods of anger, panic, or despair and is rarely relieved by periods of wellbeing. These episodes may reflect the individual's extreme reactivity to interpersonal stress."

Yes to this criterion.

"7: They may be troubled by chronic feelings of emptiness. Easily bored, they may constantly seek something to do."

Yes, in adolescence.

"8: They frequently express inappropriate anger or have difficulty controlling their anger. They may display temper, extreme sarcasm, enduring bitterness, verbal outbursts, or physical violence. Anger is often elicited when a caregiver is seen as neglectful, withholding, uncaring, or abandoning. Such expressions contribute to the feeling they have of being evil."

Yes to this criterion.

"9: They are very sensitive to environmental circumstances. Impending separation or rejection, or the loss of external structure, can lead to profound changes in self-image, affect, cognition, and behavior. They experience abandonment fears and intense anger even when faced with a time-limited separation. These are related to a need to have other people with them."

Yes to this criterion. This particular borderline behavior was the source of my abandonment phobia.

My shrink diagnosed borderline personality disorder because *I met all nine criteria* when I was a teenager and *I meet five criteria* today. Borderline originally meant people who were on the borderline between treatable mental illness and untreatable psychosis and who could slide into schizophrenia. Psychosis can involve seeing or hearing things that other people do not—like my hallucinations and voices—and developing beliefs that are not based on reality—like my instant movie star delusions. When, at fourteen, I thought I had schizophrenia, I'd been close to a diagnosis. But schizophrenia tends to strike in young adulthood, and bipolar strikes even later.

She said that tattooing and piercing are now considered to be self-mutilation only if they are done to enjoy the pain. But multiple piercings and tattoos are symbolic of borderline personality disorder, and the statistical correlation between body modifications and psychological disorders like borderline has been measured: people without tattoos or piercings were not distressed, people with tattoos were moderately distressed, and people with multiple piercings were severely distressed. I said her research is outdated because I know many millennials with tattoos, especially in creative industries, who are perfectly together. She smiled. We agreed to disagree.

She said that people with borderline personality disorder have trouble getting an education and keeping a job. It was a relief to know I wasn't alone, but I could never see myself working in an office like my dad did. We have few long-term, mature friendships and tend to choose friends and partners with similar problems. We have an increased risk of divorce and estrangement, and our family members suffer because they struggle with how to respond to our moods.

I reflected on how difficult my teenage years must have been for my parents and, for once, I felt bad for them. I had no empathy for them as a teenager, but I can see now that I caused them nothing but grief, and I helped to drive my family apart. I never used alcohol and drugs when I was young, as people with borderline personality disorder often do, but I was lucky to be living where illegal drugs are hard to get and booze costs a fortune.

She said most people with borderline improve over time,

but it takes decades. Only about half of us achieve a full-time job, a stable partner, and relief from all symptoms, especially negative emotions and social impairment. Psychotherapy improves the odds, and I'm grateful for that.

I said I blamed my parents for making me feel I was never good enough, which gave me trauma, which gave me post-traumatic stress disorder, which gave me borderline personality disorder.

My shrink advised me not to blame anyone; borderline personality disorder is not caused by obsessive parenting and is not a form of post-traumatic stress disorder. Childhood trauma is thought to be a risk factor, but borderline is not caused by trauma because *risk* does not mean *cause*. She said childhood sexual abuse was once thought to be a risk factor, but when patients in earlier studies were queried years later, many of their stories of abuse had changed. She said borderline personality disorder is mainly a genetic disorder, like bipolar disorder and schizophrenia, and it's seventy percent inheritable.

I told her about my mother's and grandmother's mood swings and how I used to think they were bipolar. As we talked about them I realized their mood swings were always caused by triggers, like when something would happen and my mom would throw tantrums or sulk for days, so it was more likely that they had mild borderline personality disorder than bipolar disorder. Mild, because they finished college, had long marriages, and raised families. I could never do any of those things. My shrink agreed, gave me the *Borderline Symptoms List*, and asked me to score myself. I scored "very high" severity in my teens and "moderate" today.

She said my borderline personality disorder may have been passed down to me by my mother and grandmother, who may have mild cases, and they may also have passed mild borderline personality disorder to my sister. No one in the family was as afflicted as me, but genetics could explain my grandmother arguing with my mom every time she visited; my mom arguing with my dad and lying to him, fighting with my sister during her final exams, and her insane obsession with cybersex; and my sister's mood swings, cutting, quitting, and breakdowns, not to mention dressing inappropriately at her graduation: all these are disordered behaviors. My dad had lived in a madhouse.

My shrink said my intelligence had worked against me during my teenage years because it allowed me to intellectualize and embrace my disorders, and it led me to take creative shortcuts that I was too naïve to know were dead ends. It *masked* my borderline personality disorder. If I had normal intelligence nobody would have said, "Lina's smart, only going through a phase" and they wouldn't have had such high expectations of me, expectations that I could not meet because of my disorders. Intelligence *multiplies* the impact of borderline on my life. The positives of high intelligence don't compensate for the negatives of severe mental illness to allow a brilliant kid to get ordinary grades. It's more like a plus times a minus equals an even bigger minus, like the way someone who is both dynamic and demented can be very dangerous. "Twice exceptional" people like me are both gifted *and* impaired.

She said not to blame my caregivers for not knowing I was mentally ill. One person in sixty has borderline personality disorder, compared with one in eighty for schizophrenia and one in forty for bipolar; not much different. Yet even though everyone knows about schizophrenia and bipolar, few know about borderline, even though a third of us with it begin self-harming by twelve and another third by seventeen!

There are 650 movies in the Internet Movie Database (IMDb) tagged with schizophrenia and 270 movies tagged with bipolar disorder, but only fifty movies tagged with borderline personality disorder. She said that as soon as it became clear I wasn't cooperating with my psychologist, I should have been sent to a psychiatrist, because they are accustomed to involuntary teenage patients and can medicate them. If only I'd seen this shrink when I was fourteen, not twenty-eight, too late to have helped me stay in my good school with my good friends and to have maintained a stable relationship with my parents.

I am slowly getting better. My *hallucinations, impulsivity, feelings of emptiness*, and *self-mutilation* are behind me. I don't ink myself as much as I used to, and now I use numbing cream when I do. My *unstable relationships, volatile anger, mood swings*, and *evil self-image* are fading. My *caregiver disillusionment, enduring bitterness*, and *righteous vengeance* for mistreatment by neglect are still with me, but I am working on them.

I understand now that with mental illness, just like physical illness, there is no proper role for apology or forgiveness, only support and appreciation.

Epilogue

Two years after my diagnosis I was stunned to turn on my computer and read this message from my sister:

"Are you sitting down? I'm in a mental hospital. I've been here two weeks, for suicide prevention. I was diagnosed with *borderline personality disorder!* And depression, ADHD, and markers of an eating disorder since my teens. It's hard to accept my diagnosis, but it explains a lot. I'm on mood stabilizers and antidepressants and on the waiting list for cognitive behavioral therapy. I must stay until my psychiatrist discharges me. I've often *felt* depressed, but now I'm *talking* about it.

In India I was almost suicidal for lack of friends, and especially after Mommy told us that if it hadn't been for us, she would have divorced Daddy. In Singapore I was happy at school, with friends and good grades, but I was miserable at home because Mommy was living for today, Daddy was living for tomorrow, and you were living in dreamland.

I started cutting my ankles as punishment for when I ate too much; my socks covered the scars. I enjoyed watching myself bleed and then painting with my blood, so I started cutting my wrists and covering the scars with arm warmers. We all have ways of dealing with our feelings, and cutting is mine. I hated the pain—it's like a paper cut but worse—because pain meant I couldn't cut deep and die, a real emo.

My college years were the best of my life; I was happy, confident, and prolific. But moving out from Daddy's to live independently, and working full time with stress and bullshit, gave me a breakdown. I was so worried about what I might do, I saw a psychiatrist. After eight months of therapy we agreed I would quit my dream job turned nightmare and work from home, Mommy's home. But I was living from commission to commission and getting carpal tunnel syndrome. I'd jumped out of the frying pan into the fire. I was going nowhere. My happiness and productivity ebbed.

When another artist job came up, in Europe, I grabbed it. I work with amazing people who make me feel welcome, but I almost broke down in the first month! It took months to get a bank account, an apartment, and a boyfriend. Stress whittled me down. My carpal tunnel syndrome returned, and I was burning out. I took a week's holiday with my boyfriend to recover, and then I was back in the funk that made me quit my previous dream job. The feelings I'd been suppressing ever since India flooded back, compounded by stagnant creativity, loneliness, and hopelessness.

Seven months into my new job, I ceased to function. I took sick leave and went into psychotherapy. But it wasn't enough. Three months later, I hit rock bottom. Nothing triggered it. One day, like checking an item off a grocery list, I decided it was time: I cut myself. My boyfriend stopped me. The first medications made me lie in bed, an unblinking goth zombie staring at the ceiling. Later medications made me cry, scream, and beg for death—so I cut myself *again*.

I need everyone's help. But my new medications work, and I feel better than I've felt in years. Meeting the ~~inmates~~, ~~patients~~, *people* in my ward, hearing their stories, sharing mine, and feeling their warmth has changed my life. They are teaching me and helping me grow. Fuck adulthood."

It was true, and it blew my mind. My sister could have died!

I quickly sent my sister a reassuring note, and we became closer than ever before. Her modeling meltdown, her book illustrator resignation, her graduation "fuck you", her self-cutting and emotional episodes—these had been acute symptoms of borderline personality disorder, feeding into her chronic depression. I felt so bad for her, but receiving her news helped me to understand her behavior during our teens much better, and to understand myself.

Borderline personality disorder doesn't just run *in* families, it runs *over* families. It flattens them.

Yet nobody knew what was going on, including the family doctor and the useless psychologist with the PhD. The thing is, when everyone you live with behaves the same way, your frame of reference gets distorted and nobody stands out—except for my dad, like a rock. We three women understood each other's feelings and didn't understand his, and vice versa, so we hated him for all he did.

Neither my sister nor I were "together," and my dad was wrong to treat us like we were. But my sister was high functioning and better at hiding her pain—until I tattooed "Pain" on her chest in 36 point sans serif. If my dad had understood the fragility of her mental health and realized that her self-expression was also a sign of distress, maybe he would have been more accepting of her pink hair, face piercings, and tattoos. Maybe he wouldn't have asked her to put on a T-shirt, and she would have stayed on speaking terms with him instead of estranging herself and adding to her emptiness.

When I was a teenager I thought my dad was critical and all over my case for homework. Now I see that he was just doing his best to give me the best chances in life by giving me an excellent education. He asked for seriousness in my studies and realism in my career plans, and he treated my sister the same way. He wanted me to excel for my sake, not his, so opportunities would open up for me when he was no longer around. He encouraged me to do what I needed to do to prepare for my dreams, and nobody was ever going to care that much about me ever again. But my definition of success didn't match his dreams for me.

My dad never understood how his support made me feel strung out, inadequate, and even more depressed than I already was. He should have realized that his dreams for my achievement made me anxious and caused me to fear that I would always disappoint him. He should have realized I was such an emotional mess that it was impossible for me to focus in school, and he should have toned down his obsession with my performance. If I'd been born to a disinterested or unsuccessful father, perhaps he would've let me be myself, in terms of choosing what I wanted to do.

And when it comes to my mom, I loved her more than I loved my dad because she gave me a lot of freedom; however, now I realize that much of this freedom was not in my best interest. She and my sister made my life easier with their acceptance of me and their refusal to hover over my homework, so we mostly stayed close and are still close, but *laissez-faire* isn't necessarily ideal caregiving for a floundering child.

My mom encouraged us to dream our dreams and do anything we wanted to do, but she was relentlessly critical and contributed to our low self-esteem, especially regarding body image. She shouldn't have left us crying in the bathroom for hours. And she had no filter! She said things to us that a parent should never say to a child. She treated us as adult confidantes when we just needed to be her children. And she would have helped the family dynamics and stability significantly if she had remained faithful to my dad.

I realize my parents and other caregivers did the best they could with the knowledge they had, and I suffered primarily because of their ignorance of mental illness, which was not their fault. My life would have been so much better if my disorder had been discovered and treated in school, and the tragedy of my life is that it was not. Even if my treatment had failed, my caregivers' expectations would have matched my abilities, instead of making me study without understanding my disabilities and ruining my school experience.

But I faced two other problems: I was disordered *and* my parents were incompatible. A mentally healthy child will not put her family through overwhelming stress. And compatible parents will cooperate to guide their teens through their toughest years. If our family had faced only one problem, then my expulsion, my mom's infidelity, my parents' divorce, our estrangements, my abscondment, my surgery, and much of my sister's suffering may have been avoided and we might still be a family of four.

During my psychotherapy I was dumbfounded to realize how effortlessly I lied to others to make the points I wanted to make, and how frequently I ended up lying to myself too. I realized how perceptive my shrink and partner had been when they questioned my interpretations. I was astonished to discover how many of my memories had become distorted over the years or were mistaken from the start, and how many had hardened into false memories that became part of my reality to protect my self-esteem. As my false memories crumble, I realize I don't need my emo reality anymore.

My shrink knows I need space from those who hurt me, and there's a reason I estranged them. We are working on helping me reconnect.

I'm beginning to understand why my dad did what he did and tell myself I am ready to forgive him, and I think I wouldn't have reached this level if I'd kept him in my life. Yet a higher consciousness is beginning to imagine that when I truly understand parenthood—why my most important caregiver did all those things he did—that there will be no need for *forgiveness*, only *acceptance*. I may never reach that higher level of understanding because I may never become a parent.

I understand I shouldn't have been so hard on my parents, blaming them for everything in my childhood and spiting my dad for my failed dreams, but I can't go back. I'm still not ready to welcome my dad back into my life, and I might have to deal with an old man's dashed hopes and expectations.

I'm grateful I didn't move to Hollywood at sixteen, because it would surely have destroyed me. But I'm disappointed I wasn't discovered on YouTube and that my novel never became a movie. Otherwise, I feel pretty good about myself these days. I self-published my novel and dozens of music CDs, and I had an acting role in a Hallmark movie.

I'm unable to live off my writing, music, and acting alone, but I live off my tattooing, along with music, blogging, and acting, and I'm so proud of that. I'm an artist and I love what I do. My partner and I live in a two-bedroom flat. I have a queen-sized bed, a car, a gym membership, a big TV, and two dogs. I have no savings but I have never been late on my rent.

I've found peace within myself, and I don't regret who I was or what I've been through. I haven't lived a life of failures; I've lived a life of challenges. I love who I am. I'm okay.

Afterword

This book would not have been written without the support of the author's friend and mentor, S.M., a retired psychologist, social worker, and human rights activist. Several years ago, after she proofread my draft 1,400 page, 1,600 image, 440,000 word family memoir for me, written as a bequest and heirloom, she wrote:

"Your memoir is a masterpiece, an eminently readable epic tale that is candid and moving, a fascinating inside look at a family that was devastated by mental health issues—an affluent, well-educated family with a father with the best intentions. Yet everything goes awry and the youngest daughter is unbearably unhappy and causes havoc for everyone around her. Even with access to the best resources in the world, the outcome was poor. It is a Shakespearean drama, addressing universal problems such as how to raise a child who doesn't want to be raised—a difficult, obstinate, 'I'm going to cut off my nose to spite my face' kind of kid. When I read about those years where you were working sixty hour weeks, I think of the things you missed and the burden of being the sole provider while dreaming of returning home with your family. It is heartbreaking to watch the girls' lives unravel after all the love and devotion and attention you poured into them, thanks to mental illness.

[Lina] is one sick puppy. Her hatred and self-harm and bullying at such young age were abnormal. Her symptoms were severe and disproportionate to her situation. Her mother opted out of her responsibilities, which compounded [Lina's] problem, and shifted all responsibility to you; then she turned both girls against you. Her sister was stuck in the middle. Sometimes nature curses us with health problems and there is no one to blame. Perhaps [Lina] had therapy on her own and blamed her family, and then the therapist guided her to create a blaming story instead of saying to her, 'We don't always know what causes mental illness, but here's what you can do to function in society.' The therapy world can be toxic. What a life you gave those girls! Around the world, a life that few other people have had. It killed me to watch the family disintegrate after India and to watch the girls go from 'I love my daddy' and 'the best parents in the world' to teenage rebellion times ten. The girls were privileged and they should be happy, but we don't always get a Norman Rockwell ending.

Have you considered changing the locations and names, removing the pictures, slashing the text dramatically, and publishing this as a novel under a pseudonym and calling it fiction? Take messages, for example, and rewrite them as narrative in first person from a female perspective; write from the [Lina] perspective as somebody older and perhaps wiser today. I think many people would be interested in reading that. I think it has real potential to be very good ...."

But distilling the *eau de vie* of a 75,000-word novel from a 440,000-word cross-referenced memoir proved to be even more difficult than compiling that original memoir from tens of millions of words and tens of thousands of source documents. And twice I gave up the project, to S.M.'s dismay. That is why this book is dedicated to S.M.: for suggesting I write it, insisting I finish it, and standing up for Lina at every step of the way.